GUNSWIFT AND VOICE OF THE GUN

Two Full Length Western Novels

GORDON D. SHIRREFFS

WOLFPACK
PUBLISHING
— EST 2013 —

Gunswift and Voice of the Gun
Paperback Edition
Copyright © 2022 (As Revised) Gordon D. Shirreffs

Wolfpack Publishing
9850 S. Maryland Parkway, Suite A-5 #323
Las Vegas, Nevada 89183

wolfpackpublishing.com

Paperback ISBN 978-1-63977-119-6
eBook ISBN 978-1-63977-118-9

GUNSWIFT AND VOICE OF THE GUN

GUNSWIFT

CHAPTER ONE

The cold wind seemed to be sweeping all the way up from the Sonora border, driving sheets of sand across the Willcox road, battering mercilessly at the lone horseman heading west. Tumbleweeds rolled swiftly across the alkali flats. Some of them brushed against the legs of the stocky coyote dun, throwing him off stride. The man himself was as blocky as the dun, wind- and sand-burned, loose, and easy in his saddle. His blue eyes were slitted against the gritty sheets that swept about him. The day before they had told him at Lordsburg that the storm was not yet in full swing, but he had shaken his head at their advice that he sit out the storm in Lordsburg where the beer was cold and the women of the cribs just the opposite.

He had left early that afternoon, causing much speculation among the bar idlers who watched him vanish into the dun world to the west. He was loco; on the run with a posse trailing him; he was after someone himself. The last was right. Boone Shattuck was after four men and he meant to kill all of them.

The dim yellow lights of Willcox winked through the storm at ten o'clock that night. The wind still moaned across the flats. For the last ten miles he had given the dun its head, letting him pick his way through the shift-ing, whirling veils of sand. Boone was sorry for the sturdy dun, but an unholy haste had driven him from Ysleta, the home station of A Company, Frontier Battalion, Texas Rangers. He had bought the dun at a corral in El Paso for a specific reason. Old-time Texas mustangers said, "If you would lead the riders, pick the coyote dun."

Emilio Estrada, cocinero for A Company, had once told Boone, "The bay dies while the dun will thrive wher-ever there is grass. The dun keeps cool amid difficulties that set the bay into a panic." Old Emilio had been right.

Boone kneed the dun into the shelter of a ramshackle shed at the town's outskirts. He rolled a smoke, snapping a lucifer on his thumbnail to light it. The flickering light revealed the twisted white scar that ran from the corner of his left eye down to the edge of his mouth. He dragged deeply on the first smoke he had had since morning coffee and eyed the dusty street ahead of him. Lamplight snowed through dirty, cracked windows. Papers and tumbleweeds blew about the streets. The wind carried the off-key tinkling of a piano to him.

Boone dismounted and led the weary dun to a sagging livery stable. The liveryman sleepily showed him a stall and the oat bin. Boone watered and fed his mount, rubbed him down, and covered him with a blanket. He took his Winchester and saddlebags and stepped out into the windy darkness. A woman across the street, looking up and down the dismal thoroughfare, turned to walk toward the center of town.

"Lookit the filly, Cass," a man said from the shadows beside the stable.

Boone stepped back into the doorway. Two men stepped out from the shadows and walked toward the young woman, swaying against the blast of the cold wind. One of them reached out and gripped her by the right arm. "Hello, girlie. How's about a drink of forty-rod with me and Cass here?"

Cass lurched a little. "Hell's fire, Billy!" he said. "It's Jonce Maxon's daughter."

Billy laughed. "I'll be damned! Old drunken Jonce! Well, she shouldn't mind drinkin' with us then, Cass."

The girl drew back but Billy hung on. Her left hand lashed out, cracking flatly against the drunk's face. Boone dropped his saddlebags and leaned his Winchester against the wall. He crossed toward the trio, freeing his tied-down Colt.

Boone stopped behind the short man. "That's enough, Billy," he said.

"What the hell?" said Billy. He released the girl, swaying as he turned, and threw a looping right at Boone. Boone blocked the blow and clipped Billy against the jaw with a right hook. Billy reeled backward.

Cass cursed and slapped his hand down for a draw. Boone freed his Colt and slapped the heavy barrel alongside Cass's head, just below the hat brim. The lanky man went down without a sound. Billy rushed in, tripped over his partner's legs and went down. Boone kicked out. The high bootheel caught Billy just behind the left ear.

Boone holstered his Colt. "Are you all right, Miss Maxon?"

"Yes." She looked down at the two unconscious men. "How did you know my name?"

"I heard Brother Cass say you were Jonce Maxon's daughter."

"I'm Marion Maxon. I was looking for my father."

"I'll take you to him."

She eyed him for a moment. "All right."

Boone picked up his saddlebags and rifle.

A tall, loose-jointed man came out of a saloon and wiped his mouth. He swayed a little as he stepped out into the street. "There's Father now," she said as she stopped. Yellow light from a store window flooded Boone's face, revealing the lean planes, the twisted scar, and the light blue eyes, startling in the deeply tanned face. Her eyes widened and she involuntarily drew back. "I don't even know your name."

"Boone. Boone Shattuck, Miss Marion."

"Thanks. Thanks for helping me." She hurried toward the drunken man and helped him across the wind-blasted street.

Boone had a clear impression of hazel eyes, a soft-looking mouth, and fine, clear skin. An oval face, framed in light brown hair and a perky bonnet. He shrugged and trudged toward the nearest saloon.

Boone pushed through the sagging doors and placed his saddlebags on a chair near the door, leaning his rifle beside it. He took off his gray hat and slapped the dust from his clothing. A dozen men were in the place. Hazy tobacco smoke lifted and wavered in cross drafts from ill-fitting doors and windows. A huge cast-iron stove stood at the back of the room. Coal-oil harp lamps swayed from their cords.

Boone walked to the end of the long bar and called for a beer. The fat bartender waddled down to him and placed the glass on the bar. "You just come in offa the road?" he asked curiously. Boone nodded. Several men looked up at him.

The bartender shook his head. "Last year two *hombres* started out from Tombstone, coming up this way, in a storm as bad as this one. They was found a week later near Dos Cabezas. Dead as doornails. Ain't no time to ride the road, brother."

"I'm lucky," said Boone dryly.

Wind scrabbled at the walls. A door banged somewhere in the rear rooms. The bartender waddled down to the far end of the bar and said something in a low voice to a man standing there. The man nodded.

Boone rolled a smoke and leaned against the bar. Jim Dobie, Wells Fargo detective in that district, was supposed to meet him in Willcox. All Boone knew about

Dobie was that he was a top man, short and stocky, with reddish hair and green eyes.

The front door banged open. The strong draft swept cards from a table. One of the players cursed and looked up angrily at the tall newcomer, then looked hastily away. The light glinted dully on a badge pinned to his loud-checked coat. He wiped his black dragoon mustache both ways. Cold eyes settled on Boone. "You," he said. "You just come in?"

The soft slap of cards and the click of chips died away. A man coughed nervously.

"Yes," Boone said.

"I'm Bob Dowling, city marshal. I got a complaint from two citizens."

"You mean those two drunks who were annoying a young woman?"

"They didn't say anything about that."

"Maybe you'd better ask them."

Dowling tried to stare down Boone. "Billy Steen got a helluva wallop," he said.

"He's lucky."

The door opened behind Dowling. He whirled and stepped back against the wall like a great lean cat. Cass came in, holding the side of his head. "That's him, Bob," he said.

"I'll have to take you in to the *calabozo*, stranger," said Dowling.

"On what charge?"

"Assault and battery."

"The Territory is changin'," Boone said quietly.

He eyed Cass. "Used to be the local boys would ride a bum like this out of town for annoyin' a lady."

A big red-faced man looked up from a table. "He's right there, Dowling," he said.

Dowling looked about the room. There was no friendship in the eyes that met his. It was obvious that he was feared and hated by all the men in the saloon.

"Forget it, Bob," said Cass.

"He'd better," said the big man.

Cass fingered the lump beneath his hatbrim. "Billy and me can handle him in our own way."

The bartender grinned. "Looks like he can handle hisself all right. Ain't no marks on him, Cass."

"Shut up, Fatty! You talk too damned much!" Cass whirled and left the saloon.

Dowling reached for a bottle of rye, drank deeply, and then wiped his mustache. "You're a stranger," he said quietly. "Now you listen to me! I'm the law here in Willcox! You keep your nose clean or I won't let you off so easy next time!"

"I hear you," said Boone.

The marshal's eyes flicked down toward the Colt. "Remember, then." He left the saloon.

The bartender wiped the mouth of the bottle. "Bastard never does pay for a drink," he said.

Boone shoved his beer glass forward. "Regular bull of the woods, eh?"

"Yen. Mean as a Nueces *ladino*. Spends most of his time beatin' up the hurdy-gurdy girls and rollin' drunks."

Fatty filled the beer glass. "Some of the boys call him the Fighting Pimp. Just you keep outa his way, mister. Watch out for Caston and Steen. They was drunk tonight, and they don't believe in turnin' the other cheek."

"Gracias! Where's the hotel?"

"The beer is on me. The hotel, such as it is, is half a block up. On the corner. None of us here like Dowling, Caston, and Steen any better'n you do. They're hard case. Useta run around with Bass Eccles!"

"That mean anything?" Boone asked.

The barkeep looked up and down the bar. "For sure he's a stranger! Never heard of Bass Eccles?"

Boone had. Eccles was one of the quartet he was

after. "Nice town you have here," he said. "With men like them runnin' about."

"Oh, it ain't the town! It's some of the people in it that makes it what it is."

Boone nodded. He drained his glass and left the saloon. He walked through the darkness to the two-story hotel, checked in, and climbed wearily to his room.

Boone locked his door and stripped to the waist to clean up. A puckered bullet hole showed at the base of his left ribs. He cleaned up and pulled on a fresh under-shirt. He placed his Colt beneath the pillow and rolled a smoke. He lowered the lamp and dropped on the hard bed.

Eight months ago the news had come to him while on a scout in the Sierra Tinaja that Perry Thorne had died in a railway holdup ten miles west of Willcox near Cochise Junction while serving as a Wells Fargo guard in the express car. Three men had done the job, stopping the train eight miles from Willcox and uncoupling the express car from the rest of the cars. They had forced the engineer to draw the lone car two miles farther west. Perry had been buffaloed into unconsciousness. The bandits had attempted to open the safe, set with a time lock. When they had failed they had set a charge of blasting powder which had lifted the top clear off the car. Forty thousand dollars' worth of mint gold, consigned to Los Angeles from Denver, had been the haul.

Boone stared up at the dim ceiling. Perry Thorne had been left unconscious in the car before the blast. A few bloody rags pasted to the shattered woodwork of the car had been the only trace found of him. Boone had imme-diately asked for a leave of absence from the Rangers. Sergeant Tobe Winkler had told him to finish the scout after six to Escobar, a pure quill *ladrone* from Chihuahua. In the fight Boone had killed Escobar but had been dropped with a fifty-caliber slug through the body. The last round in Boone's six-gun had dropped the outlaw after he had raked Boone's face from eye to mouth with a razor-edged cuchillo. The wounds had kept him in an El Paso hospital for six months while the trail in Arizona had grown cold.

Boone closed his eyes. His sister Emilie, cute as a button, Perry Thome's wife, had not even recognized Boone when she had been taken to the hospital to see him. The vacant look in her blue eyes often haunted him at night. She had been Boone's last living blood relative until she had died during the winter.

Boone reached into his saddlebags and took out a bottle of rye. He drank deeply and felt the liquor soak into his body. His resignation from A Company had gone through. His recommendation had gained him an appointment as a special Wells Fargo detective. Phil Mason, chief of the district, had been glad to get him.

Mason had briefed him on the unsolved case. Dance Younger had been seen flashing freshly minted twenty dollar gold pieces in Benson shortly after the holdup. Then he had vanished. Sim Bellam's voice had been recognized by the engineer as one of the three masked men. Bartolome Huerta, a coldblooded *bandido* from Sonora, had been seen with both men the day before the holdup, buying blasting powder at the old Acme mine. All three men had ridden into Willcox at midnight with Bass Eccles, one-time city marshal of Willcox. Bass had sworn all three men had been drinking with him all day long in his adobe two miles west of town. But Mason, as well as many other lawmen, was sure Eccles had engineered the whole deal. None of the gold, other than that spent by Younger in Benson, had ever been found.

Boone took another drink. He didn't give a fiddler's damn about the stolen gold. He wanted to put the fear of death into the eyes of those four men, Eccles, Younger, Bellamy, and Huerta, before he killed them.

CHAPTER TWO

Boone suddenly sat up in bed. The room was cold. The wind rattled the warped window casing. He listened. Something seemed to have warned him. He took out his Colt and padded restlessly about the room, wary as a lobo wolf. He snapped open the cover of his repeater watch. After midnight. He sat down at the little table and drew his saddlebags close. He took out his cleaning materials and set to work on his Colt. Cleaning his weapons always seemed to calm him.

He had finished with his Colt and was working on his double-barreled derringer when he heard a stair step creak. He stood up and cocked his Colt. Someone was in the hall, just beyond the thin door.

A soft tap hit the door. Boone did not move. The tap was repeated. "Shattuck!" a man whispered hoarsely. "It's Dobie! Jim Dobie! Open up!"

Boone reached across, unlocked the door and eased it partway open. "Come in with your hands up!" he said.

A short, well-built man, pushed through the doorway with his hands resting atop his hat. Humorous green eyes surveyed Boone. "Suspicious *hombre*, ain't you?"

"I've lived thirty years by being suspicious."

"Can I take my hands down now?"

"Easy like. Where's your credentials?"

"In my left boot."

"Set and pull it off."

Boone shut the door and locked it as Dobie sat down and removed the boot. He fished his badge and identification out of it and showed it to Boone. "Fair enough."

Dobie replaced them in his boot and pulled it on.

"Drink?" asked Boone.

"After I see your badge."

Boone grinned, took the badge and paper out of the inner pocket of his trousers. Dobie nodded, crossed to the window and drew down the tattered shade. "I heard a mean lookin' stranger got into a hassle a couple of hours ago." He eyed Boone. "You?"

"Yes. Two drunks bothered a young woman."

"Jesus! Billy Steen and Cass Caston. It didn't take you long to get into trouble."

"They don't know who I am."

Dobie scaled his hat at a hook and watched it settle and swing back and forth. "In this business, Shattuck, we don't *look* for trouble."

"I didn't agree to let a lady get molested and stand by when I signed up with Wells Fargo."

"It was a damned fool thing to do!"

The cold blue eyes held Dobie's green ones. "You didn't come here to talk about that, did you?"

For a moment Dobie looked as though he was going to get riled and then he looked at the bottle. "I'll have that drink now, Shattuck. Damned near forgot you were a Texas man."

Boone filled glasses and dropped into a chair.

"You're a marked man in Willcox now," said Dobie.

Boone touched the scar on his lean face. "I've been marked for some time," he said dryly.

"What did Mason tell you and where the hell have you been?"

Boone drained his glass. "I'll answer the last question first. I rode in from El Paso."

"With the train available?"

Boone nodded. "Everyone watches a man who gets off a train in a small town like this. No one worries much about a lone horseman."

"True enough."

"I would have been here months ago except a Mex *ladrone* nearly cashed in my chips for me."

Dobie nodded. "Perry Thorne was your brother-in-law, wasn't he?"

"As well as my best friend."

Dobie lit a cigar. "I really didn't want you on this case. This is a ticklish business. I wanted a cool man who isn't driving himself because of the murder of his brother-in-law."

Boone leaned forward. *"Let's get this straight, once and for all!* Mason thinks I'm qualified. I was told to work with you. I'm willing to. I want to get the four men who did the job. If some of them are gunned down in the process, so much the better!"

Dobie inspected his cigar. "I've done too damned much work on this case to have a gunfighter mess it up."

"Just don't get any ideas that you'll notify Mason I won't do for the job. I'll promise you that you'll be satisfied."

Dobie eyed the man watching him. A cold finger seemed to trace the line of his spine as he looked at the lean scarred face, almost as though Death were eyeing him speculatively. "All right, Shattuck," he said, "you win. I'll take your word on it."

Boone nodded and refilled the glasses. "Bring me up to date."

"I relieved Johnny B as comb two months ago. He had been recognized. I've never worked this territory before. I didn't do a helluva lot the first month. Just lazed around town, showing just enough money to let people know I was fairly well heeled. I've located Younger."

Boone's head jerked up. "So?"

"He has a small spread near the Swisshelms making out like he's an honest rancher."

The wind rattled the window casing.

"Bellamy has been seen in Gila Bend, Prescott, Globe, and lately in and around Rustler's Canyon."

"What about Huerta?"

"He's in Nacozari, down in Sonora, about seventy-five miles south of the border. One of our men went down there. He never came back."

"What about Bass Eccles?"

Dobie picked a piece of tobacco from his lip. "All we have on him is the fact that he engineered alibis for the other three. He's never really been connected with the robbery."

"What do you think?"

"None of the three who robbed the car has enough brains to pound sand down a rathole. They're rough as cobs and are killers, but stupid. Eccles is shrewd. It'd be like him to plan a big haul like that and keep his shirttail out of the manure. My God, Shattuck! Forty thousand in gold can't just vanish in this country! Dance Younger had only a few gold pieces. We know Bellamy is broke. Huerta never flashed any of the gold."

"Eccles seems to have quite a reputation around here."

"Yeah. An odd duck. Used to be city marshal here. Before that he was deputy sheriff of Cochise County. Has the reputation of a killer. When he left his job here, he got mixed up with a border gang of hardcase Americans and Mexes. Rustling, stealing, and a little high-grading. Seems as though Eccles has some high-placed amigos who keep their mouths shut and give him a hand now and then."

"Where is he now?"

"Are you familiar with Arizona?"

"I was a mulepacker with Crook back in the early 80s'."

Dobie looked at Boone with new respect. Crook's mulepackers had been hand-picked men, fighters and scouts as well as nurses for their flop-eared charges.

"Do I pass?" asked Boone.

"You'll do." Dobie scratched his jaw. "Eccles and his three sidekicks came into town about midnight and went on a hell-roarin' drunk. When the sheriff questioned Younger, Bellamy, and Huerta, Eccles swore they had been with him all day. What could be done? They were in the clear and, by God, no one around here was going to call Bass Eccles a liar."

"You didn't tell me where he was."

"In Yuma Pen. Serving time."

Boone's head snapped up. "What for?"

"Attempted robbery of a stagecoach near Pearce. Bungled the job after wounding the shotgun messenger slightly. A passenger got the drop on him and he lost his nerve. He got a year."

"Can't he be made to talk?"

"Bass Eccles? Hell no!"

"When does he get out?"

"In about five weeks. He got several months off for good behavior."

"We could wait for him to get out and then shadow him."

Dobie wet his lips. "You think he wouldn't know about it?"

"You *said* he was shrewd."

"He is. I've always suspected that he bungled that stagecoach robbery just to get put into the *calabozo*."

Boone eyed the detective. "What do you mean?"

"He's safe enough in there from his old friends."

"I don't follow you."

"Simple. I think Eccles knows where that mint gold

is. I think he double-crossed his three *compañeros* and then got sent to Yuma to be safe from them."

"It's a long shot, Dobie."

"Mebbeso, but you couldn't put a deal like that past Eccles."

"So what does he gain? They'd be waitin' for him when he gets out."

"Yeah. *If they knew when he was getting out.*"

The wind moaned about the ramshackle hotel. Sand scrabbled at the warped wooden walls. Boone rolled a smoke. Dobie stood up. "I said he had friends. Supposing;, he was let out at a time when no one suspected when it would be?"

Boone drew smoke deep into his lungs. "You think it can be done?"

"*Quién sabe?* Some years ago Bass was mixed up in the Tucson Ring. A gang of politicians, contractors, and traders, who worked machine politics to line their pockets. Selling whiskey and firearms to the Apaches. Their policy was to prevent the Apaches from becoming self-supporting so that the Ring could make profits by selling supplies to the government for them. The Indian Bureau had members who worked hand in glove with the Ring by confiscating crops, moving the tribes to barren reservations and then shifting them again when precious metals were found on land supposedly not worth a damn! Many of the members of the Ring have become respectable after making their stake. Some of them are old *compañeros* of Eccles, now in responsible territorial positions."

Boone nodded.

Dobie crushed out his cigar. "Besides, every damned lawman in the Territory would like to trail Eccles to that hidden gold. Sheriffs, U.S. Marshals, Pinkertons, and what have you."

"You forgot Wells Fargo."

"No I didn't! They're angling for the reward. Our job is to get that bullion back for the company."

Boone eyed the stocky detective. "A company man, eh?"

"Supposing an outlaw made fools of the Texas Rangers?"

"Few do, if any."

"Yes. You'd make damned sure the stain was wiped off the name of the Texas Rangers, wouldn't you? Well, Shattuck, I feel the same way about Wells Fargo!"

Boone stood up. "Supposing we planted a man in Yuma?"

"It's been tried. Eccles is slick as a greased pig."

"It's worth another try."

"We could get a man in, all right."

Boone looked at him. "Let me go."

"If he gets wise, you'll never leave Yuma alive."

"I'll take that chance."

"Let me think about it."

"Don't think too long."

Dobie eyed Boone. "Who are you supposed to be?"

"Saddlebum. Drifter."

"You look tough enough to go to Yuma with that scar."

"Thanks."

"No offense."

"Forget it."

"I still don't like it."

"Let *me* worry about it."

"Eccles is a killer. Fast as greased lightning and eleven claps of thunder with a six-gun."

"I can take care of myself."

"*If* you get out of Yuma with him. It will take planning."

"Where can I contact you here in town?"

"I'm working as jailor. Best place to pick up information."

"I don't know of a better."

"Sheriff Kelly is a good man. He's been working with

me. I'll contact him to see what we can do." Dobie put on his hat. "Meanwhile, keep out of trouble."

"What else could I have done tonight?"

"I suppose I would have done the same. Still, it makes things difficult."

Boone unlocked the door. "Who is Jonce Maxon?"

"Rancher. Has a spread near Pearce. Why?"

"It was Marion Maxon who was mauled by those two drunks."

Dobie whistled softly. "Maxon used to be a friend of Eccles years ago. They were deputy-sheriffs together. Eccles used to spend a lot of time at Maxon's place. I've heard a rumor that Jonce might have been mixed up in the robbery."

"Seems as though a lot of people were." Dobie nodded. "Well, pleasant dreams, Shattuck." Boone peeled off his clothing and crawled into bed. A picture formed in his mind of Perry Thorne.

Somehow the picture faded just before he dropped off to sleep, replaced by an oval face and hazel eyes beneath the brim of a perky bonnet.

CHAPTER THREE

The wind had died away during the night and the sun showed through a dull haze. Boone dressed quickly and swung his gunbelt about his waist. He thought of Billy Steen and Cass Caston and took his hideout gun from a saddlebag. It was a round-handled Colt double-action. Gus Schmidt of El Paso had converted it into a belly gun by shortening the original seven-and-a-half inch barrel to two inches, cutting off the hammer spur, and removing the front of the trigger guard. Boone slipped the stingy gun into his left coat pocket and left.

The hazy sun revealed the warped and faded buildings of Willcox in all their ugliness. Boone stopped at a small beanery for breakfast. A young woman sat at a corner table, her dress bedraggled and her tawdry hat hanging to one side of her head. She hiccupped as Boone glanced at her and returned his look with a stare of pure hatred. A purplish bruise showed beneath her swollen left eye.

The waitress served Boone his breakfast, eyeing him curiously. She was a plump girl with amazingly big blue eyes. "You're new in town, ain'tcha?"

Boone nodded.

Travel in' through or stayin'?"

"*Quién sabe?* I might look about a bit."

"Texan, ain'tcha?"

Boone glanced at her in amusement. "Yes."

She poured herself a cup of coffee. "My name is Lily. Some of the boys call me The Jersey Lily although I ain't never been in New Jersey in my life."

Boone grinned. "They mean Lily Langtry. She's from Jersey in England."

The girl raised her eyebrows. "Yeah? What is she? Hurdy-gurdy girl? Monte dealer? Hash-slinger?"

"Actress. A beautiful woman."

"Well, I'll be damned! All the time I thought the boys was ribbing me."

"They weren't. There's a town named after Lily down in Texas. Langtry. Not far from where the Pecos meets the Rio Grande,"

"Sure enough? Well, I never!"

"Lily!" It was the battered girl at the table.

"Comin', honey!" The waitress bustled over to the girl. "You want I should put some beefsteak on that eye?"

"To hell with it!" the woman said. "I'll wear this damned bruise until it fades away! I'll show Bob Dowling!"

Lily patted her shoulder. "You just sit tight. I'll get more coffee."

"To hell with it! Give me some whiskey."

"Now, Nelly! You know I don't serve rotgut. I'll get some coffee. Then you can lie down in my room for awhile."

The waitress came back to the counter and filled a cup. She leaned toward Boone. "She's from the cribs," she said in a low voice. "Bob Dowling beat her up early this morning."

"Nice fella."

She drew back her lips. "Him? Swaggers around town like God. Beats up the hurdy-gurdy girls. Second time in a month he worked over Nelly there."

Boone looked at the battered prostitute. She couldn't be more than twenty years old.

The waitress glanced out the window. "Here comes the skunk now."

Nelly's head jerked. She touched her bruised face.

Lily balled her fists. "He ain't gonna bother yuh, honey."

"Keep out of it, Lily," she said quietly.

The door banged open and Bob Dowling swaggered in. Boone turned on his stool and rested his elbows on the counter. Bob glanced at the girl and then at Boone. "Get back to the house," he said.

Lily raised her head. "She's resting here, Bob."

"Yen? I told you before to keep your big nose outa my business, Lily."

Lily eyed him. "I ain't ascared of you, Bob Dowling."

"Maybe you'll get a little of what Nelly got."

She laughed. "You lay a hand on me, you ugly galoot, and my brother will come alookin' for you."

"I'm worried."

"Yuh better be."

Boone shifted. Dowling turned partway toward him. There was a naked challenge in his smoldering eyes.

Lily helped the half-drunken girl to her feet. "The bed is fresh made," she said. "You can stay as long as yuh like."

Dowling reached out a big hairy hand. Boone stood up. The marshal eyed him. "She started a ruckus this morning in the Acme."

"Let her alone," Boone said.

"I've got to fine her."

"How much?"

"Ten dollars."

Boone took two fives from his shirt pocket and threw them on the table. Boone jerked his head at Lily. "Put her to bed."

Dowling picked up the bills. "You aimin' to stay long in Willcox?"

"I might."

"I warned you once last night. This is the second time. There won't be a third."

Dowling turned on a heel and left the beanery. The building shook with the impact of the slamming door.

The big waitress came back into the room. "That ornery, stinkin', no-good scum," she said. "You should see Nelly's back."

Boone smacked a fist into his other palm.

"Yeah. I feel that way, too. Dowling takes a cut from the hurdy-gurdy joints. He takes another cut from the girls. He beats them up and then fines them for disorderly conduct."

"A real bloodsucker."

"You said it. But he's leery of my brother. Say! You must be the fella he told me about. The *hombre* that beat up Billy Steen and Cass Caston."

"Your brother?"

"*Muy hombre*! A big man. Red face."

"I think I saw him last night. Wearing a gray coat and black hat."

"That's him. Eli Bell. Bob don't fool with Eli, I tell you."

Boone paid for his meal. "I'm glad somebody stands up to him."

"Eli don't get along with Bob. They useta be friends about a year ago. Ever since Bass Eccles got jugged in Yuma last year, Bob has been gettin' worse and worse. Had a falling out with Eli, too."

"Why would the jailing of Bass Eccles make Bob proddy? Were they *amigos?*"

"Useta be. Eli thinks Bass double-crossed Bob on that express robbery last year. You hear about that?"

"A little."

"Folks say Bass hid that gold and Bob was supposed to have got some of it."

"You believe that?"

She snorted. "Why, Bass, Dance Younger, Sim Bellamy, and Bartolome Huerta was in here the morning after the robbery. Been goin' the town all night. They spent the day before out at Eccles' 'dobe, two miles west of here. I never believed Bass was in on it. Bass and me was sweethearts then. Bass woulda told me, don't you think?"

Boone eyed the buxom girl. "How could he have kept it back?"

She flushed. "You see?"

"Anybody living in Eccles' place now?"

"Not since he got jugged."

Boone walked toward the jail. Jim Dobie was seated on a bench in front of it. Boone nodded.

Dobie looked up and down the quiet street. "Castor and Steen are in the Acme talking war," he said. "Take off for awhile."

"I figured I might take a look at Eccles' adobe."

"Fair enough. Follow the road west about two miles. The 'dobe is about half a mile north of the road. You won't find anything out there."

"Who knows? See you later."

Boone crossed to the livery stable and saddled his dun. He led it behind the hotel and went up to his room to get his Winchester. He headed north out of town, looking back now and then to see if anyone was behind him.

The flats were deserted.

CHAPTER FOUR

Boone topped a rise to look down on a squat adobe set in a wide hollow. He drew rein, eyeing the structure below him.

One end of the roof had sagged in. The area about the house was littered with wood, rusty tin cans, and bits of glass, tinted purple and red by the hot sun. A ramshackle shed leaned against one end of the adobe. The remains of a fence leaned every which way, surrounding about half an acre behind the house. A peeled-pole corral had been partially torn down.

Boone kneed the dun down the slope and ground-reined it behind the house. The front door sagged on leather hinges. He pulled it back to enter the low-ceilinged living room. The accumulated odors of human waste clung about him. Battered furniture stood about. Ashes were thick in the beehive fireplace in a corner. Glass crunched under his boots. It looked as though no one had lived there for a long time.

Boone picked up a stick and lifted a tattered, filthy blanket from the floor. A dirty shirt was beneath it. He walked into a smaller room. Sunlight streamed through the narrow windows. A scrawled message was on one wall, written with charcoal. Boone read it aloud:

"Within this hive we're all alive,
Good whiskey makes us funny;
So if you're dry come up and try
The flavor of our honey."

Boone grinned. The room was empty except for a fallen cot. He lifted it and looked underneath. A mouse scuttled for cover.

Boone walked into the filthy kitchen. A rusted stove was placed against the back wall and the pipes had collapsed across it, littering the stove and floor with soot. A woodbox, partially filled, stood beside it.

He walked out the back door to inspect the shed. A broken saddle hull hung from a peg. Straw still covered the hard earth floor.

Boone walked back to the house. The dun whinnied softly and thrust forward its ears, looking to the east, toward the lip of the hollow. Boone stepped into the house, crossed into the living room and stood back from a window watching the mesquite along the hollow edge. It did not move.

Boone leaned against the wall and eyed the big room. He was wasting time, he knew. Forty thousand in gold would be compact but damned heavy. He was willing to bet Keno, his dun against a chew of spit-or-drown that the gold couldn't have been hauled far from the robbery before it was cached. Mint gold was carried in small wooden boxes, sealed with wax. Boone had once acted as guard on an express train which carried twenty thousand in gold. There had been two boxes. Therefore each box must have contained ten thousand dollars. By that line of reasoning, there must have been four boxes removed from the Southern Pacific express car by the three outlaws. A real bonanza!

Boone walked back into the kitchen and poked about in the old stove. It was deep in ashes. He dumped the woodbox over and pawed through it. Suddenly he whistled. The bottom of the box was stained with melted wax. He took out his case knife and scraped at it. It was thick. Odds were that the heat of the stove, close to the woodbox, had melted the wax. But where had it come from? It was reddish. Certainly not candle wax. "I'll be go-to-hell," he said.

He refilled the woodbox, carefully examining each piece. One piece had been split in half. It was hall an inch thick. There was a dark stain on one end. He scraped at it with his knife and tasted the scrapings. Wax! He stowed the piece of wood in his coat pocket and left the adobe.

He led Keno toward the lip of the hollow, topped it and stopped short. There were six shallow marks in the loose sand. He squatted, measuring them with his eye. A man, lying prone on his belly, would have made just such hollows with elbows, knees and boot toes. Two hundred yards from the hollow he found hoofmarks. They had not been there when he had passed by earlier.

Boone swung up on the dun and headed back toward Willcox. He rode slowly. Melted wax was no real clue. Yet it was a lead...

A tall man sat in a buckboard at the edge of town, looking down the long dusty street. He jumped as he heard Keno's hoofs on the hard earth. He turned and eyed Boone with red-rimmed eyes. Boone nodded.

"You're Boone Shattuck, ain't you?" the man asked.

"Yes."

The tall man passed a shaking hand across his forehead. "I'm Jonce Maxon. Marion tells me you did her a kindness last night when she was lookin' for me."

"It was nothing," said Boone. Maxon's face was livery in color. Pouches hung below the red eyes. He had all the marks of a steady drinker. He had been a fine-looking, powerful man in his day, but the shakes had taken over.

Maxon steadied his hands. "Yeah. Nothing, he says."

Maxon's tone wasn't that of a grateful man.

"I don't get it, Maxon."

"You think I want Steen and Caston on the prod after me? I got troubles enough as it is."

"Maybe I should have let them rough her up?"

"She woulda been all right!" Maxon wet his purplish lips. "Looky here, son. I appreciate what you done, all right. Years ago I woulda done the same thing for any lady. But I was a better man then. I been sick."

Boone studied the raddled face. "You sure as hell are."

Maxon flushed. "Likker helps me along. Drives away the pains."

"So?"

Maxon swallowed. "I'm gettin' out of town back to my ranch before them two bastards come lookin' for me like they are for you. It's your fight. They give me a hard time some months ago. I ain't hankerin' to get it again."

Maxon threaded the reins through his gnarled fingers. "You wouldn't happen to have a bottle on you, would you?"

"No."

Maxon looked uneasily up the street. "I told that girl to meet me here at noon!"

Boone touched the dun with his spurs. "I'll see if I can find her for you."

"Much obliged."

A woman was standing near the hotel, looking up and down the street. The wind blew her dress flat against her long shapely legs and taut against her full breasts. Boone tethered the dun to a hitching rack.

She smiled as she saw him. "Good morning."

"It is a good morning. Your father is waiting for you at the edge of town."

"Thanks, Mister Shattuck."

"The name is Boone."

"Boone."

Boone took off his hat. "I'll walk you to him."

"Thank you. He hasn't been well. I brought him in to see Doctor Ruffin, but Dad refused to see him last night. I just can't get him to see a doctor."

She took Boone's arm as they walked. "How do you like Willcox?" she asked.

"What is there to like about Willcox?"

She laughed. "You have me there. I like the ranch much better. Run down as it is, it's much more peaceful and clean."

A woman eyed them from the doorway of a general store and then spoke over her shoulder to a man who stood behind her. They followed Marion and Boone with their eyes as they passed. Marion flushed. "Will you stay here long?"

"I'm passin' through."

"Cowman?"

"A little. Cowpoke, mulepacker, scout, drifter."

"A Texan."

"Yes."

"You've a family in Texas?" She glanced at him. Boone shook his head. "I'm the last of my family. The last of my line of the Shattucks."

"That sounds so final. *The last of the Shattucks.*"

"My father was killed by Comanches at Horsehead Crossing on the Pecos when I was a kid. My mother died of fever shortly after that. My brother Collate was drowned in the Solomon River, north of Abilene, on a trail drive. My kid sister...she died last year."

"Texas must be a hard country."

"In a way. Old-timers say it's a fine country for men and dogs, but hell on women and horses."

Jonce Maxon was standing up on the floor of the buckboard, watching them from two blocks away. A man stepped out of a saloon and started toward Maxon, saw Marion and Boone, and hurriedly stepped between two buildings. It was Cass Caston. Boone unbuttoned his coat.

"There's Father," said Marion.

Maxon touched up his teams and rode slowly toward them.

Billy Steen came out of the saloon and stood beneath the wooden awning. Suddenly he crossed the street in front of them and stopped in front of a blacksmith shop. Boone saw what they were up to. He would have to walk between them to take the girl to her father. *Why didn't the drunken fool hurry?*

Fifty yards from the buckboard, Caston stepped out into the open. The wind flopped open his gaudy cowhide vest. Marion paled. "Keep walking," said Boone.

"Will there be trouble?"

"If anything happens, you drop to the ground and stay there. Do you understand?"

"Yes. But they have guns."

He grinned. "Why, so have I."

Maxon reined in the team and looked nervously from Steen to Caston and then at Boone and the girl. "Hurry, Marion!" he called.

Billy Steen stepped out into the street. "You!" he said to Boone. "I want to talk to you!"

Boone stopped. "Let the lady go to her father," he said.

Steen glanced across the street. Caston leaned against a post. Steen swept back his coat from his left side. His right hand shot across his squat body for a cross-arm draw. Boone smashed against the girl, driving her to the hard earth. Steen fired. The crack of the Colt sounded loudly in the stillness. The slug sang thinly past Boone's head. He jumped away from the girl, ripping his Colt free of leather. Caston ran forward.

"Look out, Boone!" screamed Marion.

Boone whirled. Caston slammed his long-barreled Colt

down across Boone's gun wrist. Boone grunted in agony, dropping his six-gun, and swung from the waist, driving a vicious left to Caston's bristly jaw. Caston staggered sideways as Steen fired again. The cowhide vest jerked and dust flew from it. Caston pitched forward, gripping his lean gut.

Steen yelled through the wreathing smoke and started forward. He glanced down at Boone's fallen Colt and grinned. Boone sidled away. Steen ran forward, thrusting out his Colt.

Boone cleared his hideout gun from his coat pocket and rapped out three staccato shots. The echoes slammed back and forth between the false-fronted buildings. Steen staggered backward, dropping his pistol. Then he pitched sideways, fell heavily, twitched spasmodically and lay still. Blood spread swiftly across the front of his white shirt.

Maxon peered through the rifting smoke. "By God!" he said. "He got both of 'em!" He jumped from the buckboard, gripped Marion by the arm, dragged her to her feet and shoved her toward the buckboard. As she sat down, he gripped the reins, slapped the whip across the dusty rumps of the team and turned the buckboard swiftly, racing off to the west. Marion Maxon looked back and then covered her face with her hands.

A crowd began to gather. An aproned clerk looked down at Caston. "His tack is drove," he said.

A cowman bent over Billy Steen. "Three slugs in the gut," he said over his shoulder. "Yuh could cover them holes with the palm of your hand." He stood up and looked at Boone in awe. "Somebody better get Marshal Dowling."

Boone wiped the cold sweat from his face. It had happened so quickly he hadn't had time to think. He had done just what Dobie had warned him not to.

Dowling came up the street, his nickel-plated Colt glinting in his hand. The crowd gave way before him. "I warned you, Shattuck," he said. Before Boone could move, the marshal swung his heavy Colt. The long barrel clipped Boone over the left ear, driving him to his knees. The second blow caught him atop the head. He fought with reeling senses to get up. Dowling lashed out with a big booted foot. The heel hit Boone on the temple.

He struck the hard ground and lay still, knowing nothing.

CHAPTER FIVE

Boone opened his eyes and a ray of sunlight lanced deeply into his throbbing skull. He turned away from the window. He was in a cell. He sat up, wincing as pain shot through his battered head. He groaned softly.

"You sure as hell drove everything up the spout," said a dry voice.

Boone looked up. Jim Dobie was looking through the bars at him. "Kill two men in two minutes! Where the hell did you think you were? In some Mex *plazita* along the Rio Grande after some ladrones?"

"Shut up."

"You acted like a whiskey fool out there."

Boone gripped the bars and pulled himself to his feet. "Where's Dowling?"

"Over at Doc Ruffin's at the autopsy. The fat is in the fire now."

Boone suddenly thrust a hand into his inner pocket.

"I got your badge and papers out when they carried you in here. I'm sending them back to Mason with a request that he send me an agent who isn't all hoofs and horns, teethed on a six-shooter."

"Go to hell! You think *I* started that fracas?"

"Well, pardon *me* all to hell! You started the whole thing last night. Caston and Steen tried to finish it. By God! I'll say this for you: You're a ring-tailed roarer with striped wheels when it comes to gunplay. Too bad you can't play detective as well. You've finished yourself with Wells Fargo, Shattuck."

Boone sat down and gingerly touched his battered head. "I didn't kill Caston. Steen opened fire. I knocked the girl out of the way. Caston knocked my cutter from my hand. Steen fired as I hit Caston. Steen's slug killed Caston. I dropped Billy with my hideout gun."

"Yeah?" asked Dobie quietly. "Who saw it?"

"Jonce Maxon. Maybe the girl did, too."

"Maxon was chased by one of the boys. He claims he saw nothing. It was too quick." Boone went icy-cold.

"What about Marion?" Dobie lit a cigar. "She was half-stunned when she hit the caliche. Says she didn't see anything, either."

"They're both double-barreled liars! Anyone else see what happened? Or is this two-bit helltown full of liars?"

"No one has come forward as yet."

"So?"

"Dowling is pinning two murder charges on you."

"Why? I killed Steen in self-defense."

Dobie placed his face close to the bars. "You faced Dowling down last night and also gave him a hard time this morning in Lily Bell's beanery."

Maybe you don't know the man. *No one faces him down in Willcox.* He's the hairy bear in this burg. That cold-gutted shark will see you swing for no other reason than that you had the nerve to face him down."

"Christ!"

"You can say that again. I'll get you some jamoke. How's the *cabeza?*"

"Twice as big as it should be." He stood up and looked through the barred window. A small group of men stood across the street, looking at the jail. One of them was the big red-faced man who had been in the saloon the night Dowling had faced Boone. Eli Bell. He was talking angrily. Dowling trudged down the street, ignoring Bell and the men with him.

Boone paced back and forth. The thought of Marion Maxon refusing to stand up for him hurt him a hell of a lot more than his battered head.

Dowling stood outside Boone's cell. "I warned you," he said. "You didn't listen to me."

"I didn't kill Caston."

"The hell you didn't!"

"Look, Dowling. My Colt was knocked out of my hand. It was never fired. The belly gun was fired three times. Steen was hit three times. How the hell could I have shot Caston?"

Dowling's eyes narrowed. Boone was instantly sorry for what he had said.

"Steen was killed by me in self-defense."

"You got witnesses?"

"Jonce Maxon and his daughter."

"They claim they didn't see what happened, *hombre*."

"Maxon is a damned liar!"

"It's your word against his, Shattuck, and you ain't in any position to have anyone listen to you."

"I might have expected you to say that."

Dowling's eyes were as flat and expressionless as a diamondback's. "Don't get on the prod. Next time I'll mark you for life." He turned and walked away.

Dobie came down the corridor. "He's gone." He opened the cell door and handed Boone a granite cup of jamoke. "I heard what you said. You should have kept your mouth shut."

"I know it now."

"He has all the guns. Yours as well as Caston's and Steen's I wouldn't put it past him to frame you."

"Just because I stood up to him?"

"There's more than that, Boone," the detective said quietly. "He followed you out of town this morning."

Boone looked up. "Someone was watching me out there."

Dobie looked back up the corridor. "He goes out there now and then. Hell, everybody does. Personally, I doubt if the gold was ever there."

Boone reached in his coat pocket and took out the piece of wood he had found. He handed it to Dobie. Dobie looked curiously at Boone. "You feel all right?"

"I found that in the bottom of the woodbox out there. Notice the melted wax. There was more melted wax in the bottom of the box."

"So?"

"Gold shipments are sealed with wax in wooden boxes. Those boxes might have been broken up out there and burned. The heat of the stove melted the wax on the wood before it was put into the stove. It dripped down."

Dobie worked his mouth. "Jesus! I've been out there half a dozen times and never noticed this. You might make a detective yet, Boone."

"Yeah! With a double murder charge against me."

Dobie scratched his jaw. "You're not dead yet. Sheriff Mike Kelly is in Benson. He's coming down here on the eastbound tonight. This clue, slight as it is, is the first one we've found that indicates that the gold might actually have been brought to Eccles' 'dobe."

Boone emptied his cup. "How will I get out of here?"

Dobie took the cup. "Listen, Brasadero. When it comes to sheer brainwork, you leave it up to Mrs. Dobie's little boy, James."

"Keno."

Dobie locked the cell. Boone dropped on his bunk and rolled a smoke. He lit it and watched the bluish smoke drift and waver in the air and then flow out of the small window...

The noise of the cell door being opened awoke him.

Jim Dobie was looking down at him. "Had your breakfast brought in from Lily Bell's," he said. "Eli brought it over."

Eli Bell brought in a covered tray. "Heat the jamoke, Jim," he said.

Boone sat up. "Damned nice of you, Eli."

The big man sat down at the end of the bunk. "Lily thought it up," he said. "Besides, I want to talk to you."

"Shoot."

Boone eyed the big man. He had the same amazingly big blue eyes of his buxom sister, but it was obvious he wasn't a man to be choused by Bob Dowling.

Bell lit a cigar and watched Boone eat. "I saw Dowling last night," he said. "I was heading home when I saw him go into a deserted 'dobe at the edge of town. Ain't no one lived there for years. I was leavin' when I heard a shot. Bein' curious I took a look in a window. Bob was standing in the house with a smoking Colt in his hand. It wasn't his nickel-plated hogleg. Then he digs the slug outa the mattress he shot it into. He leaves the 'dobe then."

Boone paused. "So?"

"What did your Colt look like?"

"Sheriffs Model. Forty-four. Four-and-a-half-inch barrel. Ivory grips with a Lone Star cut into them."

Eli nodded. "That's it!"

Boone placed the tray on the floor. "What the hell was he up to?"

"Jim Dobie told me you killed Steen with three shots from your bellygun. Your Colt was never fired."

"That's right."

"Mebbe Dowling wants it to look like you *did* shoot that single-action Colt." Bell stood up and got the tray. "Thought you might like to know."

"I'm obliged, Eli."

"Forget it. I don't know you, Shattuck, but I ain't about to see Bob Dowling get away with a thing like this." The big man left the jail.

Dobie brought in the coffee. Boone told him what Eli Bell had said. Dobie nodded. "It figures. Mike Kelly is getting the coroner's jury together. I'll take you over there after lunch."

The long morning drifted past. About one o'clock Jim came and unlocked the cell. He handcuffed Boone with Mattatuck irons and escorted him to the schoolhouse. Six jurors sat uncomfortably on a long bench. Doc Ruffin, Assistant Coroner of Cochise County, presided. Sheriff Mike Kelly, a giant of a man with sweeping blond mustaches, came over to Boone. "Jim told me the whole story, Shattuck," he said.

"Did he tell you *my* side of the story?"

"Yes."

"Dowling is out to get me."

Kelly grinned. "Sit tight. You ever commit a robbery in Mohave County?"

"You loco?"

Kelly grinned. "You want to get placed in Yuma Pen, don't you?"

"Yes." Boone figured it was all too fast for him.

"Then you held up two prospectors near Squaw Peak a year ago last February. The sixteenth, to be exact, while using the name of Jack Field. You escaped from the deputy sheriff who was transporting you to Yuma in March of last year. You haven't been seen in Arizona until this month."

Boone rubbed his jaw. "You make up this tall tale?"

Kelly shook his head. "A man by the name of Jack Field *did* commit that robbery and was sentenced to Yuma. He *did* escape from a Mohave County law officer. But he'll never go to Yuma."

"How so?"

"I ran him down last week near Fort Huachuca. He resisted arrest. I killed him. I haven't had time to make out a report. Instead of reporting I killed him, I can say he escaped and headed for New Mexico, then came back into Arizona. You follow me?"

Boone grinned. "Yep."

"You play your part, sonny. Leave the rest up to Michael Francis Patrick Kelly."

"Keno!"

The inquest began. The room was filled with curious townspeople. Matilda Bennett testified that she saw Boone walking toward Jonce Maxon's buckboard with Marion Maxon. Her husband Amos testified to the same fact. They had then gone into Corby's General Store and had heard the gunfire. Thomas Fraser, teamster, testified that he had also seen Boone and Marion walk toward the buckboard, and had also seen Casimir Caston and William Steen standing on opposite sides of the street. He had then run into the shed behind Bayliss' Blacksmith Shop. He had not seen the shooting.

Coroner Ruffin then called for witnesses Jonce and Marion Maxon. Sheriff Kelly stood up. "A man was sent for them early this morning. They should be here within the hour."

Ruffin scratched his beard. "In order to speed this inquest I will call on City Marshal Robert Dowling."

Dowling was sworn in. "I was in the jailhouse office when I heard the firing. When I reached the scene of the shooting I saw Jonce Maxon and his daughter leaving the scene in a buckboard. Boon Shattuck was standing in the middle of the street. A Colt single-action lay ten feet away from him. At his feet was a double-action Colt, altered into a bellygun."

"Bellygun?" asked Ruffin.

"Yessir. A gun altered for a speedy draw. Barrel cut down, front of the trigger guard removed as well as the hammer spur. This is the weapon." Dowling placed the bellygun on the table along with Boone's single-action colt.

"Continue," said Ruffin.

"Cass Caston was lying on his face. He had been shot through the belly and was dead. Billy Steen was lying on his back near the sidewalk. He had been shot three times through the chest."

All eyes in the courtroom turned toward Boone. Dowling continued. "I was forced to subdue Shattuck and then incarcerated him in the jail. I had the bodies taken to your office. Doctor Ruffin."

Ruffin turned over the gavel to Sheriff Kelly and was sworn. His testimony, replete with medical terms, told that Caston had been killed by a slug through the abdomen. Steen had been hit three times close to the heart. Four .44/40 slugs had been removed from the bodies. Three from Steen, one from Caston. Ruffin returned to his presiding position. The door opened and Jonce Maxon came in, with Marion holding his arm. He looked deathly pale. Marion's face was drawn. She did not look at Boone.

Jonce Maxon took the stand and was sworn. "I was waiting for my daughter Marion in my buckboard, ready to go back to my ranch," he said in a low voice. "This man, Shattuck, was walking with her toward me. Steen and Caston was on opposite sides of the street. My team was nervous so I wasn't watching the three men. All of a sudden this shooting starts. When I looks up I sees Caston lyin' in the street. Steen was falling. My daughter was lyin' in the street, Shattuck was in front of her with a smokin' pistol in his left hand. I got Marion into the buckboard and drove off."

"Then you did not see who actually shot Casimir Caston?" asked Ruffin.

"No."

"But you did see who shot Steen?"

Maxon swallowed. "I said I seen Steen fallin' and Shattuck with a smokin' gun in his hand. I never said I seen anybody shoot at anyone else."

Boone looked at the gangling rancher. The man was obviously lying.

Marion Maxon took the stand. "Boone Shattuck offered to take me to my father. When we approached the buckboard we saw Cass Caston on one side of the street and Billy Steen on the other. Billy Steen stepped out and spoke to Boone Shattuck. Boone Shattuck knocked me down to protect me from the bullets. Billy Steen fired first at Boone. I saw Cass Caston run toward Boone Shattuck from behind. Mister Shattuck then had his Colt in his hand. Cass Caston struck it from his hand. Then I must have fainted."

Boone raised his head. His eyes met those of Marion Maxon. She lowered her head.

"Did you see who shot William Steen?"

"No."

"Did you see who shot Casimir Caston?"

"No"

Ruffin glanced at the jury. "That is all, Miss Maxon. City Marshal Robert Dowling to the stand."

Dowling took the stand.

Ruffin pointed at the pistols. "Did you examine those weapons, Mister Dowling?

"I did. As well as the weapons carried by Steen and Caston."

"Tell us what you found."

Dowling stepped over to the table. "This is Billy Steen's gun. A .44/40 Colt single-action. It had been fired once."

Boone's head jerked up. Maxon bit his lower lip.

"This is Cass Caston's handgun," said Dowling. "A Colt .41 caliber Lightning. It was loaded with five cartridges, the sixth chamber bein' empty. The gun had not been fired."

He's right there at least, thought Boone.

Dowling glanced at Boone. "This bellygun is .44/40 caliber. A double-action. It was loaded with five cartridges. Three of them had been fired." Dowling picked up Boone's Sheriffs Model Colt. "This is a .44/40 caliber Sheriffs Model Colt. I found it lying near Boone Shattuck. It had been loaded with five cartridges. *One of them had been fired.* That slug hit and killed Cass Caston."

Ruffin glanced at the clerk. "Do not take down that last sentence." He looked at the jury. "You will remember that William Steen, according to the testimony of Miss Maxon, fired *first,* at Boone Shattuck. Also that Casimir Caston, did, according to Miss Maxon's testimony, strike Boone Shattuck's pistol from his hand.

"Are there any other witnesses to be called?" asked Ruffin.

Kelly stood up. "Eli Bell has a statement to make."

Bell moved up the aisle and was sworn in. "I didn't see the shootin'," he said. "But there is somethin' I saw that might have some bearing on this case. Last night about midnight, I was walking home when I sees City Marshal Dowling go into the old Miranda 'dobe at the edge of town. I heard a shot. I looked in through a window. Marshal Dowling was standing there with a smokin' pistol in his hand. He lays the pistol down in plain view and digs the slug out'n a mattress he had fired it into."

Dowling rose halfway from his chair. Ruffin raised his eyebrows. "Can you identify the weapon you saw, Mr. Bell?"

Bell stood up and placed his hand on Boone's single-action Colt. "This is it. I know it by the short barrel and the ivory grips with the star carved in 'em."

Whispering started in the big room. Ruffin banged the gavel. "Did you actually see Marshal Dowling fire the shot?"

"No."

Dowling grinned.

Ruffin fingered his gavel and glanced at the jury. "If there are no more witnesses the case will be summarized."

Jim Dobie walked forward. "I have something to say," he said quietly. Dowling scowled at Dobie.

Jim was sworn. "I was in the jailhouse when the first shot was fired. I looked through a cell window. Billy Steen was standing with a smoking pistol in his hand. Marion Maxon was lying on the ground."

Jonce Maxon was in his buckboard. Boone Shattuck was drawing his Colt. The single-action. Cass Caston struck it from his hand. Shattuck struck Caston. Caston staggered away from him just as Billy Steen fired. The bullet struck Caston, killing him. Boone Shattuck backed away with no weapon in his hand. Steen approached him with his gun in his hand. Shattuck drew out his double-action, dropped to the ground to protect Miss Maxon, and fired three times, killing Billy Steen. To my knowledge, Shattuck never fired his single-action Colt and did not kill Casimir Caston. "

Ruffin looked at Dobie. "Is there anything else you have to say, Mister Dobie?"

"Yes. In shooting affairs, when the participants are arrested, their weapons are held in the jail office. City Marshal Dowling took the weapons from the scene of the shooting. This is the first time I have seen them since."

"He's a damned liar!" yelled Dowling.

Ruffin frowned. "Remain quiet, or you will be fined for contempt of this court!"

Boone eyed the jailor. Dobie had lied. There was no doubt in Boone's mind about that.

The jury left the schoolroom. In twenty minutes they returned. Dock Ruffin read the verdict. "Territory of Arizona, County of Cochise. An inquisition, holden in the county of Cochise, territory of Arizona, on the 15th day of May, A.D. 1889, before me, Jonas Ruffin, Assistant Coroner of Cochise County, Territory of Arizona, upon the bodies of William Steen and Casimir Caston, by the persons whose names are hereto subscribed. The said jurors upon their oaths, from the evidence do say that the said Casimir Caston was accidentally killed by a bullet wound from a pistol fired by William Steen, since deceased, on the 13th day of May, 1889, in the county of Cochise, Territory of Arizona. That the said William Steen came to his death by three bullet wounds from a pistol fired by Boone Shattuck in self-defense, on the 13th day of May, 1889, in the county of Cochise, Territory of Arizona."

Dowling got to his feet. "Bell," he said. "You'll pay for this!"

Sheriff Mike Kelly came close to the two big men. "Dowling, I've heard about your foul record hereabouts. If the people of Willcox have any pride they'll kick you out of that job of yours!"

"Go to hell!" said Dowling.

Jim Dobie came toward them. Dowling whirled. "Here's another damned liar!" he roared. Suddenly, as though reason had departed, he slapped his hand down for a draw. Boone jumped from his chair. He gripped the big marshal by the arm and whirled him about. His wrists were still encircled with the heavy Mattatuck irons. He swung both arms to the side and smashed his clasped hands against Dowling's heavy jaw. The marshal grunted and staggered back. Blood streamed from his mouth. He hit Dowling again. The marshal threw up his arms and turned to run. Boone smashed his hands against the back of Dowling's head. Dowling did not see the window in front of him. He smashed through the glass, hanging on the sill. Glass tinkled down.

Boone stepped back, looking at the unconscious marshal. Dobie pulled him back through the window. His face was slashed to ribbons. "Jesus," Jim said.

Sheriff Kelly thrust a long arm in between Boone and Dobie as the jailor held out the key to unlock the irons. "This man is wanted for robbery in Mohave County. Under the alias of Jack Field he robbed two men near Squaw Mountain last year. He escaped from a deputy sheriff who was escorting him to Yuma Penitentiary last year."

"Well I'll be double-damned!" said Eli Bell.

Dobie handed the key to Sheriff Kelly. "He's your prisoner, Mike."

The last thing Boone saw as Kelly walked him back toward the *calabozo* was Marion Maxon, standing beside her father, just outside the schoolhouse.

Her eyes told the story of her thoughts.

CHAPTER SIX

A cold wind whispered over Prison Hill and moaned softly through the long cell corridor. Boone shivered in the thin-striped coat and pants he had been issued, as he trudged between two burly guards down the dimly lit corridor. His scalp itched from the close shave in the prison barber shop. The harsh leather of the square-toed prison shoes irked feet that had worn nothing but boots.

The screws stopped before a barred cell door and unlocked the heavy padlock set through a thick hasp three feet from the edge of the narrow door. He removed the padlock, lifted the hasp and threw his weight against the metal bar which actuated both the inner and outer doors of the cell. They creaked open. The second screw shoved Boone forward. "In!"

Boone walked into the gloomy cell. Both doors creaked shut behind him.

"Fresh fish," a hoarse voice said from a lower bunk.

A man giggled from an upper bunk. Boone stood in a narrow cell between the tiered metal bunks, three on a side, eight feet high. He stumbled over a thick metal ring set into the cell floor.

"Any room?" asked Boone.

The man in the lower bunk laughed. "Any room in Yuma! Hawww!"

"Take the top or middle bunk to your right," a shadow said from the lower left bunk. He chuckled. "We're lucky, us short-timers. Only got three of us in here... four, counting you."

Boone threw his mattress cover and blanket into the middle bunk. There was barely enough room for an average sized man to fit into the bunk.

A squat man thrust thick legs over the side of the right hand lower bunk. "The name is Concho Bates," he said. "Two years for armed robbery." He thrust out a ham of a hand. Boone gripped it. "Boone Shattuck. One year for armed robbery. Six months for escaping before they landed me here."

Bates jerked his head. "The skinny man behind you is Benny Hatch. Two years for knifing a gambler at Gila Bend."

Benny giggled.

"Thalus Hastings," the man in the left hand lower bunk said. "A year for attempted robbery." His voice seemed cultured.

Boone looked toward the back of the cell. It was blocked by a cross hatching of thick double bars. Beyond the bars was another cell, exactly like the one he was in. "Shut up in there!" a man yelled. "We wanta sleep!"

"Go to hell, Dixie!" said Concho.

"I'll kick the crap outa you tomorrow!" said Dixie.

Concho laughed deep in his throat. "Yuh tried it two months ago. Remember what happened?"

"Go to hell!" said Dixie.

Boone made up his bunk and rolled into it. There was a rank smell in the cell; the mingled odors of sweat, urine, stale bedding, and unwashed feet.

Concho said, "Yuh got any smokin' material?"

"They cleaned me."

"Damned screws won't even let a man have a smoke at night."

"No smokin' here," said Benny Hatch. He giggled. "Anyways, *I* don't smoke."

"Clean livin' bastard," grunted Concho. "Don't smoke or drink. But don't turn your back on him when he's got a knife in his dirty hand."

Boone wriggled about. The mattress was packed and lumpy.

Thalus Hastings laughed. "It's not much worse than sleeping on the ground, Shattuck."

"It's the stink yuh got to get used to," said Concho.

Boone covered himself with his blanket. "I doubt if I will."

"You're from Texas," Hastings said.

Boone glanced down at the shadowy face, thin and ascetic in the dim light. "Yes."

"I'm from Kentucky. Lived in Texas for a time."

"Yeah," said Concho. "They had him in Huntsville for forgery."

"Nice place Texas," said Hastings.

Concho yawned. "I'm from Missouri. Show me."

Benny giggled. "You ain't seen Old Chi," he said.

"Old Chi?" asked Boone.

"Chicago. Real booming town after they rebuilt it. Nice fillies there." Benny giggled. "Once I get out of this hellhole I'm headin' for Frisco. They say it's like Old Chi."

"I'll give you a week there," said Hastings dryly. "Then you'll end up in the pokey again."

"Shut up in there!" yelled Dixie.

"Come and make us," jeered Concho. "You damned long-legged rebel."

Silence answered him.

Concho leaned out of his bunk and looked up at Boone. "Dixie is the rooster in that cell. I'm the hairy bear in this one. Yuh clean up the cell this next month and me and the boys will go easy on yuh."

"Fair enough," said Boone.

"Some of the cells have a kangaroo court on fresh fish. Dixie give a new man a going over last week because he thought he was tough. Ended up in the infirmary. He's a good boy now. We'll go easy on you, Boone."

Boone grinned in the semi-darkness.

Concho eyed him. "Hard case, eh?"

"Hard enough."

"Shut up," said Thalus Hastings. "Never let it be said that Cell Two didn't consider a man's feelings his first night away from home."

"Jeeeesus!" said Concho.

Benny giggled.

"How's the chuck?" asked Boone.

"Slop," said Concho.

"Anything to do here?"

Thalus laughed. "Mattress shop. Tailor shop. Laundry. Library. Blacksmith. Bakery. Mess hall. Supply shop. Workshops. What can you do?"

"Punch cows. Pack mules. Scout. Break horses."

"Most of the plushy jobs are taken by old-timers. Probably end up in the laundry," said Hastings.

"Ain't bad in the winter," said Concho. "Sheer hell in the summer."

The cold wind swept through the cells. Boone shivered.

Concho coughed. "Like I said: I'm the hairy bear in here, Shattuck. Don't never forget it."

Benny giggled. "Yeah, when Bass Eccles ain't in here, you are."

Boone's eyes snapped open.

"Bass ain't so much," growled Concho.

"You sure walk quiet when he *is* here," said Benny.

"I'll break your waggin' jaw!" blustered Concho

"Who's Bass Eccles?" asked Boone.

Thalus leaned out of his bunk. Short-termer. Robber. Used to have your bunk."

"Where is he now?"

"The Snake Den," said Concho. He laughed. "Eccles got lippy with Cap Ingalls, the warden. Ingalls had him thrown into the Snake Den until his time is up."

"What's the Snake Den?"

"Cell for incorrigibles," said Thalus. "Hewn out of solid granite. Right across from the cell block entrance. A bitch of a place."

"Just right for Eccles," said Concho.

Boots slapped on the concrete of the corridor. A shadowy figure stood outside the outer door. Concho waited until the guard walked away. "Bastard," he said.

Boone closed his eyes. Yuma Pen was fourteen years old. Seven prisoners had been the first contingent. Additional prisoners had built the cell blocks and prison buildings. Ten acres atop a granite bluff that pushed its way into the yellow waters of the Colorado. Now the prison held over three hundred, some of them from states and territories other than Arizona.

In two days, Kelly had taken Boone from Willcox, manacled and under guard. They had left the train at the Yuma station and Boone had been stripped of his clothing, ordered to bathe, and had his head shaved by a lifer. Captain Ingalls had given him advice on his conduct and then he had been locked in this filthy, cold cell.

If Eccles got word that Boone was an undercover man, Boone would never leave Yuma unless he was sewed into his blanket and buried on the slope near the river.

———

THE GUARDS' whistles blew just after dawn. Boone dropped from his bunk and looked about the white-plastered cell. The ceiling was arched and smoothly plastered. Some past inmate had scored the word *Libertad* in the smooth plaster. "Liberty," he translated.

Thalus Hastings yawned from his bunk. "Jesus Diaz cut that in there six months ago."

Concho spat on the floor. "Yeah. The screws figgered he was tryin' to cut through. He got a month in the Snake Den. Never come out. Went loco. They stuck him in the insane cell. I helped bury the poor bastard."

"Wouldn't have done him any good trying to get through there," said Hastings. "You see those bars between us and the next cell? Well, those bars are on each side of us and all the way up over the top. Like a cage covered with plaster. Besides, Jesus just wanted to lie in his bunk and look at the word he had inscribed." He laughed harshly. *"Liberty, indeed!"*

Thalus Hastings was about forty-five, thin and intelligent looking. His prison garb hung loosely on his tall spare figure.

Benny Hatch was a little man, like a weasel, with washed-out eyes and a hooked nose that seemed to tremble. Concho stood up and pulled back his striped coat revealing a barrel chest covered thickly with stiff black hair. His dark eyes studied Boone. "Yuh clean up good, yuh hear?"

Boone nodded. Concho balled a big fist. "I don't want no bitchin' from the screws." He clamped a big hand about Boone's left wrist. Boone eyed the hand. "Take it away," he said quietly. The man was as strong as an ox. Concho exerted more pressure. "Sure, sure," He growled. He stepped back, a naked challenge in his small dark eyes.

Boone dropped to the floor and began cleaning up the cell with a worn broom. "Sweep in the corners!" ordered Concho.

The double doors swung open and they filed out into the corridor. Up and down the rows of cells Boone heard the clank of chains. "Some of the boys are chained to that big ring you saw in the cell floor," said Hastings. "We're short-termers so they don't bother to chain us."

"Any breaks here?" said Boone.

Thalus shrugged. "Now and then. Work parties mostly. A year ago three of them tried it. The watchtower is set up over the big cistern. They have a Gatling up there. Two of the boys were killed before they got two hundred yards. The last of them made the river and drowned."

Mess was doughy mush, strong black coffee, and bristly sowbelly. The men ate noisily. There was no talking, no sound other than the clatter of utensils and the shuffling of feet on the gritty floor. A screw banged on a table with his truncheon. "All new inmates will fall in outside the door for an inspection tour." He grinned. "Welcome to Yuma Pen."

Boone shuffled out with a string of bowed men.

"We use the mess hall for a chapel," said the leading guard. "Some of you bastards could use a little Bible learning." He led them past the blacksmith and bakery and then to the supply building overlooking the town. Boone looked across Yuma. There was a small park between Prison Hill and the S.P. tracks. Slab-sided houses stood starkly out on bare ground on a ridge beyond the tracks. "Hell of a place," murmured a man behind him.

They skirted the main cell block past the building where the solitary cells were. The guard stopped and pointed to the end of a granite hill that stood up at the end of the ten-acre prison area. "Them's the women's cells overlookin' the town," he said with a grin. "Don't get any ideas of consortin' with the female prisoners." He walked along a row of doorways cut into the naked granite. "That's the insane cell there. Take a look," he invited. Boone looked into a roughly hewn cell. It was just big enough for a man. Even the low bunk had been hewn from the stone.

"Cell One is for visitin'," said the guard. "Not that you

scum can expect any visitors. Two and Three are for the violently insane. Some of you will probably end up there."

"Nice *hombre*," said a convict.

"Shut up!" roared a guard.

"Cell Four is the Mattress Shop," said the guide. "We train the boys in there to make them as uncomfortable as possible."

The leading guard stopped at a narrow door. "This is Cell Five. The Snake Den. This is for incorrigables! You get out of line, you go in there and about one outa every ten goes nuts in there. Then we shift him down to the Insane Cell. There ain't no way outa the Snake Den except through two barred doors. Solid granite all around and over your head. Remember that!"

The guard led them through a gateway set in a thick wall. "That row of cells is extra, for hard cases." He paused and pointed up. "You see them towers? Guards up there with rifles. Dead shots, every one of 'em." He led the way back through the gateway and along the work-shops to the toilets set near a squat, low-roofed tower built above a stone cistern. "Yuh see that Gatling? It covers every inch of open ground. Don't get any ideas on makin' breaks here." He pointed down a slope to a fenced enclosure. "Cemetery." The morning sun cast faint shadows behind the redwood headboards.

The guard turned to his two mates. "Take 'em back to their cells." He stalked off.

Boone eyed the rock walls enclosing the ten-acre prison tract. Men lounged about the prison yard. One of the guards spoke over his shoulder. "You can stay in the prison yard from seven A.M. until five P.M. unless you got work to do. No fighting. No groups."

Boone wandered over to where Thalus Hastings sat with his back to the wall. Concho Bates leaned beside him. Benny Hatch was idly tossing a stone up and down. "Yuh get the Grand Tour?" asked Concho with a grin.

Boone nodded.

"There isn't a damned thing to do unless they assign you to one of the shops," said Thalus. "I work in the library. Spend the day reading. Makes the time go."

"Wish that I could read," said Benny.

"Offered to teach you," said Thalus dryly.

Concho spat. "Hell's fire! Readin'! Why don't they let us have some cards?"

"Bad for the morals," said Thalus.

A man squatted not far from them, patiently knitting a bedspread. His gnarled fingers moved slowly.

"Jesse Bardolph," said Thalus. "A lifer. Makes the best bedcovers I ever saw. Sells them to visitors. Damned if I know what he does with the money, though."

Boone sat down and took off his left shoe. His heel was rubbing raw. A man rounded the corner, an angry look on his lean face. "Here comes Dixie Yates," said Benny.

Concho balled big hairy fists and looked at him. "I hope he tries to get proddy," he said.

"He's looking for Shattuck," Thalus said.

The tall man eyed Boone. Two other men watched the trio next to the wall as though anticipating something. Yates sauntered over. "Who was doin' all the jawin' last night?" he asked in a slow drawl.

"All of us was," said Concho. "Why?"

Yates' icy eyes studied Boone. "I got no bone to pick with you, Bates," he said. "It's this new fish."

Boone looked up. "I'm sorry," he said.

"He's sorry," Yates said over his shoulder. The two watching men laughed. The southerner looked at Boone's unshod foot. "Shoe pinchin'?" he asked.

Boone nodded.

"Ain't you got no manners?"

"I don't follow you, Yates."

Yates yawned. "Your feet stink. Smelled 'em plumb over in our cell. The boys asked me to tell yuh to keep 'em clean."

Men began to gather. One of them stood near the corner of the cell block, watching for a guard.

Boone pulled on his shoe. "Surprising you could smell me over your stink, Yates."

Yates went red. "You lookin' for trouble?"

Boone stood up. "No. But I don't aim to crawfish."

"Yuh forgot to tie your shoe," Yates said.

Boone looked down. Yates stepped in. His long right arm lashed out. The hard fist knocked Boone back against the wall. Yates stepped in close and drove in a hard one-two that sent Boone down.

Yates blew on his fists and looked back at the watcher. "Any screws around, Jimmy?" he called.

"Nary a one, Dixie."

Boone wiped the blood from his mouth as he got up. Yates danced about easily, shadow boxing. "Had enough?" he asked.

Boone nodded. Concho growled in his throat.

Yates looked back over his shoulder. "He's yella," he said.

Boone uncorked a driving left which clipped Yates' lean jaw, a right jab which staggered him. His left sank to the wrist in the lean gut of the southerner. His right came up short and hard, connecting solidly with Yates' chin. Yates went down hard. He bounced to his feet and rushed Boone, throwing punishing blows. Boone danced aside and Yates drove a wild blow against the cell block behind Boone. Yates screamed.

"Screw comin'," yelled Jimmy.

Yates thrust his bleeding hands into his pants' pocket and leaned back against the wall. Boone squatted beside Hastings. The guard rounded the corner. "Spread out, you bastards!" He stopped short and looked at Boone. "Your mouth is bleeding."

"Yeah."

"How'd you do it?" The guard looked at Yates.

Boone grinned. "Fell up a wall."

The guard rubbed his thick jaw. "I'll remember you. What's your name?"

"Boone Shattuck."

"The man who killed those two men down in Willcox a week ago?"

All eyes turned toward Boone. Boone nodded.

"Hard case, eh?"

Boone looked at him.

"Well, I catch any of you fools fighting and you'll end up in the Snake Den." The guard walked away.

Concho eyed Boone. "Thought you said you was in for robbery?"

"I am."

Concho jerked his head in the direction where the guard had gone. "What'd he mean?"

"I killed *one* man down in Willcox. He killed his *amigo* with a wild shot. The sheriff picked me up on an old robbery charge."

Yates paled a little, licked his abraded hand. "I ain't done with you," he said.

Benny grinned. "He wasn't done with you, neither."

The tall southerner walked away.

"You handled him right nice," Concho said.

Hastings nodded. "Watch him, Shattuck. He's mean."

Boone nodded. The words of the guard came back to him. *I catch any of you bastards fighting and you'll end up in the Snake Den.*

Concho watched Boone through veiled eyes. "I know Willcox," he said. "Who was it you knocked off there?"

"Billy Steen. Cass Caston was the other *hombre*."

"Billy Steen? I knew him down to Bisbee. He had bobcat bristles on his belly."

"He hasn't anymore."

"How'd yuh do it?" asked Benny eagerly.

"Gun hassle. Billy drew and missed. Killed Caston. I dropped Steen."

"Steen was fast with a six-gun," said Concho. "Near as fast as Bass Eccles. They was *amigos* once."

Boone looked out across the prison yard to the distant hazy Gilas. Suddenly a wild, unreasoning surge swept over him. He wanted to yell out, race for the wall and scale it, and bury himself in the sandy brushy wastes to the east.

"Don't try it," advised Thalus softly.

Boone looked at him.

"It comes over all of us the first week or so in here. Take it easy, Boone."

Boone wiped his face. "It's gettin' warm," he said.

Concho nodded. "It'll get warmer. Hell of a place. Freeze in winter. Roast in summer. I've heard it said the mercury dries up in August around here."

"Everything dries up," said Thalus. "Wagons. Men. Chickens. All the juices dry up. People creak when they walk. Mules bray only at night. The carcasses of cattle dry inside their hides and rattle like bones. Snakes find it hard to bend. Horned frogs die of apoplexy."

"Hell!" said Benny. "Listen to him!"

Concho grinned. "Heard tell of a soldier from Fort Yuma, across the river, who died and went to hell one blasting summer day. That night his ghost comes back and asks the quartermaster to re-issue his blankets. He couldn't stand the drop in temperature down there! Hawww!"

Thalus rolled his eyes upwards. "Makes me want to try for Mexico. Only twenty-six miles south of here."

"You'd never make it," said Benny.

Concho shook his head. "They got Yuma and special trackers around here. Johnny the Dip got away once with Jesse Ebbetts. They got as far as Martinez Well, northeast of here. Johnny sees Yuma trackers. He breaks for the brush. Jesse surrenders. The Yuma's didn't bother to haul Jesse back. Brung in his head in a sack. They got fifty dollars. Johnny the Dip comes back on his own.

Went loco, thinkin' about Jesse. They buried him six months later."

At noon mess Boone felt Dixie Yates' eyes on him. At supper, the lanky southerner dropped a pot of coffee behind Boone and burned his back with the hot liquid. On the way back to the cells Thalus Hastings spoke. "He'll ride you until you fight again. This time he'll try to maim you."

That night Boone lay in his bunk, the snores of the other men driving sleep from him. He thought of Marion Maxon. If Dobie hadn't perjured himself, Boone might have been sent to Yuma for life, if they hadn't strung him up instead. Maybe she had been protecting her weak father. He covered his face with his hands. Marion Maxon seemed to haunt him.

To her he was nothing but a number in the hellhole on Prison Hill.

CHAPTER SEVEN

A week dragged by. The heat began to get hellish. Summer was early. Sweat soaked the rough striped suits and then dried. There was a constant odor of urine, sweat, and unwashed bodies about the bare cells; a miasma which clung in the cell block and sickened Boone. He thought often of the days along the Brazos. At night he could hear the wild screaming of an inmate confined in one of the stone cubicles for the insane and then the yelling of the guards as they clubbed the poor wretch into unconsciousness.

Boone's solid frame began to thin out. He thought of *chili, olla podrida, enchiladas,* and *panoches* until he felt his mouth fill with water. The prison fare was coarse, prepared by convict cooks. The very smell of the mess hall was enough to turn a man's gut.

Boone was put to work in the laundry. The steaming tubs filled the air with fog. Sweat rolled from his body and dripped into the tubs with the soapy water. He looked over the stone walls at the distant mountains, and a wild urge to break free would sweep over him, almost overpowering in its intensity, but Thalus Hastings always seemed to know when it was at its worst, and his quiet voice drove away the mad desire to break free.

The sun was beating down, and the guard in charge of the laundry let them off an hour early. Boone went to the toilets to find Thalus, who had taken his turn there as orderly. The lean man wasn't there, but Dixie Yates was, leaning against the wall with two of his mates. Yates grinned. "Watch the door, Sam. Keep an eye outa the window, Jimmy."

Boone turned toward the door. Sam leaned against it, grinning at him. Yates swaggered up to Boone. "Well," he said thinly, "you ready to take it up again?"

Boone wiped his hands on his coat. "You want the screws to come in?"

"You bastard," Yates said. "I'da broken you in half if that screw hadn't horned in." He rushed Boone and drove in a stinging right. Boone covered up, blocking a hard left, and fell back. Yates circled slowly, like a copperhead ready to strike. "Yuh had an advantage the first time," he said. "Full of good chuck from outside. Yuma thinned you down to the right size."

Yates closed in. Boone straightened him with a left and brought over a whistling right which drove the tall man against the wall, stepped in, and smashed Yates' head back against the wall. Yates sagged.

"Go get him, Dixie!" said the big man at the door.

Yates drove in at Boone. Boone stopped him with jabs and hooked in a vicious right which sent Dixie reeling across the room. "Come on, Dixie!" implored Jimmy.

"Watch that damned window!" said Yates out of his smashed mouth.

Yates suddenly rushed in, stepped on Boone's right foot, and hit him with both fists to the face. Boone crashed to the floor and rolled away from Yates' smashing feet. He got to his knees and went down again from a kick to the ribs. Yates stood over him, waiting for him to get up. When he didn't, Yates started to lift him by the hair.

Boone pulled back and smashed a blow to the tall man's groin. As Yates bent forward, Boone drove up with his head and hit Yates square in the face. Blood spattered down on Boone. He jumped away. Yates yelled, pawing at his face with reddened hands. Boone hit him in the gut and drove him back against the wall. Sam left his post and rushed in. Boone whirled, caught the burly man with a right, and then hit Yates title a vicious uppercut. Yates went down, striking his neck on the edge of a toilet.

"Guards!" yelled Jimmy. "Shattuck is fightin' again!"

Sam hit Boone with a short left. Boone hung on to the big man, and they reeled about the stinking room. Sam fell over Yates' legs with Boone on top. He gripped Sam by the collar and battered his head against the hard floor.

"He's killin' my pals!" yelled Jimmy.

Boone was jerked back. Something hit hard just over his left ear. He went down into a swirling pit of blackness and knew no more...

Something was poking into Boone's pocket. He groaned. He was roughly rolled over. "Clean as a coot," a dry voice said in disgust.

Boone opened his eyes. His face was flat against a hard stone floor. He gently touched over his left ear. Blood coated the side of his head.

"It ain't busted," the voice said. "Yuh got a thick head, brother, in more ways than one."

Boone rolled over and sat up. A chain clanked. He moved his left leg. The chain clanked again. A stub of a candle guttered from a niche in the rough-hewn stone wall. A tall, stoop-shouldered man sat with his back against the wall eyeing Boone. "You sure raised hell in the craphouse," he said.

Boone winced as he moved his head. "Where the hell am I?"

The tall man laughed. "In the Snake Den. By God! You musta had a helluva fight. The screw tells me Dixie

Yates has a cracked skull and Sam Penner ain't much better off. You're a good man with your fists, Shattuck, even if yuh ain't very bright."

Boone shook his head. "I feel like they threw me off Prison Hill."

"Hawww! They sure heaved you in here."

The yellow candlelight showed on the man's bald head. The man grinned lopsidedly. "I'm Bass Eccles. Mebbe yuh heard of me?"

Boone nodded.

Eccles chuckled. The light showed his piercing black eyes. "Seems like everybody knows about old Bass Eccles."

Boone nodded. He looked about the notorious cell. It was about fifteen feet square and ten feet high, hewn out of solid rock, the rough walls blackened by smoke and covered with cobwebs. His left ankle was ringed and chained to a large iron ring set into the rock floor. Over his head was a square hole through which he could see the graying sky through many feet of solid granite.

There was a furtive movement in a dark corner. "Who's that?" asked Boone.

Eccles grinned. "Pedro Loco." He stood up with a clank of chains and took the candle from the niche. He held it toward the corner. A small man was as hunched there, wrapped in a ragged blanket, his wizened face staring without concentration at Boone.

"Who is he?" asked Boone. The mindless stare made his skin crawl.

Eccles shoved the little man with his foot. "My cell-mate until you come in. Say hello, Pedro."

Pedro did not move.

Boone looked at Eccles. "He out of his mind?"

"Yeah. Plumb loco."

Suddenly the little man began to scream thinly, his shrill voice rising higher and higher. He pointed a dirty finger at Boone. "You're dead!" he said in swift Spanish.

"Go away! You're dead! Jesus! Mary! Send him away! Covered with blood!"

"Shut up, Pedro," Eccles said.

The Mexican screamed. Eccles gripped the demented man by the neck and smashed a fist against the little man's jaw, driving his head back against the stone wall. Pedro's shrill, haunting voice cut off short. He slid to the floor. Eccles wiped his hands on his trousers. "Pedro sees things," he said. "I gotta smash him now and then. Only way I get any sleep around here."

Boone looked down at the unconscious man. Blood ran from his slack mouth. Eccles placed the candle back in the niche. "Pedro useta eat peyote. He got on a peyote jag and thought he was an executioner or somethin'. Gets his machete and lops the heads off'n his wife, brother-in-law, and a cousin. Now and agin he sees 'em starin' at him from the shadows. Three bloody heads in a row. Goes off his *cabeza.*" Eccles grinned. "Takes a good man to keep from goin' that in here."

Boone sat down with his back against the wall. "How do you stand it?"

"Me?" Eccles grinned slyly. "I got dreams, brother. Dreams. Things I aim to do once I get outa here."

"For instance?"

Eccles sat down, leaning back against the wall. "Get me a *hacienda* down in Mexico. Maybe Guatemala or Nicaragua. Get me a nice brown-skinned filly, slender in the pasterns and smooth in the flank. Mebbe about sixteen years old. Be a real *don, amigo, a real don.*"

Boone grinned. "Don't hurt to dream. Takes *dinero* for things like that. You got it?"

Eccles' eyes veiled. "I didn't say so."

"You aim to make a killin' when you get out?"

"Yeah. That's it! A killin.'"

Boone sighed. "I tried it. Held up two prospectors near Squaw Mountain. Damned near got away with six thousand in gold."

"Peanuts."

Boone grinned. "Maybe you've got a *morral* in here loaded with pesos? Where is it hidden?"

"Where is what hidden?" There was cold menace in Eccles' tone.

Boone yawned. "All the gold you'll need for that *hacienda*."

"I didn't say I had anything hidden."

"No."

Pedro groaned. Eccles aimed a boot and kicked hard against his jaw. Pedro went out again. Eccles glanced at Boone. "Where you from?"

"Texas."

"Then you shoulda been put in Huntsville."

"Squaw Mountain is in Arizona, *amigo*. In the Cerbats."

"You mean Squaw Peak."

"Same thing."

"Yeah. The screw said something about a killin' in Willcox." The dark veiled eyes studied Boone.

Boone nodded. "Had a fallin' out with two *hombres*. They went on the prod for me. We had it out."

"Real hard case, eh?" Eccles eased the ring about his skinny ankle. "Who was the men you tangled with?"

"Names of Billy Steen and Cass Caston."

"Yeah."

"You know them?"

"Useta. I useta be city marshal there."

"You're joshin'!"

"Hell no! Useta be deputy sheriff down in Cochise County, too. Everybody down there knows Bass Eccles. Didn't you ever hear of me?"

"Sounds familiar."

"Yeah." Eccles leaned back against the wall. "I only got a couple weeks to go in here."

"Then back to Cell Two?"

Eccles slowly shook his bald head. "No."

"You aimin' to make a break?"?

"I ain't sayin.'" He eyed Boone. "You must be rough as a cob. Kill Billy Steen, a good man with a hogleg. Beat up Dixie Yates and his *amigo*, Sam. Rough as a cob."

Boone waved a dirty hand.

Eccles nodded. "How long you got to go?"

"Year and a half. Year for armed robbery. Six months for breakin' away from the guard takin' me here. If I'da had any sense, I would have got over into Sonora. Instead, I circle down through Chihuahua, up into El Paso, then back into Arizona."

"Why?"

"Figured I'd head for California. I shoulda had enough sense to stay outa trouble. Instead, I tangle with Steen and Caston. I was freed on self-defense, and then Sheriff Kelly recognizes me from a wanted poster."

"Mike Kelly ain't no fool."

Boone nodded.

"Too bad. How's Willcox?"

"Just the same."

"Bob Dowling still marshal?"

Boone grinned. "He was. Perjured himself and lost his job. That's one good thing I did back there anyway."

"Yuh mean he perjured himself in a case against you?"

"Keno."

"Why?"

"I stood up to him. He didn't like it."

"Sounds like Bob, all right."

Boone looked up at the chimney hole. "Can a man fit in that?"

"Hell no! If you're aimin' to escape, play it smart, and wait until yuh get outa this hole. Fact is, yuh can't get outa here. Take it easy and wait until yuh get out."

"What then?"

"You figure it out. Now shut up. I want some shuteye."

Eccles eased down to the floor and, in a few minutes,

was snoring. Boone eyed the baldheaded outlaw. It would be so damned easy to strangle him while he slept. Pedro Loco groaned in his sleep. Boone closed his eyes. His head throbbed. The place stank. In a hole inside a granite hill with a coldblooded outlaw and a demented mass murderer.

"Hell," he said softly. "What a price to pay."

———

BOONE OPENED his eyes to stare in almost Stygian darkness. He sat bolt upright, the cold sweat of fear dewing his body. A chain clanked. There was a savage grunt. "Shattuck!! Shattuck!" The frenzied cry was cut short. Bass Eccles. Boone stretched a hand in the darkness.

"Shattuck! For God's...sake...he's strangling...me... with his...chain!"

Boone reached out and felt the thin form of the demented Mexican. Teeth gnawed at his right forearm. He set himself and struck hard. Pedro Loco gasped. The chain clanked. Boone ran his hands down the maniac's thin arms and gripped the tightly clenched hands. They were holding a leg chain twisted tightly about Eccles' neck. Boone pried at the unseen fingers. The little Mexican had the power of a much bigger man. Eccles gasped as the chain loosened. Boone went down over the sprawled outlaw, pulling Pedro with him. The rank stench of the maniac flooded his nostrils. A knee came up in his groin. A chain lashed across Boone's face starting a flood of tears. Blood ran from his nose.

Boone rolled atop the struggling madman and banged the head down on the stone floor. Pedro threw him off. Over and over they went, battling in the darkness until Boone's leg chain drew taut. He kneed his opponent in the groin and battered at the unseen face. The Mexican screamed. Eccles was silent in the darkness.

Yellow lantern light flooded the narrow entranceway. "What the hell is going on?" yelled a screw.

"Loco is out of his mind!" gasped Boone. He hit the Mexican in the gut, hammered at the thin face.

The door creaked open and the lantern flooded the Snake Den. Boone drove in a jolting right that put Pedro Loco into the long sleep. Boone stood up and wiped the blood from his face. The screw unlocked Pedro Loco's chain and dragged the unconscious man through the entranceway. Boone felt for the candle. He lit it and leaned his head against the stone wall. Fear and exertion soaked his shaking body with cold sweat. Suddenly he looked up. What had happened to Bass Eccles?

Eccles crouched in a corner with his dirty hands covering his lean face.

"Eccles," said Boone.

The outlaw did not move.

"Eccles!"

Eccles lowered his hands and looked at Boone with eyes of naked fear. His body shook. He slowly reached up and touched his abraded neck. Boone had seen men gripped by green slavering fear before, but Eccles' terror was branded on his soul, making him appear inhuman.

Boone picked up the water olla and threw some on Eccles. Eccles threw himself on the floor and shook in a paroxysm of fear. Broken sobs emanated from the terror-stricken man.

Boone heard the clanging of the cell door farther down the row as the guard threw Pedro Loco into the insane cell. Boone touched his damaged face and wiped the blood from his nose. He watched the outlaw and a stark truth seemed to stalk through the dingy stone room. Bass Eccles had a yellow streak as wide as his streak of assumed bravado. Boone filed it away in his mind. It might eventually destroy Bass Eccles.

———

"RISE AND SHINE," a voice said. "Chuck."

Boone opened his eyes and rolled over. His face was swollen. Bass Eccles squatted near the door, looking with disgust at the bowls of food in front of him. The guard eyed Boone. "How do you feel?" he asked.

"Rough."

"Pedro Loco has been raving all night. The doc says he ain't got long to live."

Eccles spat. "Hope the bastard dies. This chuck is hog slop."

"Maybe you'd like a steak?" asked the guard.

"Yeah. I'll be eating steaks, Martin, when you're still eatin' this prison swill." Quite different from the terror-stricken man who had been groveling on the floor a few hours before.

Boone eyed the outlaw. Eccles yawned. "Well, Martin, get outa here and let us eat. We like privacy."

The guard grunted and left.

"How do you feel?" asked Eccles. He did not look at Boone.

"Lousy."

"Yeah. It *was* rough." Eccles swallowed noisily. "I won't forget it, Shattuck."

"It was nothing."

Eccles touched his bruised throat. "Yeah. Nothin'." Boone finished his meal and drank the rank coffee. Eccles handed him the makings. Boone stared at the tobacco. "Where'd you get it?"

Eccles waved a hand. "I got connections."

"I guess you have." Boone rolled a smoke and lit up. He watched the bluish smoke drift up through the chimney hole. "Tastes good."

"Mexican crap. I'll buy yuh a wad of real Virginny smokin' tobacco onct we get out."

Boone eyed the lean man. He had said we.

"I ain't got long to go," Eccles said.

"Wish I could say that."

"Yuh don't have to stay in here."

Boone clanked his leg chain. "What do I do? Ask to get out?"

"Don't get funny."

Boone smoked slowly and then rolled another cigarette. "Where you headin' when you get out?"

The dark eyes glanced at Boone. "I told yuh."

Boone grinned. "Yeah. A *hacienda* down in Nicaragua, you said. With a sixteen-year-old gal. I mean, where are you really headin'?"

"I told yuh!"

"You must think I'm simple as a kit beaver."

Eccles leaned back against the wall. "Can you swim?"

"Learned how in the Brazos."

"I mean *good?*"

"Better than most cowpokes."

Eccles nodded.

"Why?"

Eccles' dark eyes were half-closed. "I don't swim worth a damn."

"I'd teach you if we weren't in this hole."

"Yuh don't have to teach me. Just give me a hand."

Boone scratched his jaw. "Keep talkin'."

Eccles got up and walked to the door dragging his chain. He peered out and then came back. "Listen! I'm gettin' out. I'll need help. Any man can down Billy Steen and lick Dixie Yates, not to mention what you done for me last night, is my man."

Boone inspected his smoke. "You forgot something. I've got eighteen months to go."

"Would you make a break if you had the chance?"

"Listen, Bass. I broke away from my guards comin' here from Mohave County. I'll do it again if I have the chance."

"Keno!"

"Give out."

Eccles squatted beside Boone. "I'm supposed to leave

here in two weeks. I ain't. I'm leaving here day after tomorrow. Oh, it'll be legal enough. They won't come after me."

"You sound like Pedro Loco."

Fear welled up in the dark eyes. "I'm all right. I kin work it so's you can go with me."

Boone ground out his smoke. "You interest me."

"Then shut up and listen!" Eccles came closer. "I kin get yuh outa here back into Cell Two with me. Leave it to me. Fact is, I got to leave here without anybody outside knowin' it. The best bet is the river."

A guard tramped into the entranceway, looked in on them, and then walked away again.

Eccles grinned. "You sit tight. I'll get yuh outa here with me in Cell Two. Until then, keep your big mouth shut."

"I'm dumb, *amigo*."

Boone studied the outlaw. Dobie had been right when he had said Eccles had connections. Maybe better connections than Jim had realized.

CHAPTER EIGHT

Boone was alone in the Snake Den. Bass Eccles had been returned to Cell Two.

Boone rolled the last smoke from the supply Eccles had left him. He knew the country well from the Salt clear down to the northern reaches of Sonora, but Bass Eccles didn't know that. Some of Eccles' conversation had revealed an amazing knowledge of the owlhoot trails of the territory and Sonora. Now and then he had dropped names; names Boone had recognized as men powerful in Arizona politics. The sly-eyed outlaw had a mind honed to a razor-edge, hiding it behind a shield of assumed ignorance, for the man could hardly read or write.

Eccles had been raised in and around Tombstone. His knowledge of Sonora was amazing. He spoke easily of Red Lopez, the *revoluntionario* of Fronteras, whose exploits had turned both Sonora and Arizona into a turmoil. He was an *amigo* of bloodthirsty Augustin Chacon, a pure quill *bandido* whose life Eccles had saved by springing him from the Tombstone *calabozo* The one thing that had impressed Boone was that Eccles was so damned sure of himself.

A guard opened the cell door and looked down at Boone. "Your time is up in here," he said.

It was the man named Martin, who seemed to be on friendly terms with Eccles.

"How so?" asked Boone.

Martin grinned. "You saved a man's life in here. Cap Ingalls is getting worried about the record of this place. Besides, we heard that Yates went after you and you was defending yourself in the craphouse." Martin unlocked the leg irons.

Boone rubbed his leg and got up. Martin followed him out into the sunny prison yard. "Eccles and his amigos are workin' down in the cemetery. Go down and give him a hand."

"No guard?" asked Boone in feigned surprise.

Martin glanced up at the tower over the cistern. "You ever see a man get hit with one of them slugs from that Gatling? Them .45-500 slugs hit like a mule. Ranges up to two miles. I've seen that thing fire up to twelve hundred shots a minute if it's served right."

"You win."

"We usually do," said Martin dryly.

Boone passed through the gate and walked down the slope to the cemetery. Bass Eccles was seated on a rock watching Thalus Hastings, Concho Bates and Benny Hatch working on two graves. He grinned slyly as he saw Boone. "Told yuh you'd get out, didn't I?"

"Sure did, Bass. What do I do?"

"Set. The boys will be done pretty soon."

Concho wiped the sweat from his face. "Grab this Irish banjo, Shattuck."

Boone looked at Eccles. Eccles grinned. "Keep goin' Concho," he said.

Concho thrust out his square jaw. "You ain't done a tap, Bass. He ain't gettin' outa this, too!"

"By grab, Concho," Eccles said. "Yuh talk as though

you was the hairy bear in Cell Two. Now that ain't right, is it."

Concho went back to work, fury in his dark eyes.

Bass spoke in a low voice. "Everything is set, Boone. Tomorrow night."

"I'm not too hot about it. The chances are too long."

"Listen! I told yuh I'd do it."

"I still don't know why you want me to go along."

The lean face broke into an infectious, friendly grin "How you talk! I like yuh, Boone."

Boone looked up at the prison, broiling under the hot sun. "I still can't see how you'll do it."

Eccles waved a hand. "Martin is corridor guard tonight and tomorrow night. No moon. Tomorrow night about eleven o'clock you get sick. Leave the rest up to me. Act it up, *amigo*. Mebbe appendicitis. Grip your belly and howl like a coyote."

Boone nodded.

Thalus Hastings got out of the grave they were working in. "Pedro Loco will sleep well here," he said. "Poor bastard won't be haunted anymore."

"Yuh talk like a damned sky pilot," growled Concho.

"How would you know?" asked Eccles. "Yuh never listened to one in your whole misbegotten life."

"Go to hell!"

They trudged up the slope to the gate and passed in. Boone looked back just before the guard closed the gate. The Colorado washed the sandy shores below them, yellow and swift, a treacherous flood. Bass had mentioned swimming. Surely he didn't intend to cross that murderous riot.

———

THE CELL WAS PITCH DARK. Boone lay on his back, looking up at the ceiling he could not see. It was close to eleven o'clock. He reached up his hand from the upper bunk he had occupied since Bass Eccles had come back to Cell Two. His fingers traced the deeply cut letters inscribed by Jesus Diaz half a year before. *Libertad!* Jesus had reached liberty all right.

Gentle snoring came from Benny Hatch's bunk. Thalus Hastings groaned in his sleep. A hand gripped Boone's right wrist. It was the signal.

Boone gripped his belly and groaned loudly. He groaned again and then cried in simulated pain. The cry echoed from the arched ceiling.

Thalus Hastings called out. "What is it, Boone?"

"My guts! That damned prison slop!" He yelled again.

Boots pounded in the corridor. Eccles slid from his bunk and lit a candle. Benny Hatch and Concho Bates looked up at Boone. Boone doubled up and yelled like a Comanche in the full of the moon.

Martin looked in through the double doors. "What the hell is goin' on in there?"

"Shattuck is sick," said Eccles.

Thalus Hastings pulled himself up beside Boone. "Where does it hurt?"

Boone wordlessly pointed to his lower right side.

"Appendicitis, I'll bet," Hastings said.

Martin unlocked the doors and came in. He looked at Boone. "Better get you to the infirmary."

Hastings and Eccles helped Boone down. He doubled over and gripped his gut. Martin stood aside. "You help him there, Eccles," he said.

"I hope the bastard dies!" yelled Dixie Yates from 72 'the next cell.

"Up your butt!" yelled Concho.

A lantern cast a sickly light. Eccles helped Boone through the ponderous corridor gate. Martin came up behind them. "The gate guard is in the can," he said softly. Boone walked beside Eccles toward the gate that overlooked the cemetery. They stopped near the gate. It was pitch black. Eccles gripped Boone by the arm. "You ready, Martin?" he asked.

"Shoot!"

Eccles smashed a hard blow to Martin's jaw. The guard went down as though pole-axed. Eccles took the keys, opened the gate and shoved Boone through. Eccles closed and locked the barred gate and threw the keys back into the prison yard. "Come on." He set off through the darkness like a great lean cat.

The prison was as silent as the grave. Any second Boone expected to hear the chattering roar of the deadly Gatling searching the darkness. Eccles slid down into a gully and started through the scrub trees, then stopped. "Wait here." He vanished into the darkness. He was back in a few minutes. "The boat is there, all right. Come on."

Boone followed Eccles through the brush. Eccles stepped into a small flat-bottomed skiff. "Untie it," he said, "shove off."

Eccles took the oars as Boone waded into the water, shoving the boat off. He stepped in. "Take an oar," said Eccles. They kept in the backwater, rowing steadily against the strong current, heading north.

Boone glanced at his silent companion. "How the hell did you do it?" he asked wonderingly.

"Shut up and row!"

Twenty minutes drifted past. Behind them lights sprang up on Prison Hill. "They're wise now," said Eccles. Strip off your pants."

Boone stripped off his trousers.

"Wedge them under the seat."

Boone did as he was told. Eccles looked over his shoulder. "Row for that sand spit," he said.

The skiff grounded. They got out. Eccles stripped off his clothing and shoved it under the rear seat. He threw the oars into the dark waters and then waded out with the empty skiff. He turned it over and shoved it out into the strong current. He waded back to shore. "Get some brush," he said. "We'll wipe out our tracks."

They crossed the spit, wiping out their tracks. On the north side of the spit another skiff was hidden in the brush. Eccles pulled a bundle from under the seat. "Clothes." He handed Boone a rough shirt and a pair of trousers, swiftly donning his own. "Get in."

Boone clambered into the skiff. Eccles carefully erased their tracks. He got into the skiff and shoved off. "Row," he said.

They pulled away from the dim spit, against the current, heading north as before. Boone looked at the silent man beside him. Eccles knew what he was doing.

The dawn was graying the Eastern sky when Eccles turned the skiff in toward a low island that bordered the eastern shore. "Get rocks," said Eccles. "We gotta sink this tub."

"Why? We can't make it across the desert on foot!"

Eccles' eyes were icy-cold in the graying light. "I got yuh out, didn' I? Get rocks!"

They loaded the shallow skiff until it was almost awash. Eccles waded out into the stream and sank the boat. He waded back. "Get into the brush," he said. "We got a long wait. I'll sleep for a spell. You keep watch." The outlaw curled up on the cold sands and went instantly to sleep.

————

LATE IN THE AFTERNOON, Boone saw dust on the east bank below them. Eccles was on his second shift of sleep. Boone gripped the outlaw's shoulder. Eccles opened his eyes. Boone pointed at the dust. Three horsemen appeared. "Yumas," said Bass.

The trackers rode slowly north, studying the ground. They passed the island. Boone glanced at Eccles. The man's face was white and set, almost as it had been the night Pedro Loco had almost killed him. The trackers disappeared to the north. Eccles yawned. "We're all right now," he said.

───────

BOONE WAS in a fitful sleep when Eccles shook him awake. "Listen," he said.

Deep shadows bordered the river. The sun was gone, dying behind the Picachos on the California shore. Down the river there came a thudding noise and the faint splash of water. "Steamer," said Bass. "Take off your shoes."

Boone wordlessly pulled off his prison shoes.

"Throw them far out," said Eccles as he heaved his footgear out into the shadowy waters. Boone followed suit. Lights showed down the river and they saw the dim white bulk of a stern-wheeler, forging against the yellow current with a steady *frash, frash, frash* of paddles. Eccles grinned at Boone. "I hope to God you wasn't lyin' about bein' able to swim. Help me shove this log into the rio."

They manhandled the thick timber into the water and began to swim, hooking an arm over the log. The steamer was forging slowly upstream. The rio was dark now, shadowed by the western bluffs.

Eccles looked at Boone. "We let go of the log when she's a hundred yards away. By grab, we gotta keep away from them paddles!"

The thudding of the engine and the thrash of the big paddles echoed from the dark bluffs. The packet forced itself upstream, curling the foam-flecked yellow water back from the low prow.

"Now!" said Eccles. He shoved away from the log. Eccles struggled desperately in the swift current, looked despairingly at Boone. Boone struck out, gripped the tall man across the chest and spoke swiftly, "Take it easy. Kick with your feet. Don't struggle!"

The steamer was fifty yards away, almost in line with

them. Eccles gasped and began to struggle. The overhang of the steamer's deck began to loom over them. Then it was on them. The hull banged against Boone's shoulder. He let go of Eccles. The outlaw went down and came up gasping and spluttering. Boone gripped him by the collar. The hull surged past, washing them up and down. Boone gripped a trailing line and hung on like grim death. The paddles thrashed steadily twenty feet from them. If Boone let go they would be swept under forever.

A head appeared over the low rail. A pair of arms reached past Boone and gripped the gasping Eccles by the shirt. Then Eccles was over the rail, kicking hard. One of his feet struck Boone on the head and pushed hard. Boone went under, clinging to the rope. He came up, spitting out silty water.

Eccles was on the deck. The man with him gripped Boone and pulled him up. Boone sprawled on the wet deck, gasping for air. The man jerked his head. "Come on." They followed him into a small cabin. He locked the door and turned up the light. "Right on time. Bass," he said with a grin.

Bass began to strip off his wet clothing. "Take a look around the deck, Frank."

Bass locked the door behind him. "Strip," he said. He took clothes from a pile on the bunk and threw them onto a chair near Boone.

Boone jerked his head toward the door. "Who's he?"

Cousin. Frank Moran."

Boone eyed the shivering man with admiration. "How do you do it, Bass?"

Easy. I'll tell yuh once we get off the steamer. She'll tie up for the night a couple miles north of here. We'll stay on all day tomorrow. By that time we'll be a helluva a ways upriver. We'll leave the steamer when she reaches Ehrenberg."

In dry clothing, Bass dropped on the bunk. "Frank

got the job as cook on here a month ago. Sure handy, wasn't it?"

"Bass, you're a genius!"

Bass waved a hand. "Connections."

Frank called through the door. "All clear, Bass!"

Boone let the man in. Frank took a bottle from a drawer and handed it to Bass. Bass drank deeply and handed it to Boone. "By grab, I needed that. What's the news from Yuma, Frankie?"

"They found Phil Martin with a busted jaw lyin' near the gate. Trackers started up and down the river. Some of them found an overturned skiff with prison clothes in it. They figgered yuh drownded."

"Damn near did." Bass laughed. "Busted Martin's jaw! Hawww! Some joke on him."

"Sure is," said Boone. He took a stiff hooker.

Frank took a drink. "I'll get yuh some chuck. We ain't carryin' no passengers this trip. Just army stores for Fort Mohave. No one will bother yuh in here so long as yuh keep quiet."

"Keno," said Bass.

Frank left the cabin. Eccles lay back luxuriously. "Travelin' in style," he said. "This is my speed. While them dumb bastards hack there think we drownded. Hawww!"

Boone rolled a smoke from a sack of makings on a small table and eyed Eccles. He was damned sure Eccles had tried to push him under after Eccles was safe on deck. The cold-gutted shark was as treacherous as an Apache.

Eccles fell asleep. He slept as peacefully as though he had done an honest day's work.

———

EHRENBERG WAS a cluster of yellow lights on the west bank. The river was dark as the Yavapai neared the little river port. "Half a mile, Bass," Boone said.

"Keno." Bass shoved a bottle into his coat pocket and slid a Colt six-shooter under his belt. He placed his hat on his bald head. "Dark enough to get off without bein' seen?"

"Yes."

"Bueno!"

Frank stuck his head into the cabin. "Get aft," he said. "Jump off as soon as we dock."

"You comin' along?" asked Bass.

"Hell no!" said Frank. "I'll quit when we get to Fort Mohave."

"O.K. I'll send the money to you at Prescott like we agreed."

Frank nodded. "Don't you cross me, Bass," he warned.

Bass looked surprised. "Who? Me? Why, Frank!"

"Just you have the money there."

"It'll be there. Ain't we cousins?"

"You'd double-cross your grandmother for a plug of spit-or-drown, you baldheaded bastard." Frank vanished.

Bass grinned. "Ain't he the one though?"

The steamer slowed down as it edged in. She bumped gently against the rough pilings. Bass darted from the cabin, leaped ashore and jumped behind a pile of freight. Boone crouched beside him. Bass peered over the boxes. "All clear. Leg it."

They ran into a dark alleyway and headed west through the little adobe town. At the outskirts Bass snatched a canteen hanging from a *jacal* wall and filled it at a well. They faded into the dimness of the desert night, slogging through the sand away from the Wickenburg road.

At the end of an hour Bass stopped and dropped to the ground. He took a hard biscuit from his pocket and handed it to Boone.

Boone gnawed at the biscuit. "If it ain't askin' too much," he said, "what the hell are we goin' out here?"

Bass finished his biscuit and rolled a smoke. "We've done all right so far, haven't we?"

"You sure as hell don't let a body into your plans."

The dark eyes were half-veiled. "I been gettin' by forty years thataway. You just keep your mouth shut and string along with old Bass Eccles, sonny. I ain't forgot you saved my life twice. Old Bass don't forget them things!"

They kept on trending to the southeast. It was well after midnight when Bass stopped and took a stiff slug from his bottle. He passed it to Boone. "We'd best get some sleep," he said. The lean outlaw seemed to be composed of whang leather and forged metal.

Several hours before dawn Eccles got up and shook Boone awake. They started off again, through low hills, hardly visible in the darkness. Suddenly Boone raised his head. "Smoke," he said.

Boone scanned the darkness with his eyes. There was nothing to see except the low humped hills. Eccles gripped Boone's arm. "Stay here," he said. He vanished. Boone squatted wearily. His feet were molded into one mass with his shoes and socks. Blisters had burst and pasted his socks to his raw flesh.

Eccles materialized in the night. "Come on," he said. "It's all right." He led the way between high walls of rock. Then they were in a wide cup of rock. A man was squatting by a fire, feeding mesquite branches into it. His high Mex sombrero cast a grotesque shadow on the rock wall behind him. A bedding roll lay to one side. A horse nickered as Boone and Bass approached the fire. There were three of them picketed beyond the fire.

The man at the fire turned. "Hola, Bass," he said.

"*Compañeros,*" said Bass. "*Como está?*"

"Good, my cousin," the man said in fluid Spanish. "I am here as you asked."

Boone looked into a broad, flat face, the Indian

strong in it. The eyes were flat and expressionless like those of a snake. A cartridge belt crossed the broad chest. The butt of a nickel-plated pistol showed from a carved leather holster.

Bass turned. "This my friend Boone," he said in Spanish to the Mexican. "Boone Shattuck. Boone, this is my cousin, Bartolome Huerta. One of the true grit."

Boone felt his skin crawl. This was the man Eccles was supposed to have double-crossed along with Sim Bellam and Dance Younger. Bartolome Huerta, the *ladrone* from Nacozari. "How is it with you, Bartolome?" he asked in cowpen Spanish.

"Very well, friend. There is food. There are horses and guns as you asked, Bass."

"Good!"

Huerta's face was pocked with smallpox pits. A thick scar showed on the upper lip, leaving a bare patch in his heavy mustache. He removed a pot from the embers.

"Mex strawberries and tortillas," said Bass.

"Tequila also," said Huerta over his shoulder.

Boone sat down on a rock. "How long has he been here?"

"Three days," said Huerta.

Boone looked at Bass. "Three horses. He expected someone to come with you."

"All he knew was that I wouldn't be alone."

"Who was coming with you if I hadn't come?"

"Concho Bates. Hawww!"

"Why didn't you take him instead of me?"

Bass sipped the tequila. "Yuh saved my life. Besides, I never trusted Concho like I do you, *amigo*."

I'll bet you do, thought Boone. He helped himself to tequila. "I'd still like to know how you did it."

Bass watched Bartolome ladle beans into tin plates. "Yeah. Yuh see, Boone, I got connections. High connections. They had to let me get outa Yuma before my time was up."

"How so?"

"I could have talked plenty about things that happened some years ago. The Tucson Ring. You've heard of it?"

"Some," admitted Boone.

"Well, I did some work for the boys years ago. I was on the inside in a lot of deals. Then when some of the boys got into big jobs they wanted to forget how they got started, and forget old Bass also. But old Bass didn't forget. He had a report writ out and sent copies to some of the boys. The other copy was kept hid. I told the boys that report would be turned over to the authorities unless I got help."

"I'm beginning to get it."

They began to eat, scooping the hot beans up with folds of tortilla. Bass talked steadily. "I had enemies waitin' for me to be released. Why, hell'sfire, they woulda been breathin' down my neck all the way to Willcox. Now, old Bass wants to live a good life from now on."

"On the *hacienda*?"

Huerta glanced quickly at Boone.

Bass nodded. "So I worked out this deal. I figgered I'd better make things look like I escaped. That was why I needed you, Boone. Now, with them findin' that overturned skiff and them prison clothes, they'll think we drownded. Frank got in touch with me a couple days afore we escaped. Frank placed the skiffs for us."

"You've got some handy cousins."

"Yeah. Yeah. Hawww!"

Boone placed his plate on the ground. Huerta threw him a blanket. Boone rolled up in the blanket and lay there listening to the low voices of Eccles and Huerta.

The flat crack of a gun awoke Boone. He threw aside his blanket and instinctively rolled behind a rock. Bass Eccles laughed. "You're as touchy as a virgin," he said. The outlaw stood beyond the smoking fire holding a six-gun in his hand. "I was just tryin' my hand again on my six-guns. Bartolome brought them for me."

Bass wore a buscadero belt, heavy with the weight of holsters and guns. "I'm tryin' out my old *dinero* winning stunt. Watch."

The empty tequila bottle hung from a string tied to a projecting rock, thirty feet away from Bass. He settled his gunbelt about his lean hips and then snapped his hands down for a double draw. The right hand Colt came up, steadied, and then flamed. Nothing happened. Bass slid the Colts back into their holsters. Again he went into a crouch and double draw. The righthand Colt roared. The string snapped. Before the bottle hit the ground the lefthand Colt splattered it through the morning air.

"Bueno!" said Bartolome. He suspended another bottle. Bass eyed Boone. "You want to try it?"

Boone shook his head. "I'm just average with a six-gun."

"Bass is the best," Bartolome said. "With six-gun or rifle. With the knife, he is almost as good as Bartolome Huerta."

Boone washed in a shallow *tinaja*. Letters were cut into the rock wall behind the water pan. "L. Biggins," he read, "passed here in '67. Mohaves on trail. May God help me." Higher up were the initials R.O. and the date 1858. To one side was a line of sharply incised letters in wavering Spanish. "There is nothing but death here in this accursed land. 1705."

"The ancient ones," said Bartolome quietly. "Several times I have seen such inscriptions. At Tinajas Atlas, the High Tanks, near the fearful Camino del Diablo. The Devil's Road, far to the south in Sonora."

Bass was saddling a gray. "Take the buckskin," he said to Boone.

"I'll need a gun," Boone said.

"I always carry two six-guns and a Winchester. You'll get a gun if you need it."

"You've got the Colt Frank gave you."

"So I have."

"I'll take it."

"It's got a rocking cylinder."

"I'll take it anyway."

Bass glanced at Bartolome. "All right." He took the old Colt from a saddlebag and handed it to Boone. Boone checked it. The cylinder was a little loose. It had five rounds in it.

He thrust it under his belt.

CHAPTER NINE

They had passed through the Kofa's, skirted the Mineral Springs, crossed the Southern Pacific tracks and the Gila, and had gone into camp five miles from Gila Bend. Bass lay on his blanket, looking up at the ice-chip stars. "One of us oughta go into Gila Bend and nose around," he said.

"Not me," said Bartolome. "I am known too well there."

"I ain't about to go," said Bass. "I'm goin' all the way to the San Pedro and beyond by the back trails. How about you goin' in, Boone?"

An idea struck him. "I might be spotted," he said.

"Sho! Sneak in, get some grub, and sneak out again."

"I don't like it, Bass."

"Saddle up," he said. "We'll wait here."

"To hell with it!"

Eccles sat up, cold fury on his face. "Git! You ride with me, you learn to take orders!"

"Si!" said Bartolome.

"All right," he said, "don't get on the prod."

"You'll learn," said Bass.

Boone saddled his horse. Bass threw him a money

pouch. "Bring a couple bottles," he said. "Cartridges. Coffee. Flour. Tobacco."

He rode slowly into town. The town was busy, and Boone suddenly realized it was Saturday night. Wagons and buckboards lined the main street. Boone tethered the buckskin to a rack at the edge of town and walked east along the main street. Boone wouldn't put it past Bass to trail him or send Bartolome along after him.

Boone made his purchases in a small general store and took them back to the horse. He tied the sack to the saddle and then remembered that Bass had asked for liquor. He walked to the nearest saloon. Boone stepped up on the porch and looked into the saloon. It was busy. He walked in, passed behind the men at the bar and stopped at the counter near the rear. "Two bottles of rye," he said to the barkeep.

"I see you've turned to heavy drinking," a familiar voice said.

Boone turned to look into the humorous eyes of Jim Dobie. "You do move around," he said.

"No more than you. I didn't know you had gotten this far."

"You knew we made the break?"

"Yes. One of our men wired at once. You're supposed to be drowned."

"Where can I talk to you?"

"I've got a room at the hotel. First on the right, top of the stairs."

"Keno. Go there."

Dobie left and Boone followed him. He stood for a time in the alleyway watching the street crowd and then he went up the stairs and rapped on the door. Dobie opened it and locked it behind Boone. "Well?"

Boone swiftly told him of what had happened.

"It seems as though we underestimated Brother Eccles. I quit my job in Willcox and came here, poking about for news. We didn't know Huerta was in the Territory."

"Don't make any moves until I find that damned gold."

"I won't."

"What's new in Willcox?"

"Dowling was ousted. He spends his time in the cribs, getting a big rake-off. Eli Bell was appointed marshal."

"A good man."

"Maybe. Eli looks out for himself."

"Where are Bellam and Younger?"

"Younger was at his ranch the last I knew. Bellam has vanished."

"I thought, from what you told me that Huerta was down on Eccles, but they seem to be real amigos. They're cousins."

Dobie nodded. "Huerta's mother and Eccles' mother are sisters. I found that out after you left. From Jonce Maxon."

Boone raised his head. "How is Jonce?"

Dobie grinned. "You mean Marion, don't you?"

"Well?"

"Jonce has been damned sick. Marion has been in town several times for medicine. She asked Eli Bell how you were."

Boone rubbed his jaw. "I know little more about the gold than I did when I went into Yuma."

"At least you're *compañeros* with Eccles and Huerta."

"Yeah," said Boone dryly. "I sure am."

Dobie said, "I have something of yours here." He thrust his hand into a saddlebag and brought out Boone's Sheriffs Model Colt and the bellygun.

Boone handed the single-action back to Dobie. "Keep this." He slid the bellygun into his coat pocket. "Eccles wants to keep me at a disadvantage."

"You can pull out, Boone."

Boone shook his head.

Dobie handed him his Wells Fargo badge and papers. Boone stood up. "I'd better get back," he said.

"What do you want me to do?"

Boone shrugged. "I think we're heading for the Willcox area. Beyond that I know nothing."

"I'll go back there."

"It's about all you can do."

Boone left the hotel by a back door and went to the buckskin. Bass was asleep when Boone returned. Huerta took one of the bottles and drank deeply. Boone unsaddled the buckskin and picketed him. He was about to go back to the fire when he noticed Huerta's claybank. The horse had been picketed at the edge of the hollow when Boone had left. Now he was on the far side of the depression. His saddle had been near the fire. Now it was lying beneath a mesquite bush. Boone went back to the fire and rolled a smoke. Eccles snored steadily.

Huerta lay back against his bedroll, drinking steadily, watching Boone whenever Boone looked away.

———

THE LIGHTS of a ranch showed through the moonlight a mile away. Somewhere behind Boone a coyote raised his melancholy voice. A cold wind searched through the draws, rustling the brush. Bartolome leaned on his rifle twenty feet away, looking toward the ranch. He held the reins of his horse and that of Bass Eccles. The tall outlaw had vanished into the moonlit brush.

Behind them lay the long trail from Gila Bend. They had traveled at night through the Maricopas to Johnson's Well, from there across Santa Rosa Wash, to the Santa Cruz. There Bass had left them to return a day later. From there, they had crossed the Tucson-Nogales Road, angling southeast to the San Pedro, and then through the brooding Dragoons to where they were now.

"Where has he gone?" asked Boone of the silent breed.

Huerta shrugged. *"Quién sabe?"*

"You know!"

"Perhaps. What difference does it make, *amigo*? An escaped prisoner need not know anything except that he is safe for the time being," Huerta said in Spanish.

The long night rides and the hidden camps had worked on Boone's nerves, honing them thin.

Eccles padded back through the silvery moonlight. "O.K.," he said, "let's go. We kin sleep in a bed tonight at least."

They rode down toward the ranch. As they drew near Boone could see the loop-holed adobe and stone buildings on a slight rise. Eccles dismounted behind the house. A tall, gangling man shambled out of the shadows. "Yuh kin put the horses in the barn," he said. "Best to leave them saddled. Yuh kin sleep in the 'dobe down in the hollow. We got vittles areadyin'."

Boone stared. It was Jonce Maxon.

They led the horses into the barn. Eccles slapped the dust from his rough clothing. "Lady in there," he said with a smirk.

Maxon looked at Boone. "Shattuck," he said nervously. "I didn't know you knew Eccles!" Maxon turned. "This man is wanted for robbery," he said. "You didn't tell me he escaped from Yuma with you!"

"What's the difference, Maxon?"

"He's wanted, I tell yuh!"

Eccles grinned. "So is Bartolome. So am I."

Maxon wiped his ravaged face. "How long will yuh stay here?"

"Until my business is done."

Maxon lowered his voice. "I got a rumor that there have been some Wells Fargo men pokin' about."

Eccles' lopsided grin vanished and a cold look came into his eyes. "Who are they?"

Maxon shrugged. "I don't know."

Eccles gripped the tall man by his corded throat and slammed him back against the wall. "You sure?"

"I swear to God, I don't know?"

"How'd yuh find out?"

"Eli Bell."

"How'd he find out?"

"When he took over as marshal in Willcox he found a badge in the desk. Locked in, it was. A Wells Fargo badge. Bell left it there. Coupla nights later it was gone."

"Who took it?"

"He don't know for sure. But Jim Dobie quit as jailor. He took his stuff from the *calabozo*. The badge was missing after that."

"Who's Dobie?"

"Who knows? Came in Willcox a couple months ago from New Mexico. Got the jailor's job. He was the man swore that Shattuck there didn't kill Cass Caston, only Billy Steen. It saved Shattuck from a rope, I tell yuh."

Eccles released the shaking rancher and turned slowly to look at Boone. Huerta slid around behind Boone.

"Dobie saw the whole hassle," Boone said easily. "He testified at the inquest. What's wrong with that?"

"Nothin'," said Eccles softly. "*Amigo* of yours?"

"No. Never saw him until I came to Willcox."

"That so? Yuh think he's Wells Fargo?"

"How the hell should I know?"

Eccles slid a hand down to his hand Colt. Boone turned so that he could see both Huerta and Eccles. He slowly opened his coat, revealing the old Colt in his belt.

Eccles eyed the Colt. "Where is this *hombre* Dobie now, Jonce?"

"He left Willcox three-four days ago. On the S.P. travelin' west."

"Where was he headin'?"

"I don't know."

Eccles rubbed his lean jaw. "Well, we better get some chuck. How's Marion, Jonce?"

Jonce flushed. "All right. It was on account of her Shattuck got into trouble with Steen and Caston."

Eccles cold eyes studied Boone. "So?"

Boone shrugged. "They were chousin' her. I stepped in."

"God," said Eccles shaking his head.

Boone slipped his hand into his left-hand pocket and felt the smooth butt of his hideout gun. "Just like I stepped in when Pedro Loco was whipping you all to hell, Eccles. Maybe I should've kept out of that, too."

"Damn you. You watch that lip, Shattuck."

"You watch yours, Eccles. I'm not hankerin' to ride the rio with you and listen to your yappin'. You get to hell outa my way, I'll leave."

Eccles paled. "Where do you think you're goin'?"

"Sonora maybe."

"No you ain't. You know too damned much."

Boone's voice was low and steady. "Listen, Eccles, I appreciate what you did for me. I played my part helping you in the raid. Call it quits."

"Yuh seen what I did to that bottle in the Kofas."

Boone grinned.

Maxon wet his lips. "I don't want no trouble, Bass."

The outlaw suddenly grinned. "Hell's fire, guess we're all tired out, Boone. Fergit it, will yuh?"

Maxon smiled uneasily. "Yeah. We got a bit of meat cookin' for you boys. Let's get into the house and take care of it."

"Sure," said Bass. "That's the way. Go ahead, Boone!"

"Why, after you, Bass, you're the boss!"

"All right, Boone." Eccles left the barn.

Huerta stopped beside Boone. "I did not like the way you spoke to Bass," he said thinly.

Boone eyed the Mexican. "So?"

Huerta tapped Boone on the chest with a thick hand. "Do not do it again, *hombre*."

Boone slapped down the hand and stepped in close. "Get into the house, you bastard. I've taken enough lip from Bass without having to take it from you."

Huerta jumped aside. His right hand slid beneath his coat and swept out with a thin-bladed *cuchillo*. Boone snatched a bucket from a hook and threw it at the Mexican. The bottom rim caught Huerta on the chin. He went down hard, blood splattering from his smashed chin. Boone picked up the *cuchillo* and thrust it in between two boards, snapped the blade, and threw the pieces on top of the Mexican.

The big kitchen was redolent with the odors of hot food. Eccles sat at the table. "Where's Bartolome?" he asked Boone.

"He'll be along."

Eccles studied Boone. "You feelin' all right?"

Boone grinned. "Sure. Why not?"

"You look like you swallowed the canary."

A woman entered the kitchen. Boone looked up into the eyes of Marion Maxon. She stepped back and glanced from Boone to Eccles. "Hello, Marion," said Boone.

"I thought you were in Yuma," she said quietly.

"I was."

Eccles laughed. "Boone and me left Yuma. We got tired of it."

Jonce Maxon loosened his collar. "I'll stay outside, Bass."

"Why?"

"Somebody's got to keep an eye open."

Eccles leaned back in his chair. "What's wrong with you, Jonce?"

Jonce did not answer. Marion spoke. "I'll tell you what's wrong! Three outlaws coming here. Supposing the sheriff finds out?"

Eccles' eyes went cold. "I've done Jonce many a favor. The least he can do is put us up for a time."

"We'll feed you and then you can leave."

"We'll leave when we're damned good and ready! You open your mouth about us bein' here, and your father will suffer. You can bet on that, sister."

The door opened, and Bartolome Huerta staggered in, holding his bloody chin. "What the hell happened to you?" asked Bass.

Huerta looked at Boone. Bass whirled. "You!"

Boone nodded. "You tell that cousin of yours that I don't take any lip from him. He pulled a knife on me."

Eccles stood up. "Lord! What have I got myself into?"

"Nothing," said Boone. "That Mex goes for me again and I'll kill him."

Jonce Maxon put on his hat and left the kitchen. Marion turned away as the Mexican dabbled at the blood on his chin. There was naked hate in Huerta's eyes. Now he would have to be constantly on guard against the Mexican.

Eccles leaned across the table. "Mebbe I oughta get rid of yuh!"

Boone shrugged.

"You'd like that, wouldn't yuh?"

"I'll stick," Boone said.

"Mebbe I shoulda taken Concho Bates along after all."

"It's a little late now, isn't it?"

Their eyes clashed and Eccles looked away. "Wash off that chin, Bartolome," he said. "You two *hombres* forget what happened. One more thing like this and I'll take a hand in it."

Huerta left the room and they could hear him splashing water in the bucket outside the door. Eccles grinned. "You're a fighter from who laid the chunk, Boone," he said easily. "Too bad you ain't got the brains to go with it."

"Like you."

"Yeah. *Like me.*"

They ate silently. The Mexican shoved back his plate and left the kitchen. Eccles said, "I'll get some sleep. You take the first watch, Boone." He left.

Marion began to clear the table. "They're no good," she said. "Leave at once. It's dangerous here."

"What do you mean?"

She glanced at the rear door. "Sheriff Kelly was here a few days ago. He'll be back. Get out of here while you have the chance."

"Why are you telling me this?"

She turned. "You can get into Mexico easily from here. It's less than forty miles. Please go."

"I won't as long as Eccles is here."

The hazel eyes held his. "There will be bloodshed here if you don't."

Boone stood up. "I'm staying."

"I warned you."

Boone opened the door. "You and your father can leave. Go to Willcox or Benson."

She shook her head. "He's ill. This is his home. No one will drive us from it."

Boone heard her sob as he closed the door.

CHAPTER TEN

A faint moon silvered the desert and streamed in through the narrow windows of the old adobe. Boone lay with his eyes open. He could hear the steady breathing of Bass Eccles across the room. There was no sound in Huerta's room, just beyond theirs.

Boone swung his legs and placed his feet on the cold floor. He took his old Colt and walked to the door of Huerta's room. The sagging cot was empty, the blanket lying on the littered floor. Boone padded back across his room. Something scraped the wall near the window. Boone stepped into the shadows, waiting.

An arm came through the narrow window. A head appeared. It was Huerta. The Mexican stared at Boone's empty cot. Then he looked quickly about the little room and withdrew his head. His feet pattered on the hard earth.

Bass Eccles moved. Boone whirled. "What did you expect?" Eccles asked in a low voice.

Boone sat down, away from the window. "I guess I was wrong in flattening him," he said softly.

"Damned fool Texan! Along the border here we don't boot them around like they do along the Rio Grande."

"They do a little booting themselves where I come from."

Bass stood up and walked into Huerta's room. He shut the door behind him. There was the sound of angry voices and then low talking. Feet scraped on the floor. Then the outer door banged shut. Bass came back into the room and dropped on his bunk.

"Well?" asked Boone.

"I've sent him south."

"Why?"

"I need both of you proddy *hombres*. Right now we can't afford to have trouble."

Hoofs thudded. Boone stood up and looked through the window. Huerta was riding south.

Bass lay back on his bunk. "We'll be headin' across the border before long."

Boone eased his hand down to his Colt. "Why Mexico? The Rurales ain't exactly happy to have *ladinos* like us underfoot."

"I got friends down in Sonora. In Durango, too. We'll be all right."

"Yeah. Without *dinero*. I don't like it here, Bass. Why are we hanging around?"

Bass spoke slowly. "We don't have to worry about *dinero*. I can get all we'll need. Trouble is, I can't get it alone. I need help. You're elected."

Boone eyed the shadowy figure. "Where is it?"

"One thing you got to get through that thick head of yours. You're too proddy. You act like you got a bug up your butt. Now you either take orders, or you can fork your hoss and dust up the road. But you won't get far. Every county law officer is on the lookout for yuh."

"We drowned. Remember?"

"Yeah. But I'm not sure they swallowed that. Mebbe somebody will talk. You either stick with old Bass or you'll be back in Yuma and this time they'll make damned sure you don't break out. You'll spend your time in the

Snake Den and end up like Pedro Loco. Now get some sleep. Tomorrow we got work to do."

Boone lay down, but he kept his hand on his six-gun until he was sure Eccles was asleep again.

———

BASS ECCLES SHOOK BOONE AWAKE. "Get up," he said, "Jonce is gone." The gray light of the false dawn showed in the sky. Eccles' face was dark with fury. "Mebbe he went into Willcox. I ain't takin' no chances."

"He hasn't got the guts."

Eccles shrugged. "Mebbe Fact is, Jonce useta be quite a man. Muy *hombre*. Afore he got to gettin' his courage from a whiskey bottle."

Boone pulled on his boots. "So what do we do?"

"Get some jamoke. You tail him towards Willcox. One of the vaqueros saw him headin' that way."

Boone slid his Colt beneath his belt. "What about you?"

"I'll stay here. You keep an eye on him if you find him."

"I'm not about to go into Willcox."

"Yuh don't have to!"

Boone went into the barn and saddled his horse. He went to the house. Marion was in the kitchen serving two vaqueros. They eyed Boone and then left after they finished eating. Boone filled a cup with coffee. "Where's your father?"

"Gone."

"Where?"

She eyed him coldly. "Does he have to leave an account of his whereabouts with you?"

"No! But Bass doesn't like it."

Her face was flushed. "Why don't you leave? There will be nothing but trouble with Bass around here. Why don't you leave?"

Boone sipped his coffee. "We've got business."

"What kind of business? My father is worried sick. Years ago he would have run Bass into the desert. He was more of a man than you and Bass put together. It's a terrible thing to see the fear in him."

"He'll be all right," Boone spoke in a low voice. "Please tell me where he has gone. Believe me, nothing will happen to him."

"I can't understand you."

He gripped Her arm. "Look. I butted into trouble in Willcox helping you. I want no thanks. But you must trust me a little."

The hazel eyes held Boone's. "All right. He's gone to Willcox. He left forty-five minutes ago."

The door banged open and Eccles came in. "Get movin', Boone," he said. He sat down at the table. "Get me some chuck, Marion."

Boone saddled his horse and rode out. A mile from the ranch he cut east and followed the base of a ridge where he could see the road. There was no dust on the winding road.

The sun came up. The buckskin plodded steadily along. Then Boone saw the buckboard standing near a wash. There was no one near it. He swung down and ground-reined two hundred yards from the buckboard. Then Boone heard the sound of digging. He walked softly to the edge of the wash. Jonce Maxon was digging steadily below. As Boone watched he saw Jonce reach into the hole and drag out a sack. With shaking hands he pulled out a bottle and uncorked it. The rancher drank deeply and then sat down on the bank of the wash.

"Jonce!"

The rancher whirled and dropped the bottle as he saw Boone. "What the hell are you goin' out here?"

"Taking a ride."

"You're a damned liar!"

Boone walked to the rancher and sat down beside

him. Maxon picked up the bottle and took a deep slug. "Marion don't let me keep the stuff in the house no more," he said.

"You take any more of that stuff and you'll have a one-way ride to Boot Hill."

Maxon wiped his shaking hands on his pants. "I need it."

"Why? Your ranch is going to pot. Marion is disgusted with you. Bass Eccles has you scared to death. Why?"

"I ain't afraid of him." Maxon could feel the liquor working in him. "I'll run him off when I get back."

"You'll get a slug in your back."

"Seems as though you know that bastard pretty well. That's *his* way all right. A slug in the back."

Boone rolled a smoke.

"Give me a quirly," said Jonce.

Boone handed him the cigarette and lit it for him.

"What's he got on you, Maxon?"

"What's it to you?" Jonce eyed Boone. "I don't figger you, Shattuck. You seemed like a right nice fella when you helped Marion. By God, I never seen such shootin' when you downed Steen."

"Yeah, you saw the shooting all right. You sure as hell didn't testify that way at the trial."

Maxon flushed. "Yuh got away with it, didn't yuh?"

Boone nodded. "No thanks to you, Maxon."

"I don't want trouble. God knows I've had enough of it. Dowling ain't one to fool with. He was out after yuh. He's sore enough at Marion for what she said. He finds out that Bass Eccles and you are at my place there'll be hell to pay. Dowling ain't yella like Eccles."

Boone rolled a smoke. "I didn't know Eccles was yellow."

"He's as treacherous as an Apache! Him and that Huerta are a pair. Appears to me yuh don't want to live long, Shattuck."

"He got me out of Yuma."

"Yeah. For his own ends, he did. Shattuck, if yuh had any sense, you'd pull leather right now and never stop until yuh was out of Arizona!"

Boone grinned. "Not while Eccles has *dinero* coming."

The bloodshot eyes studied Boone. "Yuh know about that?"

"Sure."

"Blood money."

"Forty thousand is a lot of blood money."

"I want no part of it. Not that Eccles would part with any of it."

"Then why are you helping him?" Boone gripped the man's thin wrist. "Why?"

Maxon looked up. "Some years ago me and Bass was deputies here in Cochise County. We got full of red-eye. Leastways *I* did. We were assigned as guards on a bullion shipment from Tombstone to Benson. Some miles outa Tombstone the wagon was held up. I was too damned drunk to know what was goin' on. When I comes to I see the wagon standin' in the road. The driver was dead. The bullion was gone, six thousand dollars' worth. Bass was gone, too. Out in the brush was a Mex, dead with a hole in the back of his head. I go back to Tombstone. Eccles shows up, claimin' he was disarmed. He claimed three men held up the waggin and he followed them clear down to the border and then lost them. I lost my job. So did Eccles. I tried to clear myself but it was no use."

Maxon drank deeply. "The dead Mex was Jorge Huerta. Brother to Bartolome Huerta. Eccles told me I shot him. I was scared to death of Huerta. He's Mean as hell. Eccles said he wouldn't say anything to Bartolome. He's held it over my head ever since."

"You mean that you don't know whether or not you killed Jorge?"

Maxon held up the bottle. "John Barleycorn entered

my mouth, as the preachers say, and stole my senses. You know, Shattuck, *I don't know whether I killed Jorge or not!*

"What do you think?"

"I was drunker'n a hoot owl. There was some shooting and then I passed out. Lost a good job. Lost all my friends. My wife never was the same until she died. Marion never forgave me, but she did stick with me. She's a good girl, Boone."

"Too damned good for you."

Maxon drank again. "I wasn't headin' for Willcox. I don't want Eccles to be on my back."

Boone shoved back his hat. "What about the express robbery?"

Maxon shrugged. "Bellam, Younger, and Huerta don't have the brains to pull a job like that. Eccles and Dowling planned it. Eccles alibied for them. Dowling swore they was at Eccles' 'dobe all day. Trouble is, Eccles crossed Dowling. That I know. More'n once Dowling has worked me over tryin' to find where the loot was hidden."

"You know?"

The red eyes steadied on Boone. "I think so."

"Where?"

Maxon stood up. "I'd better get back to the ranch."

Boone shook his head. "Take a ride. Go to Dos Cabezas."

"Why?"

"Do as I say, Maxon, or by God, I'll work you over!"

"All right. All right. I've had enough trouble. Maybe he'll be gone when I get back." The rancher filled the earth in on his liquor cache and took his bottle to the buckboard. He got in, slapped the reins on the rumps of his mules and drove slowly north on the dusty road.

Boone walked back to the buckskin and followed the foot of the ridge. He was almost to Dos Cabezas before he turned off. Maxon had done as had been told.

Boone picketed the buckskin in a small canyon and slept. Then he rode close toward Willcox until he reached Eccles' old adobe. The place was just as it had been when he had first seen it. He found a brushy spot two hundred yards from the adobe and dropped to the warm earth watching it. Hours drifted by.

Boone was dozing when he heard the beat of hoofs to the east. A big man rode a gray horse up, took a spade from the saddle and led the gray to the adobe. It was big Eli Bell. The marshal went into the adobe.

The sun was far down when Bell came out wiping his face and returned to the gray. Then he was gone.

Boone waited twenty minutes and then padded toward the adobe. There was a deep hole just behind the battered stove. Boone rolled a quirly and sat down in a rickety chair. Bell was like everyone else in the Willcox area, determined that the loot was hidden in the adobe.

It was dark when Boone left the adobe and walked toward Willcox.

CHAPTER ELEVEN

The ragged tinkling of a piano came to Boone on the night breeze. He walked down a dark alley-way, past the hurdy-gurdy houses. They were brightly lit and he could hear women's voices mingling with the hoarse voices of drunken men. It looked like a big night in Willcox.

Boone entered a sagging shed near the hotel and watched the wide street. He could see the lights of Lily Bell's beanery. A broad-shouldered man left the eating place and paused to light a cigar. The flare of the match revealed the broad face of Jim Dobie. The agent leaned against a post watching the street traffic. Boone left the shed and skirted the rear of the buildings and crossed the dimly lit street behind Dobie. "Jim," he called softly.

The agent whirled, dropping his hand to his Colt.

"It's Boone."

"Get off the street!"

"Where can I see you?"

"There's an empty 'dobe at the west end of town. Go there."

Boone faded into the darkness and found the adobe. In fifteen minutes Jim stepped into the darkness. "What's up?"

"Eccles is out at Maxon's. Huerta was there and Eccles sent him down to Sonora. I don't know why."

"How'd you get away?"

"Maxon left the ranch this morning. Eccles told me to follow him. Maxon is on a drunk in Dos Cabezas. I came here. I stopped by Eccles' adobe. Eli Bell was digging out there late this afternoon."

Dobie spat. "Most of the people of Willcox have been doing that ever since the holdup. You get a line on the express money?"

"No. What's been happening here?"

"Dowling has been drinking a lot ever since he heard Eccles got out of Yuma. Mean as hell. We've got to get this thing moving, Boone! I got a message from Mason. He wants action."

"He'll just have to wait."

"Supposing I go back to Maxon's with you and we run Eccles in?"

"We can't jump the gun now, Jim!"

"We're just not getting anywhere. I'd like to corral the whole bunch and beat the truth out of them."

"Take it easy. Can you get me a pair of boots and a gunbelt?"

"Sure. What size boots?"

"Ten."

"Same size as mine. I've got an old pair in my room. Your gunbelt is there, too. Stay here." Dobie left the building and vanished.

Boone rolled a smoke and sat down. Now and then he could hear the faint notes of the piano down the street.

Dobie returned and handed Boone a pair of mule-ear boots. Boone pulled on the old boots. "Pretty worn," he said.

"Best I could do."

He handed Boone his gunbelt. Boone swung it about his waist. He took the six-gun from Dobie and slid it into the holster. "Give me some cartridges." Dobie handed him a box of forty-fours. Boone filled his belt loops.

Dobie peered out the window. "Dowling saw me come out of the hotel. You'd better raise some dust out of here."

"If we move I'll get a message to you somehow but stay away from the Maxon place."

"All right." The agent left the adobe.

Boone was at the corner when he heard feet grate on the hard earth. A big white hat showed through the darkness. Boone stepped into a doorway. His back bumped the door. "*Quién es?*" someone called loudly from within the house. Boone cursed under his breath. The man in the street was Bob Dowling.

"*Quién es?*" The door was pulled open, flooding Boone with lamp light. He darted around the corner and pounded up the alleyway. Dowling yelled. Then the quiet was shattered by the roar of a gun. Boone threw himself over a fence and ran across a stable yard. He ducked into the stable as Dowling came to a halt behind the fence.

"Spread out!" yelled Dowling. "I seen Boone Shattuck!"

Boone eased open the front door of the stable and ran across the street just as two men rounded a corner. "There he goes! Hey, Dowling!"

Boone raced past one of the hurdy-gurdy houses, jumped into a doorway. He heard Dobie's voice. "He's headin' east!" The Wells Fargo man was trying to lead Boone's pursuers off the track.

Boone flattened himself against the door. It gave a little. Boone eased open the door and stepped into a dim hallway. He could hear the excited voices of women at the front of the house.

"He musta gone in one of these places," said Dowling from the alley.

Boone reached for the handle of the nearest door and

pushed it open. A slim girl whirled. It was Nelly, the girl he had saved from Bob Dowling. "What the hell!"

"Shut up," said Boone. He closed the door. "They're after me."

"Who?"

"Dowling and some others."

"I heard you broke outa Yuma."

"Can I hide here?"

She pulled back a calico curtain. "In there."

Boone stepped into the closet, in among dresses heavy with the odors of cheap perfume. Nelly dropped the hanging. "What'd you do this time?" she asked.

"Nothing. I came into town to get something."

"You damned fool!"

Boots thudded in the hallway. The door banged open. "Yuh see a man come by here, Nelly?" It was Dowling.

"I don't let *any* man come by here, Bob."

"Don't get funny!"

"I'm not. I haven't seen anyone."

Boone peered between the hangings. Men were calling to each other out in the alley and in front of the hurdy-gurdy house.

Dowling waved his six-shooter. "It was that bastard Shattuck. I'm sure."

"Then keep lookin'," she said.

Dowling looked about the shabby room. "Tell me if yuh see him." He closed the door behind him.

Nelly turned. "Wait until they move on."

She came to the hangings.

"Dowling been giving you a hard time?"

She touched a pale bruise on her face. "Yes. Someday I'll fix him."

Boone could hear the men talking as they moved away. He stepped out into the room. "I'll be on my way."

She gripped his arm. "You can stay. I'll lock the door. Won't nobody come in. They'll think I got a customer in here."

He grinned. "With those bloodhounds looking for me? No thanks."

She flushed. "Take me with you."

"On the run? Hell no! I've got to make the border."

"You got money?"

"Enough."

She came close. "Look. I got two hundred hidden. I can ride. Take me with you."

He cupped her chin in his left hand and kissed her. "No. They'll try to hunt me down."

"You could send for me."

"Maybe."

"Will you?"

He had to get out of there.

She spoke swiftly. "You send a message to Lily Bell and let me know where you are. I'll come."

"All right. All right."

She gripped him. "You will, won't you?"

"Yes! Yes!"

She opened the door and looked up and down the hallway. "Go ahead. It's clear."

Boone passed her. She touched his face. "You won't forget me, Boone?"

"No." Boone walked to the rear door, eased it open, and stepped into the filthy alley. Something bulked in the shadows across the alley. Boone started to run. Dowling jumped out and swung a length of wood at Boone. It struck him on the left shoulder. He gasped in pain and raised his Colt. The board hit him across the head and he went down on his knees, grunting in pain.

"You bastard," Dowling said. "I knowed you was in there."

Dowling's foot came up. The spur slashed Boone's forehead. Blood dripped into his eyes, half-blinding him.

The door opened. Nelly screamed as she saw Boone's bloody face in the moonlight. Dowling cursed. "Get in there, you fool!" he yelled. "I'll settle you later!"

Her right hand came up, spit flame and smoke. Dowling gripped his belly. The board clattered to the ground. The double-barreled derringer spat again. Dowling went down as the second slug smashed into him. Nelly threw the gun at the fallen man. "I did it for you!" she screamed at Boone.

Boone got up and picked up his Colt. A big man rounded the corner. It was Eli Bell, Colt in hand. "What the hell is this?" he yelled. He saw Boone. "You!"

Boone ran down the alley. Bell fired as Boone turned the corner. A horse was tied to a rack at the front of the house. Boone ripped the reins loose.

"Stop!" yelled Bell.

Boone swung up. He fired twice over Bell's head and lashed the excited horse. A gun spat behind him and the slug sang thinly over his head. Then he was on the open road, riding out.

A mile from town Boone slid from the horse and slapped him on the rump. The horse hammered west on the road. Two hundred yards from the road, Boone heard the pounding of hoofs. Four men raced past, pursuing the riderless horse.

Boone sheathed the Colt and wiped the blood from his face with his bandanna. As he slogged on to where he had hidden the buckskin he thought of the screaming girl in the filthy alley with the smoking gun in her hand.

There was a sickness in Boone as he reached the buckskin.

CHAPTER TWELVE

Boone drew rein just outside of Dos Cabezas. The moon tinted the buildings a soft silver. A dog howled somewhere at the far end of town. Boone led the tired buckskin up the one street. A buckboard was outside the only saloon. Boone dropped the buckskin's reins and stepped up on the sidewalk beneath the shaggy ramada.

The bartender was mopping behind the zinc-topped bar. One man stood at the bar. Another man sprawled across a table, his thin face in the liquor slops. It was Jonce Maxon, on a high lonesome.

Boone walked in. The bartender turned. "Rye," said Boone. He gripped the bottle that was slid toward him and filled his glass. Boone looked at Jonce. "Well, hell's fire! It's Old Jonce Maxon!"

The barkeep nodded sourly. "Drunk as a coot. Owes me for half a dozen rounds."

Boone downed his drink. He walked to Maxon and pulled him from the chair. "Come on, Jonce," he said. "I'm heading your way. I'll take you home."

Jonce opened bleary eyes. His sour breath made Boone turn away. "I gotta have another drink."

"You've got a skinful."

"One more."

The bartender spat. "He's like a gelding seeing a mare; it's all in his head."

Jonce staggered toward the bar. Boone gripped the soiled shirt. "Forget it, Jonce. Let's go home."

Jonce turned slowly. "I'm stayin' until the last dog is hung," He announced.

The man at the end of the bar turned and eyed Boone. "Looks like they didn't hang *one* dog anyways."

Boone turned away. The man knew him from somewhere. "Come on, Jonce," said Boone. The rancher whirled and drove a fist at Boone. It knocked off Boone's battered hat. The man at the bar eyed Boone and turned pale. Boone swung from the hip. The rancher went down like a falling pine. Boone slapped on his hat and carried the lean man to the door.

"He's got a tab here!" yelled the barkeep.

Boone dumped Jonce into the back of the buckboard. He walked back into the bar.

"It's him, I tell yuh!" the man at the bar was saying. "The man who killed Billy Steen. I..."

"What does he owe?" asked Boone quietly.

"Ten drinks."

"You said half a dozen before."

"All right. All right."

"I'm broke," said Boone. He reached for the old Colt in his belt.

The barkeep reached under the bar. "I got a scattergun here," he warned.

Boone grinned. "This Colt is old but it's worth half a dozen drinks. O.K.?"

"Yeah," said the barkeep sourly.

Boone placed it on the bar and walked out. "It's him," the man insisted. "Yuh better get holt of Sheriff Kelly."

Boone tied the buckskin's reins to the buckboard and climbed in. He slapped the reins down and drove swiftly out of the little town.

Jonce groaned. "Who hit me?"

"You fell."

"Christ! I *must* be drunk."

"You are, Brother Maxon, you sure as hell are."

The ranch house was dark when Boone drove the buckboard through the gate. He stopped in front of the house and helped Jonce to the ground. Boone unhitched the mules and turned them into the corral. The lights were on now in the old adobe. Boone unsaddled his horse and walked down into the hollow. He could hear voices as he neared the house. Two horses stood hipshot at the rear of the house. Boone sidled up to a window and looked in.

Bass Eccles sat at the far side of the table. Two men sat at opposite ends. One was thin of face, with a Mexican dandy mustache. His black hat was shoved back from his black curly hair. The other man was short and squat with a battered Mex sombrero pulled low over his stupid face, and the *barbiquejo* drawn taut under his fat jowls. He looked stolidly from the dark man to Bass Eccles and then back again.

"Like I said, boys. I had to leave Yuma in a hurry, so there wasn't much time to let you know where I was," Bass said.

The dark man spoke. "We knew Huerta was heading west, Bass. Sim here gets the idea Bartolome was going to meet you. Looks like he was right for once."

"I ain't that stupid," said Sim.

Eccles' dark eyes saw Boone. An almost infinitesimal look of relief crossed the crafty face of the outlaw. "Now, Dance," said Bass to the dark man. "You knowed I wasn't pullin' anythin' on yuh."

"Just listen to him!" Younger said. "Sweet as honey, ain't he?"

Sim leaned toward Bass. "We want our sugar, Bass. Yuh know damned well I can't show my face around here. I need *dinero*. Pronto!"

"You'll get your share."

"We want ten thousand apiece," said Younger.

Bass downed his drink. "Why, hell's fire, old Bass will give it to yuh."

"When will Huerta be back?" asked Sim.

Bass grinned. "I know what you're thinkin', Sim."

Sim wet thick lips. "Why split with the Mex? We can take his share and split three ways from the ace."

"I swear to God you two *hombres* is crooks."

"Listen to him," jeered Younger. He slapped a gloved hand down on the table. "Give out, Bass. Where's the sugar?"

"I'll get it."

"Get it now," said Sim. He drew his Colt and laid it on the table. His little eyes never left Eccles' face.

"All right. All right. I swear to God you fellas think I'm tryin' to do you outa it."

"*Well?*" asked Younger.

Sim nodded. "Gawd but we was taken in, Dance. This two-faced skunk gets the loot in his hands, gives us a few coins and then rushes us into Willcox. For an alibi, he says. We all get likkered up and never did see the rest of the loot."

Bass shook his head. "Yeah. If you had taken your share where would yuh be now? Six feet under with your tacks drove in tight. Younger here goes into Benson and flashes mint coins on a high lonesome. It's a wonder they didn't string him up."

Dance stood up. "All right. So I was likkered up! You got the *dinero*. Get it! Now!"

Bass waved a hand. "I'll get it. Alone."

"You will like hell," said Sim.

Bass grinned lopsidedly. "I should show you where my share is? I ain't that simple."

Dance looked at Sim. "Let him go. He won't get far."

"I don't like it."

Dance grinned. "Leave them cutters here, Bass."

"Sure. Sure." Bass drew the Colts and placed them on the table.

Dance took out a hunting case watch and snapped the lid open. "Ten minutes. No more. You don't come back, and we come lookin' for you."

"Fair enough." Bass grinned and left the house. He motioned to Boone. "Stay near the door," he whispered.

"What's your game?"

"Watch and follow my hand."

Boone nodded. He watched Bass walk past the barn. He wanted to follow him, but he could hear the soft jingle of spurs in the house and low talking.

Bass rounded the corner of the house carrying a ticking sack and went into the house. He left the door ajar. Boone eyed the three outlaws through the opening. Bass raised the heavy sack. "Here yuh are, boys."

"There ain't no twenty thousand in there," said Dance.

"I didn't say there was. I'll get the rest after you look at this."

Bass reached into his vest pocket and threw a handful of gold pieces on the table. They scattered and Sim dropped to his knees to pick up those that had rolled from the table, but Dance's eyes never left Bass. "Let's see the rest," he said.

"Sure." Bass thrust a hand into the sack. He withdrew it swiftly, gripping a double-barreled derringer. It spat fire. Dance whirled away, cursing as he drew his Colt. Bass jumped back toward the door. Sim stood up.

Boone jerked the door open with his left hand. Dance turned and fired. The slug rapped into the thick adobe. Boone fired twice from the hip. Dance fell heavily. Boone jumped into the room and swung the Colt hard. It struck Bellam alongside the skull. He fell over his *amigo*.

Eccles was crouched in the corner, eyes wide and full of fear. "It's all over, Bass," said Boone.

Bass nodded. He stood up and placed the ticking bag on the table. "Thought they had me," he blustered.

Bass picked up Sim's Colt and aimed it at Bellam. Boone gripped Bass' wrist. "Enough," he said.

There was cold fury in Eccles' eyes. "Yuh just killed Younger, didn't yuh?"

"He had a gun. He was on his feet. It was him or me. This is different."

Boone took a length of rope and bound Bellam.

He dragged the heavy man into the next room. "We'd better get rid of Younger," he said quietly.

Bass picked up the bottle and drank deeply, handed it to Boone. "There's ten thousand of the haul," he said.

"Where's the rest?"

Bass grinned.

"What's my split?"

"We'll talk about it later." Bass slid his Colts into their sheaths. "Thought yuh once said yuh was just average with a six-gun."

"I had the edge," said Boone. "He didn't expect me."

"That ain't the gun I gave yuh at the Kofas."

Boone shook his head. "I got this in Willcox along with the gunbelt and boots."

"Yuh loco fool! I told yuh to stay outa town."

"I trailed Maxon near there and lost him. I sneaked into town to look around. Found a drunk lying in an alley and took his gunbelt and gun along with his boots."

"Did yuh find Maxon?"

"He wasn't there. I found him in Dos Cabezas on a high lonesome and brought him back."

"Anyone see you?"

"There was a shooting in Willcox. Bob Dowling saw me. In the shooting, he was killed. I didn't do it."

Eccles paled. "Then they'll be after you. Why'd yuh come here?"

Boone grinned. "For my share. I've gone through a lot of hell with you, Bass. I'm not pulling out now."

Eccles wet his lips. "Then we'll have to pull leather. Let's get rid of Younger."

Boone got a spade from the barn. They dragged Younger out into the desert and buried him swiftly in the loose soil. When Eccles had turned away Boone took Younger's wallet from his coat pocket and slid it into his own. Score one for Perry Thorne.

A shadow moved next to the adobe as they approached it. "See who it is," Bass said tensely.

The shadow moved. Marion Maxon came toward him. "The shooting," she said. "What was it?"

Boone took her by the arm. "Two men. Dance Younger and Sim Bellam. Dance was killed. Bellam is in there."

She looked up at him. "I thought it was you."

"Would it matter?"

"Yes."

Boone glanced back at Eccles. "I think he wants to pull out," he said softly. "How's your father?"

"Dead to the world. I don't know how he got back."

"I brought him from Dos Cabezas."

Eccles came up to them. "Tell your father to get ready to leave," he said.

"He's staying here!"

"The hell he is. Neither are you. Get ready to move."

Boone turned. "Why?"

Eccles looked like a hungry lobo in the moonlight. "I ain't leavin' anyone behind as can talk."

"Where are we going?"

"Sonora. Pronto!"

Boone shook his head. "Leave them alone. They won't talk."

Bass rested his hands on his Colts. "We can leave them at the border. Fair enough?"

"All right," said Boone.

"Get our horses ready. Get rid of Younger's saddle and turn the hoss loose. We'll take Bellam along."

Bass went into the house.

Boone gripped Marion by the shoulders. "Listen," he said. "I'm a Wells Fargo agent assigned to the express robbery case. I've got to play along with Bass for a time."

"You lie!"

Boone took out his papers and his badge. "See for yourself."

She glanced at his credentials. "How do I know this is true?"

"You've heard of Perry Thorne?"

"The man who was murdered in the express car? Yes."

"He was my brother-in-law and my best friend. My sister died of a broken heart. They say it can't be done but it happened to her. Now do you believe me?" His face was harsh in the moonlight.

Suddenly she placed her arms about his neck. Boone kissed her. She clung to him. He kissed her again.

"Make black coffee. Sober Jonce up as quickly as you can. Do you have a gun?"

"Yes."

"Bring it with you."

Boone swiftly saddled the horses and led them outside. Eccles came over carrying three ticking sacks.

Boone went to the adobe and picked up his few articles. He picked up Eccles' Winchester and took it to the outlaw. They went into the ranch house. Jonce was seated at the table in his red undershirt swilling coffee from a granite cup. Marion was dressed in a split skirt and a fringed leather jacket. Eccles filled a sack with food and took it to the horses. Boone helped Jonce into shirt and coat. The rancher seemed to be in a daze. Boone helped him from the house.

"Where's Bellam?" asked Boone.

Eccles tightened his cinch. "He won't be along," he said.

"You can't leave him tied up like that," said Boone.

Eccles grinned. "He won't mind."

Boone walked swiftly to the house. He stopped in the doorway of the second room. Sim Bellam lay on the floor. The heft of a knife protruded from his back. Boone closed the door and walked outside. Eccles had mounted and was holding the reins of Bellam's horse.

"You cold-gutted shark!"

"Get on your hoss," Eccles said. "He woulda done the same to me. *Vámonos!*"

They rode south on the rutted road. Boone looked back at the deserted ranch buildings. Sim Bellam was dead from none of his doing. Score two for Perry Thorne. But the way of his death sickened Boone.

There were two left. The worst. Bass Eccles and Bartolome Huerta.

CHAPTER THIRTEEN

The moon was low down in the west when Bass Eccles drew rein and looked back. He stood up in his stirrups. Boone kneed the buckskin over to the outlaw. "What's wrong?"

Eccles shrugged. "Nothin' just had a feelin'."

"What kind of feeling?"

"Like we was bein' followed."

Boone looked north. Far behind them was a naked ridge. A lone horseman topped the ridge and rode slowly down into a hollow. Boone rolled a smoke. "So?"

Eccles scowled. "I don't trust no one."

"I figured that," said Boone dryly. He glanced at Bellam's horse, heavy laden with the ticking sacks. There was a chance he could drive off the packhorse. But Jonce Maxon was in bad shape, sagging in his saddle.

"Get offa the road," Eccles said. "Follow that wash up ahead to the east. I'll come along."

Boone rode up to Marion. "Off the road," he said.

He took Maxon's reins and led his horse into the wash. A quarter of a mile from the road he drew rein. An adobe perched on the lip of the wash with a faint road trending north and south from it.

Maxon shivered. Boone looked at the girl. "Take him

into that adobe. If we have time we can make coffee. Wrap him in a blanket."

"Where are you going?"

"Back to the road."

She looked toward the road. "Be careful, Boone."

"I'm safe enough."

"While you were riding behind us he asked me if I had ever been in Mexico. He told me how beautiful it was."

"So?"

"Before he went to prison he asked me to marry him. I refused. He told me he was rich and that he'd take care of my father."

Boone laughed. *"Him?"*

"Maybe Dad and I could ride off now."

"Your father wouldn't get far."

"We can try."

"No. Stick it out. I'm working for a slowdown. This may be it."

She took Jonce into the abandoned adobe.

Boone slid from his horse and climbed the bank and circled away from the wash. He came out on the road a hundred yards from where he had left Bass Eccles. The outlaw was out of sight. A horse nickered from the brush.

The packhorse was tethered to a mesquite bush. Eccles was gone as though he had vanished from the earth. Boone drew out his knife and cut into one of the ticking sacks. He thrust his hand into the bag and touched stones. Swiftly he cut into the other two sacks. Stones.

Something grated behind Boone. He whirled. A gun flashed from the brush. The slug whipped along the side of Boone's skull. The earth and sky whirled as he went down. The gun flashed again. The slug picked at Boone's jacket. He rolled over and over into a hollow. Boots thudded against the hard earth.

Boone painfully drew his hideout gun. A shadow

formed in the brush. He fired twice. He heard Eccles curse. Boone crawled deep into the brush, ripping the cloth and skin from his knees. He was sure he was going under. Eccles crashed through the brush, fired twice. Boone jerked as a bullet slashed across his left bicep. Blood ran down his arm and dripped from his fingertips as he crawled into a low overhanging bank, pressing himself as far into it as he could.

There was no sound other than the wind. Then something grated not ten feet from Boone. A tall shadow fell on the earth. Eccles passed by not ten feet away with cocked Colts in both hands. He stopped and looked about and then his face changed into an expression of deep-seated fear. He scuttled through the brush and ran off.

Boone closed his eyes. It was as though a powerful drug had been pumped into his system. Lethargy took over and then he knew no more.

———

The sun was warm on Boone's face as he opened his eyes. A sharp twinge of pain shot through his skull. His throat felt as though a dry hand was constricting it.

Boone rolled out onto the ground and winced as his wounded arm hit the hard earth. His left hand was caked with blood. He touched the side of his head. It had been a damned near thing.

Boone sat up and bowed his head in pain. Then he got to his feet, staggering a little as he tried to get his bearings. The sun was well up. He walked up to the lip of the hollow. He could see the adobe to the east. Slowly he approached the building. He walked to the doorway and pushed aside the sagging door. The big room he looked into was empty of life.

Boone walked in and leaned against the wall. A terrible thirst gripped him. Boone walked out the back door and looked down into the wash. The floor of the wash was trampled with the marks of many hoofs. The trail led up the bank of the wash and off into the thick brush.

He rolled a smoke and lay on the floor smoking slowly until he felt better.

Eccles had turned on him like the lobo he was. But who had been the lone horseman on the road behind them? Then it came to Boone. Bartolome Huerta, possibly. Eccles had fixed Boone's clock. Then the thought of Marion in Eccles' hands hit Boone like a blow. He forgot about the gold and Perry Thorne. He stood up and put on his hat and then slogged toward the road under the beating sun.

It was late afternoon when Boone saw the adobe set back from the road. A bearded man came out of the building and looked curiously at him as he staggered toward the adobe. He raised a rifle. "What do you want?" he asked.

Boone raised his hands. "I've been shot," he said.

The man came forward. "God," he said. "You look like a haunt."

"I was held up," he said.

"Come on into the house."

Boone followed the man into the house and sat down in a chair. The man eyed him. "I'm Warren Byles," he said. "Prospector. Let me take a look at them wounds."

Boone closed his eyes as Byles removed the bandages. "Clean," he said. "When did this happen?"

"Last night about five miles from here."

"So? Who did it?"

"Bandit."

Warren got a pan and bathed the wounds and then treated them. He bandaged them neatly. "Useta be a medical orderly at Fort Bowie," he said. "Do a good job if I say so myself."

"Thanks."

"I'll get some chuck. Start you with coffee."

Boone sipped the hot liquid. Warren busied himself at the fireplace. "Got some sonofagun stew left over from last night. Fair enough?"

"Anything will do, Byles."

The prospector set out the food and watched Boone eat. "Funny thing last night," he said. "Four people come by, riding like hell. Couldn't sleep. I heard the horses coming and walked outside. One of them bastards took a shot at me."

"What'd they look like?"

"One was a young woman. Real tall, *hombre*. Shorter man looked like a Mex. Another man, hanging onto his saddle horn. They had a packhorse with them carrying some sacks."

Boone stopped eating. "Sacks?"

"Yeah. Ticking sacks. The tall mean-looking bastard was the one that shot at me. I wonder why?"

"Guess they didn't want you to get a good look at them."

"Funny thing. I was sure I knew the *hombre* that shot at me."

"Bass Eccles."

Byles paled. "My God! That was him all right!"

"You know him?"

"Hell yes!" Byles smashed a fist into his palm. "I knew him in Tombstone. I was working for Wells Fargo then, as bullion guard. I never trusted him when he rode along even if he was deputy sheriff."

Boone eyed the bearded man. "Wells Fargo?"

"Yeah. Damned good job."

Boone slid a hand into his pocket and took out his credentials. Byles' eyes widened as he saw the badge. "By God! You after Eccles?"

Boone nodded.

Byles got a bottle from a cupboard. "I thought Bass was in Yuma."

"He was."

"They ever pin that express train robbery on him?"

"He engineered it."

"I'll bet he did." Byles filled two cups.

"Last night he turned on me near that old adobe beside the wash and shot me down."

"That's like him."

"Byles, will you go back there with me?"

"Why?"

"I want to look around."

"Keno. I'll get my horse and my pack mule. You can take the horse." Boone refilled his glass.

Byles led the horse and mule up to the front of the adobe and slid his rifle into its sheath. Boone weaved a little as he walked out to the horse. They rode north.

Byles led the way off the road into the thick brush to the old adobe. A hundred yards from the house he found three mounded heaps of stones. He knew they came from the ticking sacks, yet Byles had said the packhorse had been heavily laden with ticking sacks. Behind the rock knoll he found a place where the soil had been disturbed. Byles looked at him. "See if you can find something to dig with," said Boone.

"There's an old spade in the brush."

Five feet down Byles struck wood. He threw out several pieces of thick wood covered with reddish wax. He pulled a small tin box from the hole. He handed it to Boone. Boone pried it open with the spade. A battered dollar watch was in it. It suddenly dawned on Boone that the outlaw's perverted sense of humor had planted a horse on whoever would dig in the emptied cache.

Byles wiped the sweat from his face. "Well?"

Boone squatted. "The gold was here. There's no doubt about that. The sacks Bass brought here were full of those stones. He emptied them and filled the sacks with the loot. Forty thousand worth, Warren."

"Chihuahua! And I've been living within five miles of a fortune all this time."

Boone swayed a little.

"We'd better get back to my place."

Back at Byles' adobe Boone lay down on the cot. Byles shook his head. "You should have rested," he said. "You look gaunt as a gutted snowbird."

"I feel like it. Byles, will you do something for me? Wells Fargo business?"

"Sure."

"Take a message to Willcox. To a man named Jim Dobie. He's another Wells Fargo detective. Get him back here as fast as you can."

"Certainly!"

"There's a lot of reward money out for Eccles. You'll get in on it."

"I can use a new grubstake."

"You'll get it." Boone took paper and pencil from the table and wrote swiftly telling Dobie of what had happened. He looked up at Byles. "I'll need your horse."

Byles rubbed his jaw.

"You'll be taken care of."

"Take what you need. Where will you be?"

Boone lay down again. "Naco. If I leave there I'll leave a message with the *alcalde*."

Byles took the message. "I'll ride my mule. You ain't in any shape to travel, Shattuck."

Boone looked up at the prospector. "I'll follow Bass Eccles clear to Nicaragua if I have to."

Byles looked at the drawn face, with the long scar accentuated against the pale skin. But it was the cold blue eyes that told him further talk was useless.

CHAPTER FOURTEEN

The shadows were deep in the twisted streets of Bisbee when Boone tethered Warren Byles' sorrel to a rail half a block from the lamplit Wells Fargo office. He plodded wearily toward the light. His head still ached and his left arm was stiff.

Boone stopped on the boardwalk in front of the office. A thin man was seated at a desk, his face shaded by a green eyeshade. Boone opened the door and walked in. The man looked up quickly and dropped his right hand below the desk. "Can I help you?" he asked. He glanced at the wall clock. "It's almost closing time," he added uncertainly.

"You the Wells Fargo agent?"

The man grinned. "I wouldn't be sitting here going over these damned reports if I wasn't, would I?"

"I'm Boone Shattuck. You alone?"

"Yes."

Boone slid his hand into his coat. The agent raised his head quickly. "There's nothing here," he said.

"I was working with Jim Dobie up in Willcox. I'm after Bass Eccles."

"Bass Eccles? He's in Yuma."

"He got out last week."

The agent leaned back in his chair. "Where's your credentials?"

Boone placed them on the desk. The agent nodded. "I'm Charley Corson. You must be all right. You wouldn't known about Jim Dobie if you weren't. What's your problem?"

"I need money and information."

"I can give you money. What do you want to know? Why did you come here?"

"Where else would Eccles and Huerta go? He's in Mexico by now."

Corson stood up and pulled down the shade. "You figure on following them?"

"Yes."

Corson eyed Boone. "Last year one of our agents, Danny Crook, followed Bartolome Huerta down into the Rio de Bavispe country. He didn't come back."

Corson felt an ivy finger trace the length of his spine as he looked at the man facing him. The room suddenly seemed cold despite the warmth of the night. Corson looked away. "Eccles has friends in Sonora. You'd be spotted."

"My beard is growing. It'll hide this scar."

Corson was about to say that nothing would hide those eyes but he thought better of it. This was a different man than Danny Crook who had been purely after the reward money. There was some primal urge driving this strange man on into Sonora after two of the toughest men in the border country. "I said Eccles had friends, Shattuck."

"He also has enemies. A man like Eccles always has enemies."

Corson shrugged. "There is a man in Naco. Hilario Chavez. He always has information to sell. He has no love for Bartolome Huerta. You can find him in the Cantina of the Doves almost any night. He's cagey."

"I'll find him."

Corson placed his papers in a file. "What else do you need?"

"A rifle. Winchester .44/40. A good saddle and a good horse. Money for clothes and some supplies. A place to sleep."

"You want me to get the stuff?"

"I'll get it. You give me the *dinero*."

Corson opened a cash drawer. "How much?"

"Five hundred will do."

Corson counted out the bills. He locked the drawer. "Get a room at the St. Elmo. They don't ask questions there. I'll nose around town tonight. Look for me about midnight."

Boone left the office. Corson watched him from the open door, shook his head and then locked up for the night.

Boone entered a general store. He bought a good used Colt Peacemaker and a Winchester. As an afterthought he also purchased a Remington double-barreled, over-and-under derringer and a box of .41 caliber cartridges for it. He completed his purchases with some tinned food, flour, tobacco, and a canteen. He led the sorrel to a livery stable and then went to the shabby St. Elmo where he got a room.

He was asleep when Corson tapped at the door. The agent dropped into a chair and opened a bottle. He filled glasses and lit up a stogie. "Huerta was seen here in town some days ago. Heading south. Later he was seen again, heading north. No one has seen Eccles. A teamster told me he saw four people riding south, east of town, a day or so ago. A tall thin man, obviously sick. Another tall man, dark-faced. A Mex. A young woman. In a helluva hurry."

Boone nodded. "Eccles and Huerta. The sick man was Jonce Maxon. The woman, his daughter Marion."

Corson studied Boone. "Why are Maxon and his daughter with Eccles?"

Boone sipped his drink. "Eccles was afraid Maxon would talk."

"It would be like Eccles to kill him to keep his mouth shut."

Boone looked up. "Eccles is making a play for the girl."

"So?" Corson downed his drink. "Seems to me you've got more than company interest in this deal, Shattuck."

"I may have." His eyes grew dark.

"Take it easy. I've located a good horse for you. Jimmy Logan, at the livery stable will let you see it tomorrow. I've got a good Frazier hull you can use. I'll tell Jimmy to let you have it."

"Gracias."

Corson stood up and reached for the bottle. "Leave it here," said Boone.

Corson withdrew his hand. "Get some sleep," he said. "You need it."

Boone nodded. The agent left the room. Boone downed two quick slugs and dropped on the bed. His hand traced the bruised area on the side of his head.

CHAPTER FIFTEEN

Boone slowly rode the bayo coyote gelding through the wide dusty streets of Naco, lined with shabby one-story adobes and *jacal*s. Faded signs advertising merchandise, liquors, and beers were sprawled across the fronts of some of them. The *ranchito,* a noisome area of brothels and saloons, was full of life. Pianos tinkled off-key. A guitar strummed from one of them. A ragged parrot squawked from a cage hanging in front of one of the cantinas. A crude painting of a dove showed on the facade of the building. Boone tethered his horse.

Boone's spurs jingled as he walked into the dimly lit cantina and sat down at a rickety table. A girl, hardly more than sixteen, swayed up to him, wiggling her full hips, letting her *camisa* drop from a smooth brown shoulder. Boone shook his head and ordered *aguardiente* from the waiter. He eyed the men in the place as he drank. A night's sleep had done him good. Corson had sent a message to Hilario Chavez that morning.

A little man sat at a table ten feet from Boone, idly picking at a battered guitar. His liquid eyes lifted and looked at Boone, then he stood up and walked to Boone's table. "Perhaps the señor would like a *cancione?*" he asked in his native tongue.

Boone nodded. The little man softly played and sang La Raza de Bronce Que Sabe Morir. The Bronze Race That Knows How to Die. The Mexican tribute to the Yaquis and Tarahumares. Boone nodded and tossed him a coin. He shoved the bottle toward the little man, who filled a glass. "You are Senor Shattuck?"

"Yes."

"You are visiting Sonora?"

"In a way."

"Hunting?"

"Perhaps."

"It is not a good hunting season...for game."

"I do not hunt game, Hilario."

"So? That is odd. Is it women you hunt? Gold? Silver? Perhaps the Lost Tayopa Mine?"

"None of those."

"Anastacio Madera has a fine chart showing the way to El Naranjal, the fabulous lost mine. I can get it for you for a few pesos."

"No."

Hilario filled his glass. He looked about the dim cantina. "Perhaps you seek Bass Eccles and Bartolome Huerta?"

"Perhaps."

"Good!" Hilario sipped his liquor.

"Huerta is perhaps a friend of yours, Hilario?"

"That *bazofa?* Mother of God!"

Boone rolled a smoke. "Where are they?"

"Who knows?"

"You have not seen them?"

"Not I. But they have been through here."

"So? Where did they go?"

"Of that I am not sure. It is said they went to Tres Jacales."

"Where is that?"

"Near the Rio Magdelena, not far from Pitiquito."

"Is it far?"

"Yes. Many leagues."

"You are sure?"

Hilario nodded.

"How do you know?"

"My brother Jesus is a Rurale under Colonel Kosterl-itzky. He told me."

"How do I get there?"

"It is dangerous. They are hard men. They have many friends. Outlaws."

"I will go."

Hilario eyed the cold-eyed gringo sitting across from him. "Why do you go?"

"I want Bass Eccles."

"And not Huerta?"

"Yes."

"To kill them?"

"Perhaps."

Hilario smiled. "Good."

"Why do you hate them, Hilario?"

Hilario plucked at his guitar. "I had a sister once. A child. Pretty as the mountain flowers growing beside the rushing streams. She was my pet, you understand, for my father and mother were killed by the Yaquis. For a time I rode with Augustin Chacon, the great bandit. Huerta was one of us. I was but a young man. There was a time when the Rurales chased us. We separated. Huerta and I fled into the Sierra Madre to my village, where we were safe. Or so I thought. Huerta saw my sister. I watched him like an eagle. Then one night I went down the mountain to see if the Rurales were about. I was caught. Someone had informed on me. For a time I was in the prison at Hermosillo. When I was released I came home." Hilario stopped talking and refilled his glass. He tossed it down.

"So?"

The Mexican leaned forward. "Huerta had taken my

sister. A child. She died in Nacozari from a beating he gave her."

"Why did you not kill him?"

Chavez spread out his thin brown hands, palms upwards. "I was no longer one of Chacon's men. The Rurales watched me. Huerta had many friends in the mountains. So I came here. The Rurales pay me for information. Your officers do likewise. It is a good life. Dangerous, but easy. I wait for a chance at Huerta. I am patient. I say to myself: Hilario, someday a man will come who will look for Bartolome Huerta. He will want to kill him. I will help that man. You are that man."

Boone rolled another cigarette and handed it to the Mexican. Then he rolled another for himself. "You will tell me the way to Tres Jacales?"

"It is a hard road. Past Cananea to the headwaters of the Rio Magdelena. Thence to Imuris, Magdelena, Santa Ana, by a fair road. Then westerly to Altar and then Pitiquito."

Boone nodded. "What do I owe you?"

Hilario looked hurt. "You will pay me when Bartolome Huerta dies beneath those guns you carry. *Por favor*, Mister Shattuck, let him die slowly and tell him about Hilario Chavez so that he knows I helped you. *Por favor?*"

"Yes. *Por favor*."

"Good!" Hilario took another drink. "Then perhaps we will meet again?"

"Let us hope so."

"Go with God!"

"Go with God, Hilario." Boone watched the little man leave the cantina. He finished his drink, paid his tab, and left.

CHAPTER SIXTEEN

B oone squatted in the shade of his horse, a
cigarette pasted to his lower lip, eyeing the
thread of dust which rose on the rough trail
below him. His eyes never left the lone horseman riding
steadily and directly toward the low mounded hills where
Boone was waiting. Boone had traveled about a hundred
miles in the four days since he had left Naco, seeing no
one except occasional *paisanos* on the yellow roads. They
had all told him he was on the road to Pitiquito, without
a doubt.

The sun beat down on the parched earth, forming
shimmering veils that hurt the eyes. A ragged buzzard
soared on motionless pinions high above him. A *zopilote*,
like a scrap of charred paper floating in the cloudless sky.
Boone eyed the repulsive bird of carrion. He was waiting
with spidery patience for something. Something or
someone.

Boone stood up and led the horse into a hollow. He
poured some of his water into the hollow of his hat and
let the bay drink. His water was low. He allowed himself a
sip and corked the canteen. Then he walked up the slope
and dropped in the shade of a naked shaft of rock. The

horseman was a mile away now. Boone slid the rifle forward and levered a round into the chamber.

The man was close enough for Boone to see he rode wearily. The dust threaded away from the hoofs and was raveled by the hot wind.

The man rounded a turn and looked up. Boone gripped his Winchester and then relaxed his grip. There was something familiar about the stocky figure. "I'll be damned," he said softly. "Jim Dobie!" He stood up and waved his hat. Jim slid from the saddle, jerked his rifle from its sheath and slapped his gray on the rump. The gray trotted off into the brush. Dobie jumped into cover.

"Jim!" yelled Boone. "It's me! Shattuck!"

Dobie came slowly out of the brush and plodded up the trail followed by the tired gray. "God," he said. "I'm parched!"

Boone walked to his bay, got the canteen and handed it to Dobie. Dobie looked at the horse. "All right?"

Boone nodded. Dobie watered the gray. "Where's the next water?"

"*Quién sabe?* Pitiquito can't be far away."

"*Sta bueno!*" Dobie drank sparingly. He looked at Boone. "I'm dehydrated."

Boone grinned, wincing as a lip cracked. "You'll live."

"You look chipper enough."

"I'm part lizard."

Dobie squatted in the shade and took out a long nine. He lit it and watched the bluish tobacco smoke drift off. "Hilario Chavez told me you had headed this way. I've been riding like hell."

"Foolish in this country."

"Maybe so. But I've come to take you back with me."

"No go."

Dobie's green eyes went hard. "I wired Mason. He told me to stay out of Mexico and keep you out."

"I'm here."

"We'll go to Pitiquito and then head back."

Boone lazily leaned back against the rock. "You'll go back alone."

Dobie withdrew the cigar from his mouth. "You'll obey orders! There's hell to pay! We lost Danny Crook down here. The Guardia Rurales did nothing about it, claiming they should have been notified he was one of our operatives."

"That would have saved him?"

Dobie shrugged. "I doubt it. The fact is that the Mexican Government has no extradition deal with us even if we located Eccles."

"Tough."

Dobie closed his eyes. "What do you expect to do when you find Eccles?"

"Kill him."

"You will like hell!" Dobie threw away his cigar. "We want him back in Arizona!"

"You've got a fat chance of getting him there. He has the gold with him."

"It's more than the gold! There were valuable papers in that express car. If you kill Eccles they'll be lost forever."

Boone shrugged.

Dobie stood up. "Let's get to Pitiquito." He looked up at the sky. "Filthy thing."

"He's probably waiting for you, Jim."

Dobie whirled. "What do you mean?"

"You're not used to the desert. They seem to know. I didn't see him until you showed up."

"You're loco with the heat!"

"Perhaps." Boone picked up his rifle. "Let's go. *Vámonos!*"

They rode to the west in the face of the hot sun. Now and then Boone looked at the agent. He was far gone with the heat and thirst.

They met the *paisano* in a bend of the trail. The old Mexican took off his great hat. "Jorge Esteban, *servidor de ustedes,"* he said in the old phrasing.

Boone leaned on his saddle horn. "Greetings, friend," he said. "How many leagues to Pitiquito?"

"Not many. Perhaps an hour's ride."

"Thank you."

"It is nothing. Follow the trail." The old man hesitated. He eyed them closely. "It is not a good place at this time, sirs."

"How so?"

"There are bandits there. There has been some killing. Mother of God! I fled from the town. I return to my barranca where I can be at peace with my goats."

"Bandits?" asked Dobie.

"Yes. Yes. Some of the men of Chacon. The place is a veritable nest of eagles! Rape, killings, drunken revels. You must not go there. The Rurales are not within many leagues."

Boone cursed. Dobie slowly wiped his red face. "There is water nearby?"

"Yes. In the hills to the north. There is a fork in the trail a league from here. Turn right. Father Joseph is there at the little ruined mission. A good man. There is water there and shade."

Boone tossed the old man a few coins. "Thank you, friend."

"Thank you. It is nothing." The old man watched the two dusty gringos ride into the sun. "*Ay de mi*, Pablo," he said to his shaggy burro. "These Americans are mad. To travel into the Gran Desierto at this time of the year."

The tumbled ruins had almost reverted to the earth from which they had been built. Boone drew rein on a rise and studied the little mission. A thread of smoke arose from the far side of the ruins. A pair of burros grazed on a patch of greenery near a pile of rocks. Dobie sagged in his saddle. "If there isn't water here I'm done for."

"Take it easy. Someone is there." He spurred the flagging bay down the slope. The sound of the clashing hoofs brought a robed man to the front of the ruins. A padre. He shaded his eyes and watched them. Boone drew rein near him. "Good day, Father," he said politely. "There is water?"

The padre nodded. "Yes, my son. In the tanks there."

Dobie slid from his horse and ran awkwardly across to the rocks. He dropped on his belly and began to drink.

The padre shook his head. "He will be ill."

"You are alone?" asked Boone.

"Yes. Some of my laborers have gone into Pitiquito for supplies. They will return tomorrow."

"Some of Chacon's men are in Pitiquito."

The padre held up his hands. "Then there will be trouble!"

Boone led the bay to the water and let him drink a little. Dobie raised his red face and then suddenly rolled away from the rock pan to retch out the water he had taken in.

Boone sipped a double handful of water and went to the old padre. The man was sitting in the shade of a brush ramada, watching the sun die in an agony of rose and gold to the west. "Is it not beautiful?" he asked.

Boone squatted beside him. "And deadly."

"Yes. It is so. Where are you going, my son?"

"We are looking for three men and a woman."

The padre eyed Boone. "Three men and a woman came here some days ago. Two men and a woman left."

"What do you mean?"

"Come." The padre got stiffly to his feet and led Boone across a rise to a level space. The ground was mounded with desert rocks. A cemetery. A fresh mound was at one side surmounted by a crude cross. "This man died here. There was nothing we could do. An American."

"What was His name?"

"An odd one. Jonce Maxon."

Boone took off his hat.

"You knew him?"

"Yes."

"He is with God. He was suffering terribly."

"The other three?"

The padre looked off to the northwest. "They rode that way. They said they were going to Puerto Penasco. I rode after them to tell them it was the wrong trail. The tall American cursed me and told me to mind my own business. They went into the Gran Desierto. The Camino del Diablo."

"The Devil's Road."

"Yes. The trail followed by Padre Kino many years ago. A place of heat and thirst. Death is the only inhabitant." The padre looked speculatively at Jim Dobie. "The wings of death have brushed him close."

They walked back to the abandoned mission. "What do you do here, Father Joseph?" asked Boone.

The padre wiped his face. "Many years ago this was a mission of the church as you can see. The Apaches and Yaquis raided it constantly. In time the people here were wiped out. The Franciscans abandoned it. An effort was made to rebuild it in 1822, but shortly after that time the Franciscans were expelled from Mexico after Mexico won her independence from Spain. This place was forgotten. I received permission to dig into the ruins for relics of the past."

"It is hard work?"

"Yes. Very hard. My men complain of the heat and the loneliness."

They sat down under the ramada. "The woman who was with those two men, Father Joseph, how did she look?"

The padre made a pitying gesture with hands and head. "Her eyes were dry when we buried her father. She asked for my help saying she was with those men against her will. Later, the American told me she was his sister and was not well in the head. I did not believe him but what could I do?"

Boone nodded. "You do not know where they went?"

The padre shrugged. "Into the Gran Desierto, as I said, possibly to reach the Colorado by the Smuggler's Trail. The trail leads from Quito baquita, south of Ajo in your United States, thence north, thence west to Las Playas, thence northwest through Tinajas Altas, the High Tanks, to Yuma in Arizona Territory on the south side of the Gilas. It is in our records in the mission at Hermosillo that Father Kino used such a trail."

"You have been on it?"

The Mexican nodded. "Yes, as a much younger man. Our beasts died from lack of water. We almost died. Three of us made the Colorado." The padre shook his gray head. "A strange land, almost unreal, as though on the moon or a distant planet. There are voices there that speak to a man's inner soul and tell him strange terrible things. A man must put his trust in God out there or lose his reason. A man is alone, yet not lonely, for he is close to God in that terrible place. Do you believe in God, my son?"

"Yes, Father Joseph."

"It is well. You will need him."

"Do you think I will go out there?"

The old man smiled. "Two gringos, as my people call you Americans, ride out of the desert, with ready weapons. They ask about those that have gone before, not with anxiety for loved ones, but with hate in their souls. You seemed sorry for the death of that man who died. The two men that were here were in great haste to bury him and move on. So it was obvious that *they* did not feel sorrow for him. When I told you of the frightened young woman it seemed as though Satan himself stared at me from those cold eyes of yours. Yes, you will follow them. There will be more violence."

Jim Dobie lay in the shadow of the tanks, now and

then raising his head and dropping it back. He was through.

Boone watched him. "Tomorrow I will leave. My friend cannot go on. Can I leave him here?"

"Certainly."

Boone nodded. "I will pay you."

The padre shook his head. "I will accept nothing. A donation for the church perhaps, if you can afford it. For me...nothing. He is one of God's children."

Boone made a bed for Jim inside the old ruin. Boone helped him to the bed and lowered him. Dobie opened his eyes. "This stops us, Boone."

Boone leaned against the wall. "You. Not me."

"My orders were to bring you back."

Boone laughed. "You're lucky if you get back yourself, Jim."

The sick man tried to get up. He was a company man, all right. Boone walked outside. The sun was gone and already the desert was cool. The old padre was preparing food.

"Let me help you."

The old man smiled. "No. It is a simple pleasure to cook a meal and serve you. Do not deny me, my son."

Boone walked to the cemetery and looked down at the grave of Jonce Maxon. He placed a gayly striated stone on top of the pile of rocks, and returned to eat.

CHAPTER SEVENTEEN

The fire crackled in a corner of the ruined room, casting grotesque shadows on the walls. The night wind soughed about the ancient walls of the mission. Boone methodically checked the small keg Father Joseph had given him. It seemed sound enough. Before him, on a square of cloth, lay the dried fruits and meats which the old padre had traded to him for the last tins of food which he had brought from Naco. He glanced at Jim Dobie. The detective was asleep. It had been a close call for him.

Boone packed his food into his saddlebags. He carried the keg to the rock pan and filled it, letting it sink beneath the water to swell tight the seams. He had his two canteens and the one big one Dobie had brought along.

The padre was asleep on his pallet in the old sacristy. Boone passed softly through the dim room, faintly lit by the firelight from the next room. Boone examined the map that the padre had given him. The thing that puzzled him was why Bass Eccles had traveled west instead of south. The padre had known vaguely of a place called Tres Jacales, but, as he had said, it was a common enough name in Mexico.

Boone gathered his gear together. His saddlebags, guns, canteens and spare clothing. He eyed his boots and then looked at Dobie's. A spare pair of boots might be necessary. He pulled the boots toward him, slipped off his own and tried on Dobie's. They weren't a bad fit.

"What the hell do you think you're doing?"

Boone looked up. Jim was up on one elbow, eyeing his boots on Boone's feet. "You won't need them for a time, Jim," he said quietly.

"Damn you! You'll return with me to Bisbee!"

Boone pulled off Dobie's boots and put on his own, then leaned back against the wall. "Maybe you don't remember what I said back in Willcox, Jim. I told you I was out to get the four men who did the job. Two of them are dead. There are two left."

Dobie shifted his hand beneath his blanket. "You've worked with the devil's luck!"

"I'm breaking the case, Jim. I went to Yuma to befriend Eccles, which I succeeded in doing. I helped force him into the open with the stolen gold."

"Yeah! Where is he now? Out in the desert heading for freedom!"

"He's trying to reach the coast, I'll swear. Something drove him west."

Dobie rubbed his forehead. He was a damned sick man. "Look, Boone. We can wire ahead to Yuma and San Diego for our men to be on the lookout for him."

Boone shook his head.

Dobie lay back. "You don't give a fiddler's damn about Wells Fargo. This is a vengeance trail for you, Shattuck."

"Marion Maxon is in his hands."

Dobie raised his head. "So that's it?"

"Yes."

"What do you think has happened to her by now? In the hands of those two skunks?"

Boone stood up. "I aim to find out."

"You're loco! One man can't go after them."

Boone eyed the sick man from lowered brows.

"Damn you! You're no longer a Texas Ranger!"

Boone shook his head. "It's no use, Jim. Padre Joseph will take care of you. You'll be all right."

Dobie flipped back his blanket. The firelight glinted on his cocked Colt.

Boone's Winchester leaned against the far wall. His Colts were in the corner on his bed. But beneath his left sleeve was the Remington derringer, clipped to his wrist. "You can't hold me here all night like this, Jim," he said.

"I'll get the padre to tie you up."

"I doubt it."

There was a slight touch of madness in the tired green eyes. "You called me a company man once. I am. Enough of a company man to obey the orders of Wells Fargo, and to hell with the Texas Rangers."

Boone suddenly shoved his left foot beneath his saddlebags, lifting them and throwing them at Dobie Boone hit the floor as the Colt crashed, rolled over, and jumped to his feet as Dobie tried to clear the heavy leather bags from about his head. Boone launched a kick that caught the detective behind the right ear. Dobie sagged down and dropped the Colt. Boone snatched it and looked up into the pale face of the padre. "It is nothing, Father Joseph," he said. "The sun and thirst have made him slightly mad. He tried to stop me from leaving."

The padre crossed himself. "I do not understand. Perhaps the sun and thirst have made him mad. Yet there is a more terrifying madness in you. I am afraid for you, my son."

Boone gathered his gear and weapons together and walked out into the moonlight. He saddled his bay and slung the saddlebags into place. He lashed the keg into place and slid his Winchester into its sheath. The old man came out behind him. Boone pressed some bills into his thin hands. "For the church. You will take care of him?"

"Of course."

"Goodbye then, Father Joseph."

"Go with God, my son."

Boone led the bay toward the faint trail, which led over a rise. He glanced at the lonely cemetery as he passed. At the top of the rise he looked back. The padre, a strange hunched figure in black, had his head bowed as though praying.

Boone gigged his horse and rode down the slope in the moonlight.

CHAPTER EIGHTEEN

The desert was a moonlit sea, dappled by deep pools of shadow in the hollows. The mountains to Boone's right and behind him, were dim hulks in the distance. The sands were still warm beneath his feet. The wind sighed across the wastes, setting the mesquite, ocotillo, and occasional yucca into swaying motion. There was no sign of man to be seen.

It was several hours before dawn when Boone stopped and tethered the bay to a stunted growth. He dropped on the ground and instantly fell asleep.

The false light of the first dawn showed in the eastern skies when Boone awoke. He swung up on the bay and rode northwest toward the mountains, which showed faintly in the dawn light.

Noon found him crossing a rippled area where now and then a saguaro lifted its forked arms. His eyes picked out the trail winding up the slopes of a low range of hills miles ahead of him.

It was late afternoon when he was in among the sand hills. Higher and higher he went until suddenly the trail rounded a conical hill, and he saw the *jacal*s below him, already in the shadow of the hills to the west of them. Boone dropped the reins and walked forward to study the little settlement. There was no sign of life. A ghost town.

Boone led the tired bay down the twisting trail. He left the horse in a hollow and withdrew his Winchester from its sheath. He padded forward and then stopped short. Four of the buildings were of adobe. Two of fieldstone. But three of them were definitely *jacals,* formed of upright poles set into the hard earth and plastered with adobe. *Tres Jacales*.

Boone eased forward, keeping to the deep shadows, peering into each building as he passed. They were all empty. Beyond the last building lay a dead horse with bloated belly. The eyes and soft parts of the carcass had been torn by beaks and claws. The stench from the body closed about him as he passed it. On a low rise he saw an obelisk, cut from desert stone, with the once-sharp edges rounded and smoothed by the sand-laden winds.

He came close to it and peered at the incised letters written in Spanish. "The inhabitants of Tres Jacales killed by the Yaquis," he translated. "November 10th, 1881. Christians, for the sake of God, pray for their souls."

Boone looked at the mounded graves beyond the obelisk. There were many. He leaned on his Winchester. There was an intense loneliness about the place. A brooding loneliness that seemed to reach out to engulf his soul.

The water was behind the town. Rock pans surrounded by humped rocks. The water was low but palatable. Boone went back for the bay.

The hollow was empty.

The hoof marks led off to the south. Boone trotted after the stray. He topped a rise which gave a clear view of miles of desert. The bay was not in sight, nor could he see any tracks on the rippled sands.

Boone bent forward and followed the tracks which showed faintly on the hard earth, windswept and barren.

Then they vanished. A cold feeling came over him. He whirled swiftly.

There was no one there.

Boone climbed the low hills behind the town. He shook his head and walked down into the town. Then he heard the muffled stamp of a hoof in the largest of the buildings. He walked toward it, leaned his Winchester against the outer wall, and walked in. The bay whinnied from the darkness. Something hard pressed against Boone's back. He jerked a little as something penetrated his skin and a trickle of blood worked down his back.

"*Gracias*, gringo," someone said behind Boone.

Boone raised his hands. "What do you want?"

"Mother of the Devil! It is you!"

Ice seemed to form in Boone's stomach. Bartolome Huerta!

"Drop the gunbelt, gringo!"

Boone lowered his hands and unbuckled his gunbelt. His double-action Colt was in one of his saddlebags. He had removed his wrist clip with the derringer in it because a heat rash had formed under it during the day. It too was in his saddlebags. His only weapon was the knife he had purchased in Naco, formed from a file, slim and deadly, which he carried in a soft leather sheath in his right boot.

"Walk outside, gringo."

Boone walked outside. He looked back over his shoulder. Dimly he saw the broad flat face, the flat reptilian eyes, thick ragged mustache, the smallpox pits. Huerta stepped back. A curved knife was in his brown hand. The deadly gutting knife; the saca tripas.

Boone eyed the Mexican. He had been through hell from the looks of him. The face had thinned out. His clothing was ragged and tattered. He wore no gunbelt.

Huerta grinned in the dimness. "I saw you coming, you garbage," he said thinly. "There is a score we must even, pig!"

An icy trickle of sweat ran down from Boone's armpits as he eyed the dull gleam of the curved knife blade. "Take the horse, Huerta," he said. "Why kill me?"

The Mexican reached up and touched the scabbed scar on his chin where the bucket thrown by Boone at Maxon's ranch had struck him. "Son of a goat," he said. "Do you think I forget this?"

"Where is Bass?" asked Boone.

Huerta jerked his left hand, pointing west. "In the hills."

"Beyond town?"

"No. Miles from here. It is there I go when I have finished with you."

There was a bitterness in Bartolome's tone. Boone looked closely at him. "You got your share of the gold?"

Huerta spat.

"You have fallen out with Bass then?" asked Boone.

"Yes. The scum sent me back to scout. When I returned to the waterhole he was gone with the food and the water kegs."

"And the gold?"

"Of course!"

"Supposing I help you trail him? You can have your share of the gold. I want the girl."

Huerta threw back his head and laughed. "Do you take me for such a fool?"

The bay showed at the door of the old building, looking past Huerta at Boone.

"I am not dead! I lived through the desert although my horse died. I'll follow him to Tinajas Altas and kill him. I'll take the gold and the gringa girl!"

The bay edged forward and nudged into Huerta. He jerked his head sideways. Boone closed in, smashing at Huerta's chin. Blood flew from the crusted scab. The Mexican went back against the wall, swiping at Boone with the wickedly curved *saca tripas*. It swept over his head. Boone stopped and whipped his knife free from its boot sheath.

Huerta circled swiftly, grinning with pain. This was his game. The ripping of guts. "Ha, gringo," he said. "You have the guts to face me with the knife?"

"I'm here."

Huerta's movements were sinuous and graceful, his body relaxed. The curved knife leaped in and slashed through Boone's left sleeve drawing a thin trickle of blood from the forearm. Boone retreated. Huerta moved in. The *saca tripas* lanced in but Boone leaped aside, countering with a hard thrust which Huerta easily avoided.

Their breaths came harsh in their throats. The desert had taken a bigger toll of their strength than they had realized.

Boone swung up his blade and Huerta leaped in, ripping up with the blade but his foot rolled on gravel and he staggered sideways to regain his balance. Boone's blade drew blood from Huerta's left side, just over the hip, a ragged slashing blow that drew a flow that stained Huerta's dirty shirt. He gasped as he shuffled away, weaving and swaying, watching Boone's cold eyes.

They closed. In a swift interplay of clashing blades, Boone felt the *saca tripas* pink his chest before he threw the panting Mexican back. The bloodstain was big on Huerta's shirt now, black in the darkness of the shadows.

Huerta moved steadily. He grunted as he thrust out his blade, trying to get the offensive, but Boone was always just out of reach. There was no doubt in his mind that Huerta was by far the better man.

Huerta tried a sweeping slash, spinning about as he turned away, offering his broad back for an instant. Boone feinted and jumped back. The *saca tripas* swept up from below in a wicked ripping movement.

Their wrists crossed. Strength flowed from the straining bodies. Boone felt Huerta weaken. He threw him back with an upward rip of his *cuchillo*. It sank deeply, grated against bone and then was free, spraying blood against Boone's face.

Huerta coughed and moved back. There was fear on his face now, his left hand clasped to his gut.

Suddenly the Mexican stopped, coughed again. The *saca tripas* clattered on the baked earth. His eyes were wide in his head.

Boone threw away his knife and balled his fists. The left caught Huerta in the gut over his left hand. The right smashed under the scabby chin, snapping back his head. Huerta's skull bounced from the wall behind him. A crushing right shredded his knuckles and pasted Huerta's lips and teeth together in a bloody mass. Huerta sank down against the wall. His breath bubbled in his throat.

Boone stepped back looking down at the wounded man. He seemed to see the thin face of Hilario Chavez before him and hear the soft voice of the informer. "*Por favor, Mister Shattuck, let him die slowly and tell him about Hilario Chavez so that he knows I helped you. Por favor?*"

"Huerta," said Boone.

The Mexican's voice seemed to come from far away. "Curse you!"

"Do you remember Hilario Chavez?"

"That...*bazofa?*"

"Yes. The man whose sister you murdered. He was the one who set me on your trail."

Huerta coughed and sagged sideways. Then he opened his mouth. Blood flooded down through his bristly beard and dripped blackly onto his dirty shirt. Then he was gone.

Boone picked up his rifle and knife. He led the bay away from the dead man, the horse shying and blowing at the smell of blood. Score three for Perry Thorne. Boone did not look back.

The *zopilotes* would take care of Bartolome Huerta.

CHAPTER NINETEEN

T wo days of hell lay behind Boone. He plodded through a weird valley. To each side were tilted masses of rock, layer on layer of vari-colored stone, slanting up toward the west like the prows of half-sunken ships, half immersed in a sandy sea.

The bay was far gone, limping from innumerable cactus needles in his legs. Now and then Boone tried to remove them, bloodying the bay's legs and his hands, sometimes extracting the barbs from the horse flesh only to drive them into his own.

The valley was a maze of cacti. Barrel cactus, prickly pear, cholla, deer horn, catclaw, elephant ear, hedgehog, and fish hook. Lizards scuttled for cover at his slow approach. Hawks veered away. The trail had long since petered out on rock flats, but some animal instinct kept him moving on. The salt sweat irritated the bullet graze and knife slash on his left arm. Blisters had formed on his feet and had broken, pasting socks, feet and boots together in an aching mass. But it was the horse he worried about. He walked most of the time. The horse was used for his gear.

There were black specks in the sky. Specks that moved slowly. It was impossible to make out what they were without a glass, but Boone knew. *Zopilotes*. He had seen them hovering over Tres Jacales the day after he had left there, now and then swooping low and disappearing from sight.

There was nothing of man to be seen. Not like the trails of Arizona or Texas where a worn shoe, a scrap of dried out harness, the ashes of a fire, an empty bottle bluing in the hot sun, might be seen. Nothing.

Far ahead of him, dimly purple on the horizon, was a rising line, as though of an island seen across many miles of a motionless sea.

He reached the end of the tip-tilted ships of the desert, the striated rock layers. He found himself trending to the right. Lost men walked in circles.

The sun was a molten blade against his neck. He pulled up his collar and buttoned it about his lean corded neck. Sweat worked down his body, pasting his shirt and undershirt against him. A slow itching feeling came over him. He drew in a deep breath which seemed to come from an oven. He shook his head and dropped the reins of the bay. He squatted in the meager shade of the horse, wetting a rag of bandanna which he placed in his mouth, sucking the moisture from it.

"A strange land, almost unreal, as though on the moon or a distant planet. There are voices there that speak to a man's inner soul and tell him strange terrible things. A man must put his trust in God out there or lose his reason. A man is alone, yet not lonely, for he is close to God in that terrible place. Do you believe in God, my son?"

Boone raised his head. "Yes, Father Joseph."

"It is well. You will need Him."

Boone jerked his head and looked over his shoulder. There was nothing behind him but the bay.

Boone stood up and gripped the reins. He plodded on, a gaunt lath of a man, his eyes slitted against the glare of the sun's rays reflecting from the whitish earth.

The wind began to rise with a hissing sound, blowing

against Boone and the weak bay. Sand particles sifted down his collar, up his sleeves and into his shirt front.

There was a yellowish haze about the molten, brassy sun. A sickly color. Far ahead was a naked ledge of rock, thrusting itself up like a great knife blade from the yellow-white surface of the ground. Boone plodded on, dragging now and then at the reins. By the time they reached the ledge the desert had vanished in a haze of swirling sand.

Boone found a cleft beneath the ledge big enough for himself. The bay stood with lowered head, half in the cavity. The wind moaned like a soul in torment. Boone removed his saddle, saddlebags and canteens from the bay and stored them in the back of the cleft and settled down. The storm might blow itself out as quickly as it had come.

Boone awoke to thick darkness. He pulled the stifling blanket from his head. His boots were half buried in drifted sand. He pulled them free and crawled out into the windy night. The sand storm had died out. The moon shown faintly over the far mountains. The bay was gone.

Boone went back to his gear. He slung his canteens over his shoulder after re-filling them from the keg, which had started a leak. He carried the remains of his food supply in his pockets, his Winchester in his hand. He started northwest again through the windy dimness.

———

THE *ZOPILOTES* HAD BEEN JOINED by their gruesome allies, the vultures. There was little to distinguish them from each other at the great height at which they soared except for the white spots under the wings of the vultures. It didn't really matter, thought Boone, as he slogged up an incline of loose powdery sand.

He looked up to see the swiftly soaring shadow sweep down on him. He threw himself to one side as the *zopilote* shot over him. The odor of carrion hung in the still hot air of the afternoon. Boone raised his rifle and then lowered it. Spots seemed to dance before his eyes. But the spots were alive, soaring patiently. They had time. The desert was theirs.

He plodded on until, at last, he stood at the crest. He did not believe what he saw.

Across an area of jumbled black rock rose a steeply pitched slope of black lava. Beyond that were low mounded hills. Beyond them rose the dim mountains which had always seemed at an impossible distance for him to travel.

He slogged down the far side of the dune and entered the malpais. Jagged lava rock cut at his thin boots. Higher and higher the black rock rose until it was many feet over his head as he plodded through a labyrinthine passage. The sweat burst from his body and soaked his stinking clothing.

He rounded a turn and stopped short. A horse lay on the baking rock. It was the mount Bartolome Huerta had brought to the Kofas to meet him and Bass Eccles. They had passed that way.

It was late afternoon when he left the malpais and dropped beneath a creosote bush. His boots were in tatters. He patiently wrapped them with strips of his stinking shirt. One canteen was full. He walked on again.

The earth was all a haze, one with the sky. Joshua trees raised their gaunt hairy arms in supplication to the pitiless sky. Tortured growths of a tortured land.

Boone wiped the sweat from his face and looked west. A thread of smoke flung against the sky. Boone raised his head. Then he saw the second thread of smoke rising from a gaunt peak. A third rose from a range of hills to the north. *Yaquis.*

CHAPTER TWENTY

Boone lay prone on a rocky rise looking off into the velvet darkness to the west. Somewhere between him and the heights ahead of him must be the Yaquis. *The Bronze race that knows how to die.* He had seen two of them move across the rocky area ahead of him through the darkening shadows just after he had seen the smoke signals.

This was their country. The Sierra Madre of the North. The Apache and the Yaqui are cousins. A Yaqui mother quiets her child by saying the *yori* will get him. Not ogres or witches, but yori...the *White foreigners. The Americans.* Al Sieber, the German-born Chief of Scouts for Crook, Howard, and Miles, had once told Boone a Yaqui saying used by the mother of a Yaqui child. "The *yori* killed your father. The *yori* killed your grandfather. The *yori* killed my father. Son, kill the *yori*. Never trust them."

The desert was awakening to its nocturnal life. Yaquis were hunting *yori* and Boone was hunting Yaquis.

Boone set off slowly through the darkness, planting each foot carefully, rifle slanted across his chest; eyes, ears, and nose tuned to the night sounds. Ahead of him the dim bulk of the mountains showed.

The moon showed wanly in the eastern sky when Boone caught the odor of horses. A horse whinnied softly not a hundred yards from him, upwind. Boone froze as he heard the soft padding of feet. A shadow moved across an open space. There was no mistaking the lank black hair and the loose easy stride of the Yaqui. The Yaqui vanished toward the horses.

Boone made his way through the tumbled rocks and thick brush. In half an hour he could see the faint light of the fire. Now and then the silhouette of a horse showed against the glow. Three Yaquis squatted beside it. He worked his way forward, up through rocks and boulder still hot from the day's sun.

The moon was up high when he reached a level area five hundred feet above the desert floor beneath him. The fire was concealed by a ledge of high rock.

Boone padded across the level area and looked up at an almost sheer wall of rock, broken and crumbling. Beyond it was the bulk of the rugged mountain, thrusting great gaunt shoulders into the night sky. He sipped a little water, dying for a smoke, but knowing better than to light one.

He found a great crack in the low escarpment, a fault which had been widened by tumbling rocks. He worked his way up it in darkness until he reached the top. The area before him was lit by the faint moon.

There was no movement other than the rustling of the brush. Then the odor of a horse came faintly to him. Boone placed his rifle on the ground and took out his knife. He slithered across the ground moving to a higher area. He stopped there and lay flat, testing the night.

A faint ringing sound carried clearly to Boone. The metallic sound of a shod hoof. Then Boone saw a horse's head arch against the light of the moon. A shadow moved. A tall figure appeared, gripped the horse's halter and led the animal into the darkness. The man wore a hat. A white man.

Boone slid forward down the face of the rocks and got to his feet. He worked on and stopped at the lip of a hollow. To one side a ruined rock wall showed. A naked shoulder of rock thrust into the area. Boone went to it and eased around it. There were two horses picketed back in a large opening. The moonlight picked out the dim outline of a tumbledown rock house, the doors and windows black with shadow.

One of the horses snorted and shied. The other horse whinnied sharply. The door shadow thickened. A tall man appeared with a rifle in his hands. Boone watched him. Bass Eccles.

Eccles walked to the horses and spoke quietly to them. He faded into the shadows toward the lip of the level area. Boone heard the faint clicking of rocks as the outlaw moved down the slope.

Boone walked to the slope's edge. Eccles was a hundred yards away walking toward the edge of the escarpment. Boone padded toward the ruins and flattened himself against the wall. Something moved inside. Someone was coming to the door not five feet from Boone.

A shadow appeared. Boone raised the knife. Then he lowered it. "Marion," he said softly.

The girl whirled and raised a pistol. The double click of the hammer sounded clearly.

"Marion! It's Boone! Boone Shattuck!"

She stood still eyeing him across the raised pistol. "He's dead," she said. "Who are you?"

Boone raised his hands and stepped out into the moonlight.

She stared unbelievingly at the gaunt man who faced her, dressed in filthy undershirt and ragged trousers. She saw the hollow eyes and the thick growth of beard. Then she lowered the pistol and ran to him. He took her in his arms. The odor of sour sweat-soaked clothing filled his nostrils, but it seemed sweet to him. She clung to him. "I don't believe it," she whispered. "It's impossible."

"Are you alone with Eccles?"

"Yes. He got rid of Huerta,"

Boone looked across her shoulder. Eccles was not in sight. He led her into the dark building. "Where are the Yaquis?"

She raised her head. "Below us. Bass said they are in the pass behind us, too. They followed us for a full day. We rested here thinking we had shaken them off but they showed up in the afternoon."

"How many of them?"

"We saw at least six. There may be more."

Boots clicked on the hard earth. Boone pushed the girl back. "Keep quiet," he said.

Boone flattened himself against the wall. Eccles stopped outside. Then he came on and stepped into the room. "I could see a fire," he said to the girl. "We can't make a break. They're probably in the pass, too."

Boone stepped forward and placed the tip of the knife against Eccles' back. "Stand still, Bass," he said thinly. "This *cuchillo* may slip if you move."

Boone felt the tall outlaw tense. "Shattuck."

"Yes. You thought you killed me, Bass. You were never more wrong in your misbegotten life."

Eccles raised his hands, still holding the rifle.

"Take the rifle, Marion," said Boone.

She took the Winchester. Boone reached around Bass and took his two six-guns. He stepped back, cocking one of the six-guns. "Turn around," he said.

"For Christ's sake, Boone! Don't shoot! You'll rouse them damned bushy-headed devils."

"They won't jump you at night. You know that."

Eccles shifted. "Yeah. Yeah. But they're out there like prowling wolves waitin' for dawn."

Boone looked at the dim figure of the girl. "What about water?"

"There's a rock pan behind the house. There's very little in it."

"I'm going back to get my rifle," said Boone. "Hold this gun on him."

Eccles tilted his head to one side. "Look, Boone," he said. "I won't cause no trouble. Yuh got to help us."

"I will, Eccles. Then you and I will have an accounting."

"Anything you say!"

Boone walked outside and went to his rifle. He looked over the escarpment. A man stood on a rock looking toward the old ruin. A Yaqui. He vanished even as Boone watched.

Boone went back to the old house. Behind it, cracking the mountain wall, was a deep path of shadow. The pass. It wasn't very wide, a channel of darkness from which a cool night wind soughed.

Boone stepped into the house with cocked rifle. Eccles was leaning against the wall. Boone walked to the corner where a dim eye of fire glowed in the beehive fireplace. He threw some wood on the fire. It flickered up. He turned to look at Marion. She was thin with privation, her eyes hollow in her face. Eccles squatted by the fire. He looked up at Boone. "What do we do?" There was undisguised fear in his voice.

Boone lowered the hammer on his rifle. "Sit tight until before dawn. Then we'll go after them."

"We're better off here!"

"With a dozen of them waiting? You ever fought Indians?"

"No."

"Well, they don't take chances. They'd never rush you."

"I don't liked it!"

"They don't know I'm here."

"Then you go!"

Boone felt for the makings and rolled a smoke.

"What were you trying to do up here? Kill yourself and the girl?"

Eccles wiped his face. "Chacon knew I was back in Sonora. They followed us to Pitiquito. I couldn't go south. He has men operatin' clear down to Soyopa. The Rurales were lookin' for me in the Sierra Vallecillos on a tip. I fingered I'd fox them all by headin' west on the Camino del Diablo."

"Heading for where?"

Eccles squatted on the floor letting his long arms dangle over his bony knees. "Maybe San Luis. Gulf steamers come up there to discharge cargo for the Colorado River steamers."

"You'd be spotted right away."

"Maybe. Anyways I figgered I'd head for Ensenada and get a coastal steamer outa there headin' for Mazatlan, Tuxpan or maybe even Panama."

"Your money won't pay your way through the Yaquis."

Eccles bowed his bald head. "Yeah."

"Wells Fargo may have men in San Luis."

"I've foxed Wells Fargo. I ain't worried about them."

"That so?"

Eccles' head snapped up. "What do you mean?"

"Nothing."

Eccles rolled a smoke and lit it with shaking hands.

Boone leaned back against the wall. Marion was in bad shape. Her eyes never left Boone. "Why is Chacon after you?"

Eccles took the cigarette from his cracked lips. "I offered him a split. Bartolome told me Chacon figgered on taking the whole kit and caboodle."

"Diamond cut diamond, eh?"

"What the hell does that mean?"

Boone grinned. "Takes a thief to rob a thief."

"To Hell with this loco talk! How do we get out of this mess?"

Boone stood up. "Before dawn I'll leave here, find a

good shooting place. You and Marion will have to hold this place. Can they get behind you?"

"Down the pass."

"I'll cover that, too."

Eccles rolled another smoke. "You help me get out of this, Boone, and I'll split."

"*You?* I'm thinking about her."

Eccles looked up. "We're all in it now."

"Where's the gold?"

Eccles jerked his head. "In the corner."

Boone looked at the full ticking sacks. "If we have to pull foot we'll leave it behind."

Eccles jumped to his feet. "Not on your life!"

Boone grinned. "It may cost you your life."

Marion stood up. "Don't go out there, Boone. He isn't to be trusted."

Boone went to her. "He'll have to stick with us. Yaquis have some clever ways of torturing white men. I don't think Bass wants to be the subject of one of them."

Bass cringed. "I'll play the game."

Boone handed the girl his rifle. "Are you tired?"

"I couldn't sleep, Boone."

"Then watch him while I get some sleep. I'll need it." He stooped and kissed her cracked lips.

"Very touching," jeered Eccles. Boone dropped on the floor and placed an arm across his burning eyes. He went to sleep instantly.

CHAPTER TWENTY-ONE

Boone looked up into Marion's dim face. "It will be dawn soon," she said.

Boone shivered in the cold. She handed him a cup of coffee. "This is the last," she said.

"You take it."

She shook her head.

Boone sipped the strong brew. Eccles was asleep in the corner with his head resting on the plump ticking sacks. "How did he treat you?" asked Boone.

She leaned her head back against the wall. "All right. He never touched me until we came up here."

Boone lowered the cup. "What happened then?"

She placed a hand on his arm. "He thought we were safe. Last night he tried to make love to me. He promised me everything if I would."

"So?"

She touched the front of her clothing. It had been ripped from neck to waistline and roughly pinned together with thorns. "I couldn't fight anymore. Then we heard the horses neigh. He went to look and saw the Yaquis. He forgot all about me then."

Boone eyed the sleeping outlaw.

She drew a blanket about her shoulders. "Do you think we can get away, Boone?"

"Yes," he lied.

Boone stood up and took the Winchester. "I'll leave now. Keep out of sight. Shoot only if they rush you." He lifted her face with his free hand. "You must remember something."

"Yes," she said quietly.

He picked up her Colt and checked the cylinder. "There are six cartridges in here." He placed the heavy gun in her slim brown hands. "You must save one for yourself if necessary. Do you understand?"

She looked down at the Colt. "Are you trying to say goodbye to me, Boone?"

"No. But do not let them take you alive."

Boone left. It was still dark, a whispering darkness, the wind moaning softly through the pass and rustling the brush. He padded to a place where he could see both the lip of the escarpment and the pass. He could cover the level area in front of the ruined building. He dropped to the ground and lay still. He wondered who had ever built such a place.

The sky lightened almost imperceptibly in the East. It was cold. Boone half-cocked his rifle. He had twelve rounds in it. He drew out his two Colts and loaded the empty cylinder chambers on which the hammer normally rested. Twelve more rounds. He touched the derringer clipped under his undershirt sleeve. Two rounds. One for himself if they broke through on him.

It grew lighter. Boone stared at a bushy head for minutes before he realized it was a bush instead of a Yaqui. Somewhere, high in the dark pass, an eagle screamed. It was answered from below the escarpment. Almost a perfect imitation. A set feeling came over Boone. Kill or be killed.

Two *yori* were at the old ruin. A man and a woman. The man might die quickly or be saved for torture. The woman would be used until she was a screaming, thrashing wreck on the ground. War the Yaqui way.

Silently through the brush they came.

One minute the escarpment was empty. The next minute three shadowy figures were there, slipping toward a pile of scattered rock. Something moved in the pass. Two more.

Boone wet his dry lips. He eased the Winchester forward. There was no movement at the house. Boone's heart thudded against his ribs.

Another Yaqui showed beyond the house, standing behind a tall bush. Now the sky was lighter. Ready for the swift, deadly rush on silent feet.

The three Yaquis behind the rocks stood up. Boone rested his cheek against the scarred stock of the rifle. He took up the trigger slack. He squeezed off. The rifle spat and pushed back against his shoulder. He levered another round home, sighted and fired again before the echoes died away on the rock face. One Yaqui was down. The second thrashed about. The third was staring at Boone's position. The slug took him fair on the breastbone, driving him back over his two mates.

Boone turned. A Yaqui was scuttling for cover in the pass. Boone fired. The impact of the heavy slug drove the buck forward on his knees. The second slug plowed into his back.

Two warriors bounded from the brush, trying to reach the escarpment. A rifle flashed from a window. One of them went down. The other stumbled over him. Another bullet sent him to the House of Spirits.

Six down. Boone reloaded. Smoke drifted across the level area. The horses screamed like frightened women. One of them jerked back. His picket pin flew through the air and clattered on the hard earth. He buck-jumped toward the escarpment, crashing through the brush. A Yaqui jumped out of his way.

Eccles and Boone fired simultaneously. The Yaqui

sprawled in death. The frenzied horse plunged down the escarpment in a rattle of stones and gravel, striking hard far below.

The echoes died away. The Eastern sky was light, bringing into relief the sharp crags of the eastern mountains.

One of the Yaquis thrashed about, his legs locked from a shattered spine. Boone stood up and walked forward. Eccles came out of the house. He walked to the Yaqui and fired at three feet. Bits of hair and skull flew away from the smash of the soft-nosed slug.

Boone looked down the escarpment. Three Yaquis were riding fast away from the base of the steep slope. Boone pumped his Winchester dry after them, forcing them to scatter. It was all over.

Eccles grinned. "We did it," he said.

Boone nodded. "One horse left. Marion can ride him."

Eccles' face tightened. "What about the gold?"

"We'll bury it."

"Hell no! It goes."

Boone threw aside his Winchester and dropped his hand to his Colt. The holster was empty. Then he remembered he had left both of his six-guns lying back at his position.

Marion came out of the house and ran to Boone. "Thank God."

Boone looked across her shoulder at Eccles. The tall outlaw held his Winchester at hip level, pointing toward them. His face looked like a death's-head. "Get away from the woman," he said thinly.

Boone gently pushed her back.

"Get into the house," said Eccles.

Boone walked toward the house. He stepped in.

Eccles prodded him in the back with the rifle. A cold trickle of sweat worked down Boone's sides.

"Stand in the corner with your back to me," said Eccles. "Get them hands up high."

"He saved our lives!" called Marion.

"Shut up! Get that hoss."

She led the horse to the front of the house.

"Get them money sacks. Tie 'em onto the horse." She did as she was told.

Eccles stepped back. "The canteens are full," he said. "Marion, you lead that horse up the pass."

"No!"

"Git! Git, or I'll shoot."

She came closer to Bass. "Let him go and I'll go with you."

"Git!"

She led the horse past the house, the hoofs clashing on the gravel.

Boone stared at the wall. His hands were up high. He hoped to God Eccles didn't notice the bulge at his left wrist under the filthy undershirt sleeve.

"You and me might have gone places together, Shattuck. We'd of made a good team."

Boone almost reached for the derringer.

Eccles spat. "I guess I'm just a lobo," he said. "I like to make you poor bastards work for me and then take the loot."

"You haven't a chance, Eccles."

"I've done all right so far."

"Yes."

Eccles shifted. He cocked the rifle.

Boone spoke over his shoulder. "I'll make a deal," he said.

"Go to hell!"

"Listen, Bass. Wells Fargo knows you've come this way. They wired ahead to Yuma. They have agents from Yuma down to San Luis. You can't go south, Chacon is ravaging the country."

"How do you know?" There was fear in his voice.

Boone thought quickly. "A Wells Fargo man was at Naco."

"You're a damned liar!"

"I waylaid him and took his badge and credentials. They're in my pocket."

"Turn around."

Boone turned to face the muzzle of the rifle. There was fear in Eccles' dark eyes.

"Reach down easylike," said Bass. "Get them credentials."

Boone slid his right hand into his pocket and took out the badge and the folded paper. He handed them to Eccles. Eccles held the rifle in his right hand, finger pressing against the trigger. He glanced down at the badge. "Yeah. This is the real thing." He fumbled with the paper and unfolded it. He read the name on it and his eyes widened.

Boone kicked out. The Winchester barrel went up and the gun roared. Eccles cursed and jumped back. Boone gripped the barrel in his left hand and forced it up. Eccles smashed a fist at Boone's face. The blow half-stunned him. He went back against the wall. Eccles let go of the rifle and jumped back, clawing for his Colt.

Boone ripped the derringer from its clip and cocked it as Eccles' Colt came up. Both weapons roared. Something slammed Boone back against the wall. He went down and rolled away as Eccles fired again. The slug screamed from the packed earth floor.

Boone's right shoulder was numb. He jerked the derringer with his left hand from his right and fired from the noon.

Eccles jerked, staggered back. His eyes were glazing even as he fired for the last time. The Colt dropped from nerveless fingers as Eccles hit the wall and slid to the floor over the ticking sacks. He opened his mouth and a flood of blood poured from it, soaking into the sacks.

Boone bent his head and touched his own right shoulder. His hand came away stained with blood. The slug had plowed just over the bone, cutting a deep furrow. His gut moiled.

"Boone!" Marion stood in the doorway. She looked at Eccles and then ran to Boone, cradling him in her arms. "You're hurt bad!"

He looked up at her. Her eyes were wet. "It's all over, isn't it, Boone?"

"Yes. We'll rest awhile. Then head for Yuma."

She touched his gaunt face. "And then?"

He grinned. "Why we'll head for Texas, honey. Where else?"

She kissed him hard. He drew her close with his left arm and then suddenly forgot the pain in his right shoulder as he crushed her to him, feeling the softness of her. The bloody trail of death was over. A new life would begin for the two of them. The hate was out of him now. The desert had burned the impurities out of him. Somewhere on the desert below them a thrasher lifted its rich song to greet the morning sun.

VOICE OF THE GUN

CHAPTER ONE

Sloan Sutro came up the narrow winding trail through the lower Mountain Meadows country, riding his tired coyote dun and leading a pair of dusty burros trotting steadily along under big diamond-hitched kyacks. Sloan drew rein at the top of the trail, slid from the saddle, and felt for the makings, never taking his eyes from the scene spread out before him.

In the far background rose the Wolf-Fanged Mountains, with patches of snow still in some of the deeper hollows. The timber line etched itself across a huge sunlit talus slope almost as though drawn with a gigantic straightedge by a master hand. The pines swayed in the fresh thrust and drive of the clean wind, and the soughing melody carried down to the lean, tired man who had ridden so many miles to return to the one place in the Southwest where he wanted to make his home. It had taken Sloan Sutro time to get back to this one place, but now he was here to stay.

The Mountain Meadows country started at the near edge of the wide belt of timber, dotted here and there with bosques and mottes of fine trees standing proudly erect on the green carpet of the meadows. The sun reflected from a small clear lake and the waters of a swiftly rushing stream that emerged from the lower end of the lake. The gay music of the rushing waters mingled with that of the fugue of the pines and spruces and the constantly murmuring wind. Beyond the widest of the meadows was a strange wonderland of rocks just below the vast panorama of the mountain backdrop. The distorted and weirdly shaped rock formations were tinted yellow, salmon, buff, red and bright pink in various shades and nuances. Here and there, the dark and mysterious mouths of caves and clefts showed against the brilliant coloring of the rocks.

Sloan slowly rolled a quirly while he scanned the scene. It had not changed since his first unbelievable and delightful view of it some months ago. Pines, firs, and spruces were intermingled with swaying clumps of white-stemmed aspens and birches. Nature had spread flowers with a lavish hand—silene, larkspur, verbena, golden helenium, columbine, Indian paintbrush, iris, and penstemon.

Sloan lighted his cigarette, and as he did so, he saw a small bear waddle across a sun-dappled clearing, carefully avoiding a porcupine. Somewhere in the woods, a turkey gobbled. The coyote dun whinnied sharply as he smelled the fresh water, and the sound startled a white-tailed deer who leaped a mossy log and vanished silently into the woods.

The log buildings were situated on a low grassy knoll set in front of the vast jumble of turreted, spired, and battlemented rock formations. Riding closer, he saw a low house, fair-sized barn, several small outbuildings, and what remained of a sagging, peeled pole corral. From what Sloan could see, the buildings were in fair repair. He nodded in satisfaction, looked at the weary dun, and said with a tired grin, "I think we've come home Tango."

He led the three animals up the gentle slope, enjoying the soft feel of the grass beneath his worn boot soles, boot soles that too often had felt the hellish heat of the naked desert floor burning up through them. He unsaddled the dun, unloaded the two burros, then slapped them on the rumps, raising a cloud of thin dust that drifted between the trees. The three animals buck jumped a little, then streaked for the stream. They wouldn't stray very far that day, at least. Who'd want to stray from such a place anyway? He'd have plenty of time to repair the corral.

The sun flashed on the house windows as he started toward the log structure, and something made him halt and drop his right hand to the worn walnut butt of the Colt that was holstered low down and tied to his muscular thigh. He stood there for several minutes with the wind whipping his faded bandana about his brown and corded throat. Then he shook his head. "Not a blessed soul for at least ten miles," he said. "What the hell is the matter with you, Sutro?"

But the habits of years are not easily forgotten by outlaws and lawmen. They are always alert or they die quickly. Sloan did not walk directly to the low roofed porch but rather side-stepped behind a thick tree to study house and barn. Buck Kelso said no one lived there, nor did anyone live there since Simon Kelso, more familiarly known as 'Old Man' Kelso, died on his land with a bullet between his eyes. The last time Sloan was there, he had not entered the buildings. He had captured Buck Kelso in the tangled labyrinth of rocks behind the buildings. No one called the place home now. But still...

Sloan walked to the porch. No one knew him in this remote part of Arizona Territory unless it might be by hearsay. It wasn't likely, for the Rio Blanco Valley was almost a world apart in Eastern Arizona. It was wedged in between huge mountains to the east and the wild Apache Reservation to the west, a long strip of land more or less isolated from the main east-west travel routes that traversed the easier desert country north and south.

A fresh cardboard sign had been tacked to the front of the house beside the front door. "Property of the Rio

Blanco Ranching, Mining, and Development Company," he read aloud. He spat, then ripped the sign from the building and rolled it up. He walked around the side of the house and opened the rear door with a rusty squealing of hinges to enter the kitchen.

The big kitchen range was covered with a patina of dust and scaling rust. Transients had used the place, leaving broken bottles and hacked tin cans lying on the floor and on the filthy table. He walked into the living room past the single bedroom. A huge and rugged fireplace dominated the room. The dusty furniture had been supplying rats and other small creatures with nesting materials. Their scattered droppings littered the floor. Other animals, of the two-legged talking variety that proudly leaves its filth wherever it goes, had left their litter in the comers. Sloan wrinkled his nose. "Animals," he said disgustedly.

The place had possibilities. It was well built and the roof seemed sound. There was plenty of time for him to get it ready before the rains came, followed by the heavy snows of those elevations. He was used to the loneliness of the deserts and sterile mountain country in other parts of Arizona and in New Mexico and Texas, as well as parts of Mexico. But that was different. He had hardly settled at any place for more than a few months at a time. His work always kept him on the move, and he liked it until he suddenly realized that a man must have a home. This would be his home. He knew it and knew it well. He couldn't say why, but it was so.

He walked outside and watched the animals. The horse was grazing, one of the burros was rolling on its back, while the other meditated knee deep in the clear sparkling waters of the stream. Sloan rolled another cigarette and walked across the grassy meadow, through a fringe of trees to stand at last where he could see the great valley of the Rio Blanco spread out before him. Here and there, he could see thin threads of smoke arising. The sun glinted on water. Far up the valley, there was a cluster of buildings, the town of Rio Blanco.

It was a beautiful place. The words of Buck Kelso came back to Sloan. *You ain't never going to find a prettier place to live, Sutro. Scenery-wise, that is, but some of the people living there have made it into a pocket-sized edition of hell, and likely it ain't changed much since then. I'll never go back; you've seen to that, Sutro. They'll hang me, but you can go back there. But you always got to walk a tightrope in the Rio Blanco Valley, Sutro, and that ain't easy. Not for a man like you, it ain't.*

He walked back to his new home. He was bone-tired and had been for weeks, more because of his mind than because of his body, but he couldn't sit there in the dappled sunlight like an old man warming his thin blood. He got a doublebitted axe from one of the kyacks, honed it, peeled off vest and shirt, gunbelt and hat, hung them on the corral fence, then walked into the nearest stand of timber. He needed fresh poles for the corral, but before he made one stroke of the axe he did something that surprised himself. He studied the stand of timber to see where it needed thinning; the act of a man who knew he might live in such a place for a long time, perhaps for the rest of his life—natural or otherwise.

It was a good place to put down roots for a trans-planted Texan whose adult life had been one of move-ment and adventure, always moving on, trying to forget some of the past. The odd insistence of Buck Kelso that Sloan buy the place had finally borne fruit. It was a pecu-liar quirk of fate for a doomed outlaw to sell his land to the man who had tracked him down and captured him on that very land.

Under other circumstances Sloan Sutro and Buck Kelso might have become good friends. Their qualities were much the same. Their hard-earned skills with weapons and fists could have been used to uphold the law or to break it. Sloan had chosen to uphold it; Kelso to break it.

Sloan stepped back and eyed a straight pine. Why had Buck Kelso left such a place? It was his home. He was born and raised there. He had talked of the place almost as a man talking about the woman he loves; the *only* woman he had ever loved. Why, then, had he chosen the owlhoot trail? Sloan shrugged, raised the axe, and swung it against the tight bark of the pine.

The sharp, clean blows of the axe rang across the meadows and echoed from the mountainside with a musical quality all its own. The feeling of sweat was gratifying to Sloan as he worked steadily. When he had a neat pile of poles, he paused to wipe the sweat from his lean face. It was then that he knew he was no longer alone. He turned slowly to see the young woman seated on the top rail of the corral, hat hanging at the nape of her lovely neck, from the *barbiquejo* strap that drew a sharp dark line across her skin. There was a vague uneasiness in Sloan Sutro at the thought it brought back to his mind, only *that* time it had been a horsehair reata drawn tightly about the strong neck of a *man*.

He picked up the poles and carried them beneath his left arm, the axe in his right hand, as he approached her. The sun slanted down through the treetops, and dust motes whirled about her as though enchanted by this vision that had come to such a lonely place. "Hello," said Sloan easily.

She smiled. "Hello," she answered in a throaty voice. She glanced down at the poles. "You handle an axe like a lumberjack."

He smiled. "I've had to use an axe at times," he said.

Her eyes were hazel with dancing flecks of gold in them, reminding Sloan of a German drink he had once seen in a plush Denver bar that had gold dust swirling about in it. Her hair was honey-colored, and her skin seemed to have a golden tint to it. A real golden girl, thought Sloan.

"Seen enough, stranger?" she quietly asked.

Sloan flushed beneath his tan. "I beg your pardon," he said quickly.

She slid from the top rail. "Forget it," she said. "I'm Julie Landres."

"Sloan Sutro," he said, studying her to see if his name would mean anything, but there was no indication that she knew him.

"Camping here tonight?" she asked.

"Tonight and perhaps a great many other nights, Miss Landres. It is *Miss* Landres?"

"Yes," she said quickly. "No one lives here, of course. I guess it's all right. Buck Kelso hasn't lived here in about three years." She laughed suddenly. "It isn't likely he'd be back to bother you."

"No... he won't be, Miss Landres."

She lowered her eyelids. "You know Buck?" she asked.

"Yes."

"Friend of his?"

"Not exactly."

"What do you mean by that, Mr. Sutro?"

A jay chattered angrily from a tall pine.

"I knew Buck," he said quietly.

"That sounds like past tense, Mr. Sutro."

He nodded. "Buck Kelso is dead."

Her breath caught in her throat.' "Are you sure?" she said slowly.

"Positive."

Her eyes searched his face. "How do I know you are telling me the truth?"

He walked to the corral, threw the poles inside it, then picked up the shirt and vest, taking a wallet out of the shirt pocket. He removed a folded paper and turned toward her. "Buck Kelso sold me this place, Miss Landres," he said. "That was less than a month ago. It's legal and proper like," he said.

Strange thoughts made themselves known on her face. "Does anyone around here know about this?"

"Not to my knowledge. I came through Caballo Pass and haven't seen anyone for three days, excepting you, of course."

"You intend to stay here?"

He looked at the vista before them, with the sun slanting down like rays from the windows of heaven. "I hope so," he said softly.

She tilted her head to one side. "You are sure that you own this place, Mr. Sutro?"

He tapped the paper. "This will, stand up in *any* court. Buck Kelso saw to that, Miss Landers."

"You don't look like a rancher, Mr. Sutro."

"I've worked cows in my time."

"You still don't look the type."

He smiled faintly. "Is there a type? If so, what would you call me?" He shrugged into his shirt and buttoned it, then reached for his vest. Her eyes flicked up and down him. "Well?" he asked. He put on the vest. Her eyes settled on the left hand side of the vest just above the heart area. The vest was of dark gray material, but it had faded from desert suns and winds. There was a dark patch above the heart area; a place where something had shielded the material from fading.

"Lawman," she said quickly.

"You have sharp eyes."

"I've seen your type before, Mr. Sutro. Some people around here call them 'hired killers' as well as other unmentionable things."

He nodded as he reached for his hat. "Thanks," he said dryly.

"But you, you're not here on business?"

"Private business, Miss Landres."

"Such as?"

He swept out a hand to encompass his land. "To make a home perhaps. I don't know. It isn't easy for a man like me to put down roots."

She smiled faintly. "Do you think you'll be able to put roots down here?"

"Why not?"

"Buck didn't tell you much about Rio Blanco, did he?"

"A little."

"Did he say anything about the Kelso-Bylas feud?"

"He didn't call it a feud." Sloan remembered Buck's warning. *But you got to walk a tightrope in Rio Blanco Valley, Sutro, and that ain't easy. Not for a man like you, it ain't.*

"You might have a pig in a poke here, Mr. Sutro."

"I'll wait and see."

"How much did it cost you?"

He glanced at her with an annoyed look.

She waved a hand. "Come on, Mr. Sutro," she said quickly. "This is no time to be subtle."

"All right," said Sloan. "I think I paid enough. Three thousand dollars' worth, Miss Landres."

"I'll give you five thousand cash for the place."

He felt for the makings, then looked at her. "I suppose you think I conned Buck out of the place. That wasn't so. It was *his* idea, Miss Landres. I really can't say why I agreed to the deal." He hesitated with the sack of makings in his hand.

"Goon," she said. "Roll one for me, too. Does that surprise you, Mr. Sutro?"

He shook his head. "Seems like nothing about you surprises me, Miss Landres."

"Julie," she said.

"Julie then." He rolled two smokes and casually placed one between her full red lips, snapping a lucifer on a thumbnail to light it for her. She drew in the smoke deeply and blew out a perfect ring. "Left my damned smokes with my horse," she said. "He strayed. I heard you chopping and couldn't resist coming to see who it was."

"You said five thousand dollars," he said thoughtfully. "Why that sum?"

"It's two thousand more than you *paid* for the place."

"Yes." He lighted his cigarette and eyed her through the wreathing smoke. "That's what Buck said the place was worth. Exactly five thousand dollars."

She flushed. "Well, you'd still make a profit."

"It's not for sale."

"Three thousand dollars made this place a steal."

He couldn't help but let a faint smile trace its way across his hawk's face. "Yes. That's very good," he said.

"Buck Kelso is dead. A lot of good that three thousand dollars did him. Probably gambled it away or blew it on a woman," she said bitterly.

He shook his head. "Buck Kelso never saw a cent of the money. Our agreement was that I would pay off any of his debts. It amounted to about three thousand dollars."

"That doesn't sound like him."

"I said he was dead," Sloan said quietly.

"How did he die?"

The jay chattered noisily. Sloan looked away from the young woman. "Buck Kelso was lynched in Vista Springs some weeks ago."

"I knew he'd end up with a rope about his neck."

"You don't mean that, Julie," he said.

She looked down at the ground. "No, I don't." There was a catch in her voice.

"Buck said he was the last of his line. He wanted me to have the place, for some reason of his own. I had been here once, and liked it. After what happened in Vista Springs I knew it was time for me to settle down somewhere. To forget being a lawman."

"You might forget being a lawman here. There are other things that will not be forgotten. A man will have to *hold* this land, Sloan, not just settle peacefully upon it."

"I think I can hold it."

She glanced toward the house as though expecting to see something.

"The sign?" he asked. "I tore it down. Someone was in a right hurry to take over the place. It's *mine,* Julie."

She drew in on the cigarette. "That wasn't exactly diplomatic of you, but so long as I am the only one who knows about it, I guess it's all right."

"It is my place, Julie or will be as soon as Buck's debts are paid off."

There was an odd look in her lovely eyes. "Six thousand, Sloan," she said quickly.

"No."

"I won't go any higher."

"It doesn't make any difference."

"You might be sorry."

"I'll take my chances on that."

She looked past him. "There's my horse." She whistled shrilly. A dainty appaloosa mare splashed across the stream and trotted to her. She swung up into the saddle. "Do me one favor," she said. "If you decide to sell, consider my offer first, will you?"

"Why not?" he smiled. "That's a lot of money, Julie."

"You'd be much better off to take my offer now, Sloan."

"No."

She shrugged, then glanced about the meadows, almost as though someone might be eavesdropping. "I don't think you quite know what you are up against, Sloan."

"I'm staying, Julie."

She shook her head in resignation. "Well, it's your problem, Sloan. I have an idea. One more thing: Don't tell anyone, *anyone* you understand, that I offered to buy the place."

"No," he said.

She swung easily up onto the appaloosa and looked down at him. "I like you," she said frankly.

"Gracias!"

She rode a few feet, then drew rein and turned in the

saddle, resting a gloved hand on the cantle. "You were a long way from your guns, Mr. Sutro, when I came up behind you."

"So?"

She looked down at his lean waist. "You haven't got a gun on you now. Take my advice. *Wear your Colt and keep your Winchester handy. Adios,* Sloan!" She dug her heels into the mare, and the dainty creature bounded like a rubber ball, racing toward the stream to leap it cleanly. The rush of air swept Julie's hat from her head and the sun shined on her hair, turning it into living gold until she vanished into the pines, leaving the echo of thudding hoofs behind her.

Sloan shrugged. He picked up his gunbelt and swung it about his lean waist with practiced ease, cinching it, then buckling it, settling it down on his thigh. He looked down the worn walnut butt of the sixshooter. "And I thought I'd be able to walk around here without you," he said. He shook his head. He had lived by the gun for a long time and he had thought its voice was stilled for the rest of his life. But Julie Landres thought differently.

He walked to the house and set to work in the kitchen. By the time the sun had vanished in the west he had cleaned the room and prepared a simple meal of beans and bacon. He made his bed in a corner, then went outside and rounded up his animals. He led them into the barn and wedged the door shut. As he walked toward the dark house he heard a faint screaming sound like that of a woman in dire terror, but he knew what it was.

A cougar was on the loose in the thick timber and he had smelled the animals.

Before he went to bed he walked to the rim of the meadowland and looked down upon the dark valley of the Rio Blanco. Here and there lamplight dotted the darkness like topazes cast carelessly on black velvet. The faint bittersweet odor of wood smoke came to him on the night wind. It was a beautiful place, but Buck Kelso had said it had been turned into a pocket-sized edition of hell. Sloan rolled a cigarette and lighted it, strolling slowly back to his house. There was another, more famous place of wondrous beauty that was turned into a hell—Eden.

CHAPTER TWO

The sun was up high when Sloan Sutro's horse clattered over the plank bridge that spanned the north fork of the Rio Blanco, to enter the town named after the river. Rio Blanco had been placed, perhaps with unconscious taste, in a setting of beauty. The mountains formed a magnificent backdrop east and north of the town, while beyond the foaming river, the great oval valley fell away in successive folds and ridges to the hazy blue-green escarpment on top of which perched Sloan's new holding.

But man made fabrications had hashed up the beauty of the scene. Ugly, scabrous frame structures lined both sides of the wide dirt street. Here and there was a log structure, which seemed more fitting in that setting. On a hill just north of the town the supreme insult to the natural setting had been placed, like an excrescence on the nose of a lovely woman. A huge pile of a house complete with wooden turrets, a captain's walk, heavy stiff fringes of wooden gingerbreading and a wide veranda complete with horrible looking furniture in the style of the East and Midwest. "Jesus God," said Sloan as he eyed the monstrosity.

A woman looked curiously at him as he rode past. He

tipped his hat. "Where can I find the office of the Rio Blanco Ranching, Mining and Development Company, ma'am," he asked.

She pointed up the street. "White frame building at the corner of Main and Spruce," she said. "Can't miss it. Right across from the Bascomb House."

"Thank you, ma'am."

"You must be a stranger here," she said. "Asking for the Rio Blanco Company."

"I am," he said politely, then touched Tango with his spurs to make him move along a little faster.

He tethered the dun to a hitching rack and looked at the company building. It was a dandy. A saloon held the post of honor at the corner and the sun flashed from the stained glass of its windows and its polished bat-wing doors. There were other businesses along the wide board sidewalk beneath the porch that stretched the full length of the building, all of half a block.

Sloan wiped his mouth and eyed the batwings, then shook his head. He walked toward an entrance behind which was a wide stairway leading up to the second floor of the building. He slapped some of the dust from his clothing, then walked up the stairs expecting to find himself in a hallway but instead he found himself in a wide office full of roll top desks behind which eye-shaded men worked steadily, the scratching of pens and the rustling of paper reminding Sloan of mice moving about in a hayloft and, by God, most of the men behind the desks had a mousey look about them, at that.

A young woman sat at a desk behind a low wooden railing in which a swinging gate of ornately carved wood was set. She looked up at Sloan. "May I help you?" she asked. Her blue eyes appraised him quickly and seemed to like what they saw. After all, she spent most of her time in this varnished museum with older men who were hardly more than automatons.

"I'd like to see Mr. Garth Bylas," he said.

Her eyes narrowed. She stood up. "Your name and business please?"

"Sloan Sutro. The business is of a private nature."

She hesitated. "Mr. Bylas would hardly receive a person who did not have an appointment, Mr. Sutro."

He took off his hat and rested his big hands on the railing. "Ma'am," he said quietly, "I think Mr. Bylas will see me. It won't take long."

She eyed the hard gray eyes and the lean hawk-face, and although a shiver went up and down her lovely little spine, she seemed to get a delicious thrill out of this timber wolf of a man. "I'll see what can be done," she said. She walked with slightly swinging hips toward a glass-enclosed office, and although Sloan didn't realize it, she was watching him by reflection through the glass, and saw his appreciative and appraising perusal of her hips and ankles.

Sloan rolled a cigarette after she vanished. He lighted it and leaned against the railing, catching a frowning glance from one of the eye-shaded mice behind a desk.

She of the gently rolling hips came back with a man in tow. A man in a black suit and white shirt, with black tie, squared spectacles, from which a ribbon depended, and a frosty look in the eyes behind the spectacles. The girl smiled faintly. "This is Mr. Jonas, our office manager," she said. "Mr. Jonas, this is Mr. Sutro."

Sloan nodded, taking the cigarette from his lips. "Jonas," he said politely.

Jonas' cold eyes flicked up and down Sloan, appraising *him,* as Sloan had appraised the girl. "Business please?" he asked in a dry voice.

"It's personal with Mr. Bylas."

"I am afraid that Mr. Bylas can't see you, Mr. Sutro. I handle all secondary business here."

"This is personal with Mr. Bylas."

Jonas flushed a little. The big wall clock ticked on, with the sun glinting from the polished brass pendulum.

"I said that I handle all secondary business here, Mr. Sutro."

"What makes you think it's secondary business, Mr. Jonas?"

Some of the clerks looked up to eye Sloan.

Jonas looked up and down Sloan again. "Well, Mr. Sutro, I'd hardly say a man, such as yourself, would be in *a position* to talk with Mr. Bylas on equal terms. Come now! What is it? I haven't all day, sir!"

The girl flushed a little. She bit her full lower lip and glanced from Jonas to Sloan and back again.

Sloan leaned forward. "I haven't all day either, Mr. Jonas. Now you run along and tell Mr. Bylas that Sloan Sutro wants to see him right quick."

Jonas' face reddened. "Why, you..."

Sloan's face tightened. "Take it easy," he said softly, and his native Texas drawl seemed to be a little more pronounced.

Jonas glanced to right and left. This man was making a fool out of Ernest Jonas right in his own bailiwick. Most of these leather-skinned, slow-spoken men who came in from the ranges and the mines, smelling of horse and cow manure, sweat, and cheap tobacco, not to mention cheap liquor, took damned good care not to rile *Ernest Jonas.*

It was then that Sloan noticed one of the white-collared mice glancing anxiously toward the glass-enclosed office from which Mr. Jonas had appeared like a rabbit out of a magician's hat. The door was still partly open, and whoever was standing behind it listening had evidently forgotten that the sunlight was *behind* him. Sloan squinted his eyes. The name on the glass part of the door was Garth Bylas, President.

Jonas reconsidered. "Kindly leave your name and the nature of your business here with Miss Corday," he said frostily, "and I'll let you know when Mr. Bylas can see you."

Sloan shook his head. "I came here to see Garth Bylas on a matter of business, and I aim to see him this morning."

The clock ticked on, and Sloan could see the bitter venom of hate in the little eyes of Jonas. The man turned on a heel and walked away. Sloan dropped his cigarette into a gaboon, smiled at Miss Corday, swung open the gate, then followed Jonas up the aisle. Jonas turned suddenly, and his face went pale as he looked up into the lean, tanned face of Sloan Sutro. "Get out!" he snapped.

"Move out of the way, *amigo*," said Sloan gently.

Jonas raised a shaking hand. Sloan slid big hands beneath the man's armpits, lifted him easily and set him to one side, then walked on toward the office. One of the clerks tittered, then froze as he caught a glance from Jonas.

Sloan saw that the shadow behind the glass had disappeared. He tapped on the glass. "Mr. Bylas?" he called out.

"Yes?"

"Name of Sloan Sutro. I have private business with you, sir."

"Concerning what?"

"Money."

There was a moment's hesitation, then a low laugh. "You know the way to get to meet Garth Bylas. Come in, Sutro!"

Sloan opened the door and walked into a big bright corner office. A broad-shouldered man sat between two huge walnut desks, leaning back in a heavily padded leather swivel chair. He was in his early forties and had gone a little into flesh, but Sloan could tell that Garth Bylas had been a fine figure of a man in his earlier days, and still was for that matter. His eyes were a blue-gray, surprisingly light for his tanned face, and his nose was magnificent. A fine dragoon mustache of the same silken quality as the man's thinning light brown hair covered his full upper lip. Bylas nodded. "Sit down," he said. He shoved a cigar box across the desk. "Cigar?"

"Thanks." Sloan selected one, cut off the tip with the silver cutters lying on the desk, then leaned forward to accept a light from the big hand of Garth Bylas, noting the fine diamond ring on his finger.

Sloan hung his hat on a rack, then settled into a large leather armchair, blowing out a cloud of smoke as he did so, much to the amusement of the big man seated behind the desk. "You have a way about you, Sutro, I must say," he murmured.

"I thought I was in Arizona Territory, not Wall Street, when I came in here, Mr. Bylas."

Bylas waved a hand. "You can see my position, Sutro. I have many and varied interests and I can't see every man who comes in here. Evidently you're a stranger here?"

"I am. But I won't be for long."

The eyes narrowed. "That so? What's your line? Ranching? Mining? Business? Bylas leaned forward. "No," he said softly. "By God! I think I know, Sutro! I should have figured it out!"

"So?"

"A hired gun?"

Sloan took the fine cigar from his mouth and eyed it. "I used to be, in a sense."

"Hashknife Outfit? Lazy L? Who did you work for? John Chisum? Slaughter?"

"I worked for Cochise County, Mr. Bylas, and before that for the City of El Paso, and before that, I was with the Frontier Battalion of the Texas Rangers."

"By Judas! A lawman!"

"Past tense," admitted Sloan quietly.

"What do you mean?"

"I'm not here in any official capacity, Mr. Bylas."

There was almost a look of relief in the man's eyes. "No? Then why *are* you here?"

"I brought a message and something else from an old enemy of yours, Mr. Bylas."

"So? Who?"

"Buck Kelso."

The big hands closed spasmodically and the man's tongue tip appeared suddenly beneath his thick mustache. The man had been startled, but he wasn't afraid. Sloan saw the right hand slide slowly from the desk and vanish beneath the edge of it, and all the while the hard eyes never left those of Sloan Sutro.

"You can forget about that hideout gun, Mr. Bylas," said Sloan quietly. "I'm not here to do a job for Buck Kelso. At least not the kind of job you *think* I may have come here for."

Their eyes seemed to feint and maneuver, trying for a winning hold, then Bylas smiled faintly and brought his hand up from beneath the desk. "Your cigar has gone out," he said.

Sloan nodded and then lighted the fine weed.

"Where is Buck Kelso?" asked Bylas.

"In Cochise County. Buried in Boot Hill outside of Vista Springs."

There was a look of relief in Bylas' eyes and it suddenly came to Sloan Sutro that Garth Bylas, as powerful as he was, had feared Buck Kelso, for Kelso was a man who would fight at any time and any place, with friends at his side, or alone, and preferably the latter. But it was a certainty that Bylas feared that type of man, for he evidently knew that he could handle other men and groups of men by the weight of his power and his hired gunslicks.

There was no doubt in Sloan's mind that Bylas had plenty of hired guns to back him up and was always looking for more of them, as evidenced by his first belief that Sloan was one of them. But the lone wolf could come and go at any time and try to kill like his namesake, and no matter how many of them Bylas could have run out of the country or drygulched there would always be another one of them, and one of them might get him despite his protective wall of hired guns. It was a thought to remember, and Sloan Sutro neatly tucked it into the mental file he kept on such matters. Such little items had been useful before.

"How did he die?" asked Bylas at last.

"Lynched, Mr. Bylas."

Bylas laughed shortly. "That figures."

Sloan should have let it go at that, but that was not his way. "*Mistakenly,* Mr. Bylas," he said quietly.

"How do you know?" asked Bylas sharply.

Sloan leaned forward. "I mortally wounded the man who later confessed the crime for which Kelso had been accused. I had suspected all along that Kelso was innocent, otherwise I would never have delivered him into the hands of his lynchers. I had trailed him for weeks and caught him here in the valley."

Bylas' eyes narrowed. "*Where* in the valley?"

"On his own land. It was a long hunch, but I was right."

"Quite a job to get Buck Kelso. How many men did you have with you?"

"I was alone."

Bylas studied Sloan with new respect. "Well, although it is hard to say, the death of Buck Kelso was long overdue. The man was a habitual criminal. One way or another he would have died as he lived—violently."

"Before God, Bylas, I wish I had let him go!"

"What difference does it make now?"

Sloan touched the place where his deputy sheriff's badge had been pinned. "It made a difference here, Bylas. You see, I liked Buck Kelso!"

The whistle blew stridently at the sawmill up the river. Bylas took out a heavy gold hunting case watch and snapped open the lid. "Three minutes slow," he said with pursed lips.

"Change it then, Mr. Bylas."

The hard gray eyes came up and held Sloan's eyes. "The whistle is three minutes late, Mr. Sutro, not my watch."

In that one sentence Sloan had the complete picture of the man. Garth Bylas made the rules in Rio Blanco; *he* ran the country. It was what Buck Kelso had said.

"I have a luncheon appointment in twenty minutes, Sutro," said Bylas. "You said you had a message from Buck Kelso and something else as well."

Sloan nodded. He took out his wallet and removed a thousand dollars in hundred dollar bills from it. "One thousand dollars, Mr. Bylas. The exact sum of money owed you by Buck Kelso."

The eyes flicked down at the money, then up at Sloan. "How do you happen to be handling this?"

"Kelso was wanted for murder. I trailed him and got him. I believed he was innocent of the crime. He was. But somehow he knew he was reaching the end of his trail. There was a lot of ill feeling fanned against him in Vista Springs. A bunch of drunks broke into the jail while I was gone. They strung him up. It was just as much murder as the crime for which he had been accused. Before that, he had sold his property to me, with the condition that I take the money and pay off his debts. This I did, and with the payment of one thousand dollars owed to you, Buck Kelso's slate is clean."

The eyes narrowed again. "He sold his property to you? The land and buildings at the south end of this valley?"

"That's right."

Something seemed to slam into Bylas' guts with the impact of a forty-four. A sickly color spread beneath his tanned skin.

Sloan smiled. "The debt is paid. I'll thank you for the deed of land, which Buck had put up for collateral."

Bylas' breath came harshly in his throat. "There may be some legal technicalities here, Sutro. I..."

"You had already put up your sign on the property. A little hastily, I'm sure. The property is now mine."

"You're not a rancher, Sutro?"

"I have worked cattle. The land is good and there is fine timber on it. I have not yet decided what to do with it."

"I'll give you four thousand dollars for it."

"It's not for sale."

Bylas smiled. "It is possible that I could take legal action to possess that land, Sutro. I had an option to buy it, you know."

"May I see it?"

The clock ticked for five seconds. "It was a verbal deal, Sutro," said Bylas quietly.

It was Sloan's turn to smile. "Come, come, Mr. Bylas. I can't buy a thing like that. Buck Kelso is dead. I paid for the land. I paid off his debt to you. *The deed,* Mr. Bylas."

"I'll give you five thousand dollars for the land."

"I was offered six thousand just yesterday."

Bylas stared at Sloan. "By who?" he demanded.

"I am not at liberty to say."

"I see. It might just be possible that I can take legal action on that verbal deal with Kelso."

"You have witnesses, of course?"

"It seems to me, Sutro, that you're a little short with me. You don't aim to fight Garth Bylas, do you?" Bylas leaned forward. "I'll give you six thousand dollars, spot cash, here and now for that land."

Sloan stood up. "I'll think it over."

Bylas also stood up. "Do," he said politely. "But one piece of advice, if I may: don't take too long."

"Thanks for the advice. I don't like to be rushed into things, Mr. Bylas."

Bylas nodded. "You said that Kelso had sent a message for me. What is it."

Sloan dropped his cigar into a gaboon. "He said he thought the last laugh would be on you and that he would surely know it from beyond the grave." Sloan smiled. "And now a receipt for that thousand dollars and the deed, Mr. Bylas."

For a moment their eyes clashed and then Bylas sat down, wrote out a receipt, and thrust it toward Sloan. "The deed is not available right now, Sutro. I'll have it sent up to your place."

Sloan shook his head. "I want that deed right now, Mr. Bylas. I'll wait."

Bylas' eyes were as cold as ice. "As you will. What did Kelso mean by that message of his?"

"I really don't know, Mr. Bylas. He said you would know. Perhaps not right away, but in time. And now the deed, Mr. Bylas."

Bylas stood up. "Will you wait here?"

"I'll be downstairs, in the Bijou. I don't want to wait too long."

For a moment Bylas' temper almost broke loose. "Why, you...I ought to..."

Sloan smiled. "Good day, Mr. Bylas."

Mr. Jonas was seated at his roll top desk. He looked up and tried to smile. "So now you are the owner of the Kelso place, Mr. Sutro." The man had ears like an Apache to have overheard the conversation in Bylas' office. He glanced toward the office. The door was closed. "I know of an interested party who might consider paying you seven thousand dollars for the place."

"You, Mr. Jonas?"

Jonas flushed. "Just remember what I said. Keep it to yourself, Mr. Sutro."

Sloan walked to the gate and looked down at the pretty receptionist. "Lunch, Miss Corday?" he suggested.

She was startled, but before she could compose

herself and answer, Mr. Jonas loomed up. "I'm afraid you will have to postpone that luncheon, Miss Corday. I have some work for you to do and it cannot wait."

"I'm sorry, Mr. Sutro," she said.

"Some other time," he answered. Mr. Jonas couldn't keep hobbles on her all the time.

"I'll hold you to it, Mr. Sutro," she said.

He walked downstairs. There was more than just a feeling of opposition against him. For some reason that land was important to quite a few closemouthed people. But the land now belonged to him. There was a stubbornness in Sloan Sutro that some people might call plain cussedness, while others, knowingly, would say it was downright independence. There was a difference.

CHAPTER THREE

Sloan walked into the Bijou and almost whistled aloud. It was quite a place, almost as fine as the Oriental or the Crystal Palace in Tombstone. It was high toned. Polished mahogany bar, brass rails, and spittoons, brocaded wallpaper, polished crystal ware, a few oil paintings. The bartender and the waiter were in white jackets.

Sloan walked halfway down the bar. "Rye," he said to the bartender.

"Yes, sir." The man expertly whipped up bottle and glass, and just as Sloan reached for the bottle, the waiter tapped him on the shoulder. "There's a lady wanting to talk to you, mister," he said.

Sloan turned and saw Julie Landres seated in a rear booth, but this time she was dressed in fashion, with a pert little hat on her golden hair. Sloan took off his hat and walked back to the booth.

"It didn't take you long," she said with a smile.

"To come to town or come in here, Miss Landres?"

"Both," she said. "What are you drinking?"

"Rye," he said. He eyed her a little more closely and realized she was carrying quite a bit of liquor.

"Bennie," she said to the waiter, "bring that bottle over here and bring another glass."

Bennie touched his lips with the point of his tongue. "How about some luncheon first, ma'am?"

"Dammit! Get that bottle!" She studied Sloan. "I suppose you think I've been drinking?"

"It's none of my concern, Miss Landres."

"You're always *so* polite! Do you ever get angry?"

"Sometimes."

"I'd like to see it," she said.

"I hope not, Miss Julie."

"Did you reconsider my offer?"

"The place is not for sale."

Her gold-flecked eyes were half closed. "Did you get a better offer?"

"Perhaps."

"You know very well you did! Who made the offer?"

"Mr. Garth Bylas."

She paled a little, then she leaned across the table and spoke quickly in a low voice. "You kept your word, didn't you? About not talking about *my* offer?"

"I didn't tell anyone."

Bennie brought the bottle and glasses. Julie's hand shook a little as she raised her glass, downing the strong liquor without a tremor. "That's better," she said and refilled her glass.

"Go easy, Miss Julie," he said.

"Go easy, yourself! You might just have to keep your senses about you before you leave this town today, Mr. Sutro!"

"What do you mean by that?"

She tilted her head to one side, and the pert little hat shifted askew. "My God," she said softly. "You really don't know, do you? You're not stupid and certainly not a coward, but you really don't know, do you?"

There was a subtle change in the atmosphere of the

place. Sloan turned and saw a tall man, dressed in gray broadcloth, striding purposefully toward them. Julie looked up and paled again. She glanced uncertainly at Sloan."

"Come on home, Julie," the man said quietly.

"Let me alone, Dave!"

Sloan stood up. "She doesn't want to leave, mister," he said quietly.

"Keep out of this, Sutro."

"You know me, then?"

"*I do.* Come on now, Julie!"

She looked up archly. "Mr. Sutro invited me to have luncheon with him, Dave, dear."

Dave turned to look at Sloan. "She's been drinking, Sutro. I'm not blaming you for this. Julie gets ideas when she drinks."

"May I ask who you are?" said Sloan.

The man didn't wear a belt gun, but he didn't look like the type who would go around unarmed. "Dave Landres," said he.

"Julie's brother?"

Julie laughed.

Dave turned slowly. "Julie! Get up and come on home!"

"No."

"You crazy fool!"

Sloan had the man by the front of the coat, and he hit him once across the mouth with the back of a big hand. "Mind your manners, Landres!" he said sharply.

Landres broke loose, stepped back, wiped his left hand across his bloody mouth, then snaked his right hand inside his coat. Sloan stepped in close, gripped Landres' right wrist with his left hand, drawing his own Colt at the same instant to ram the muzzle into Landres' belly. Landres whitened. His cold eyes bored into Sloan's, but he was too surprised and too sick to fight now. He slowly withdrew his right hand from inside his coat, and Sloan released the wrist. Sloan stepped back and holstered his gun.

Landres saw his chance and could not resist it. He snaked his right hand in again, trying to reach his hideout gun. Sloan swung his left hand, catching Landres hard across the side of his neck, then followed through with a short, smashing right jab that drove Landres back against a table. He fell heavily to the floor, fully conscious but unable to move.

"Oh, my God!" said the bartender as he vanished beneath the mahogany.

Julie tittered. "What happened, Davie, dear? Have you met a better man than yourself? A man *faster* than Dave Landres?"

The waiter helped Dave to his feet. Landres took out a silk handkerchief and wiped his mouth, but his eyes never left Sloan. "I may have forgotten my manners in talking to Julie," he said softly, "and for *that,* I apologize. But you've made a bigger mistake, Mr. Sutro, and that mistake will not be forgotten."

Julie downed her drink and stood up. "I'm leaving," she said a little thickly. "This is no place for a lady."

"You head home, Julie," said Landres sharply.

"We'll see about that," she snapped back as she walked toward the side entrance.

Landres started after her, then saw the look on Sloan's face. "Let me pass, Sutro," he warned, "*or this time I'll kill you—*"

"Let her be!"

Landres' eyes narrowed. "Don't you know who she is?"

"She said she was Miss Julie Landres. That's all I know."

"Miss Landres? My God! You're either a complete fool or a complete stranger in this valley."

"Maybe a little bit of both," admitted Sloan. "Just who is she?"

"She's Mrs. Julia Landres, my brother Harry's wife."

"I didn't know she was married, Landres."

"She can be a bit of a hellion. If it was Harry who came in, there would have been a shooting scrape. It won't sit well with Garth Bylas either."

"How so?"

"Julie was Julie Bylas before she married my brother. Garth Bylas' only sister. Take my advice. Get out of this valley and stay out of it!"

"I intend to stay, Landres."

The man nodded shortly, reached inside his coat, then flicked his eyes at Sloan's ready right hand. "I have something for you from Garth Bylas. The deed to your property." He withdrew the paper and handed it to Sloan.

Sloan nodded. "Mr. Bylas kept his word. I'm sorry about the mix-up with Julie, Landres."

Landres turned away, walked a few feet, then turned again. "Get out of the valley, Sutro. Get out of it *or be buried in it.*"

Sloan walked to the bar and rapped on it as Landres left. "You can come up now," he said. "Get me a rye."

The bartender came up and poured the drink. "I never seen the like of that since Buck Kelso faced down Landres in here three years ago."

"Buck Kelso was pretty good," admitted Sloan.

"You can bet on that! Wasn't anyone around here could beat him, drunk or sober. That night he was owly-eyed drunk, and still, Dave wouldn't draw on him. Harry Landres was here, too, and he couldn't get Dave to face Buck. Dave always claimed Buck was too drunk to know what he was doing. Lot of people thought otherwise."

"What about Harry? Why didn't he face Buck?"

The bartender grinned and looked at the waiter. "You hear that, Bennie?"

"Yen. That's pretty good, Charlie."

"What does that mean?" asked Sloan curiously.

Charlie sniffed. "Hell! Harry Landres talks big, but he

ain't got Dave's guts. Beats me why Julie ever married Harry."

"She's got spunk," said Bennie.

"She sure has," said Sloan drily.

Bennie nodded. "She never forgot Buck Kelso," he said thoughtfully.' 'Rough and tough as he was, he was her man. But Garth Bylas stood in the way. At that, he might have been better off with Buck for a brother-in-law than what he's got now. Wonder where Buck is these days?"

"Dead," said Sloan quietly. "Lynched unjustly by a mob in Vista Springs."

"Who had the guts to round up Buck and arrest him?" asked Charlie.

"I arrested him," said Sloan.

Bennie looked at Charlie, and Charlie looked at Bennie. "You bought property in this valley?" asked the waiter.

"Yes. The Kelso place. That was the deed I got from Dave Landres."

Charlie whistled softly. He poured another drink for Sloan. "Drink up," he said. "This one is on Charlie Priest. Hell of a name for a bartender, but it's my name all right."

"Why the generosity, Charlie?" asked Sloan with a smile.

"I think there are going to be big doings in Rio Blanco Valley, Mr. Sutro! Big doings! Yes, sir!"

When Sloan left the bar, he noticed men standing on the corners of Main and Spruce, covertly eying him. He thought he knew why. He had easily handled Dave Landres, and the news had traveled fast. It might have been a good thing for his morale that he didn't hear the short conversation between Charlie, the bartender, and Bennie, the waiter. It went like this: "How come you bought him that drink, Charlie?" asked Bennie curiously.

"I liked the way he faced down Dave Landres, Bennie."

"That all, Charlie?"

"Well, look at it this way: if he stays alive in the Rio Blanco, I'm honored to buy him a drink."

"And if he doesn't?"

Charlie shrugged. "Then I bought that drink in advance memory of a damned good man!"

It was dusk by the time Sloan Sutro finished his business in town and rode slowly toward the bridge. On the second floor of the huge frame building at the corner of Main and Spruce, Garth Bylas stood in his unlighted office, watching Sloan. The man's face was alternately lighted by the glowing of his cigar as he drew in on it, then plunged into darkness again. He waited until Sloan was out of sight. "Mr. Jonas!" he called out.

"Yes, sir?" said the office manager from the doorway.

"Send a man to my ranch for Rio Yarnell."

"Yes, sir."

Bylas worked his cigar from one side of his wide mouth to the other. He looked to the south, across the darkened valley. "Well, Mr. Sloan Sutro," he said softly, "we'll soon see just how tough you really are."

CHAPTER FOUR

Sloan unloaded the sack of supplies from the horse and then turned Tango into the corral. It was a pleasure to breathe the free and quiet air of the heights after his experience in Rio Blanco that day. Maybe Bylas had been bluffing, but Sloan was not too sure about that. Sloan had hurt him several times in the two places he would suffer the most, his pocketbook and his pride—in that order. Garth Bylas would not forget easily. He ran the Rio Blanco Valley, and he had not taken over the driver's seat without smashing more than a few tough opponents. He'd do it again and again, and as long as he was able to.

Sloan finished his evening meal, carried his new lamp and broom into the living room, and set to work cleaning it up. By the middle of the evening, the room was clean, and a fire was in the fireplace. He looked about and nodded. A little extra time and a lot of patience, and he'd have his new home looking nice. He grinned to himself. He had a good idea of what his blessed mother would have said. "All you need, Sloan, is a woman's hand on your reins. Man needs a woman to be whole."

That reminded him of Amy, and the thought sent him to the kitchen to rummage for one of the bottles he brought from Rio Blanco. He filled a tin cup with rye and sat down to load his pipe with rough shag.

Amy of the dark hair and the lovely dancing blue eyes. They had been married just six months when the team had run away with her. The thought of him picking her up while her lovely head hung limply like that of a rag doll made him drain half the liquor in the cup. It was that which had sent him out into the harsh world of the Southwest. It was that which had driven him on and on, without a place to call his own, for wherever he went and saw a man making a home, with his wife working beside him, it spurred Sloan Sutro on to the loneliest of places and the loneliest of thoughts.

He leaned back in his chair. Amy Louise Pomeroy was her name. He half closed his eyes and thought of Julie Landres, nee Bylas. What made a drunk out of such a creation of womanly loveliness? She had loved Buck Kelso. The problem was plain enough in retrospect. Garth Bylas was a big man, and Buck Kelso was a little man, property wise. As men, they both had their faults, but Sloan would have coppered his bets on Buck Kelso rather than Garth Bylas.

Sloan wondered how a man like Garth Bylas spent his lonely hours. Surely, he must know how much he was hated. Buck Kelso had filled in much of that detail for Sloan. Strangely enough, Sloan didn't hate the man—not yet, in any case.

He drained his cup and walked out onto the back porch, then stepped from it to kneel and scoop up a handful of loose earth. "What makes you so valuable?" he asked thoughtfully.

It was just then that the rifle flashed from the dark woods, and the slug keened past Sloan's head to slap into the thick log wall of the house. He hit the dirt as the gun cracked again, its echo racing after that of the first shot. The slug bored a hole through Sloan's new tin bucket that hung from a peg on the porch.

Sloan cursed as he bellied close to the bottom of the wall, slid around behind a huge log that had been hollowed into a watering trough, then behind the house. Both of his guns were in the house.

The rifle flatted off, again and again, ripping into the logs, shattering two windows, splintering the rear door panels, striking the bucket, driving it from the peg, bouncing it crazily along the ground until it rolled down a slope and out of sight. Slugs whipped through the shattered windows and struck the huge kitchen range to sing eerily off and strike into the walls. A last shot smashed the lamp, scattering burning oil over the kitchen floor. The flames began to lick hungrily at the dry wood.

The acrid odor of burnt powder hung in the quiet air. The burros began to bray. The burning floor threw a crazy, dancing light against the walls and ceiling of the kitchen. Sloan bellied along the side of the house, in through the front door, and managed to snatch his Winchester from its corner. He threw a bucket of water over the floor and, by luck, managed to douse the flames. The stinking smell of wet burnt wood and kerosene hung heavily in the house.

He bellied out through the front door, then down the slope toward the base of the knoll, where he crouched behind a fallen log, eying the skyline west and north.

It was too damned quiet. He could hear the rippling stream and the murmuring trees. The burros had stopped braying. Sloan wet his lips and waited; Winchester loaded and cocked. Minutes ticked past. Then he slit his eyes. There had been a swift and furtive movement amongst the trees to the west, near the road that led down into the valley. He snapped up his rifle and fired three times, levering the rounds through as fast as he could, then he rolled over and over, holding up the rifle until he was near the edge of the stream before the last echoes died away.

A man cursed. Sloan fired at the sound, then crawled

along the stream until he could see the top of the road-way. It was quiet again, almost as though nothing had happened, but the stench of powder smoke still hung in the air. Sloan worked his way back to the house, reached in through a shattered window and got his gun-belt heavy with holstered Colt, buckled it about his waist, then faded into the darkness behind the barn and into the woods.

The mysterious quiet indicated one of two things. He had either killed his attacker or had driven him off, unless the man was lying low, waiting for that quick killing shot. But Sloan knew that such a marksman could have easily killed or wounded Sloan with that first shot. It was probably nothing but a hurrahing, and a good one, at that.

He worked his way back to the house. One half of him wanted him to load up and clear out of there, standing not upon the way of his going; the other half, the dominant half, put out its horns and rattled its hocks, and that was the half that made Sloan take rifle, soogans, along with a bottle of whiskey up on the rocky slope behind the barn, to wait for morning.

A spattering of rain awakened him. It was dawn, with a weeping sky. The wind thrashed and moaned through the swaying trees. He crawled from his damp soogans and pulled on stiff boots. He eyed his house. It looked outright lonesome down there. It needed a fire going and a friendly scarf of smoke rising over the shake roof, beaten down by the cold rain.

He carried his gear down to the house and dug out his slicker. He left the house again, passing behind the barn, to enter the woods as before. A swirling and eerie-looking mist hung in the wet timber.

He stopped behind a thick-boled tree to eye the narrow trail that vanished into the wooly mist of the lower slopes. There was no sign of life, no sound except for the wind. He padded down the slope, taking care to avoid the wet and noisy passage through the brush. His eyes began to ache with the effort of trying to pierce the opaque mist. Every now and then he turned quickly to look behind him, but he saw nothing but the dripping brush and the wet, dark trunks of the trees.

Then he heard the sound, drifting to him through the whiteness of the mist. He stopped short and raised his rifle. The sound came again. He waited, ready to fire instantly.

"Aah...aah...aah..." The eerie sound seemed part of the weird-looking mist. It died away.

Sloan moved slowly, one careful step at a time, peering from side to side like a great and lean hunting cat. The sound came once more, closer this time.

Sloan moved on until he could see something lying in the thick brush beyond the winding trail. A man, face downward, trying to raise himself, only to fall flat again, while a tremor ran through his body. "*Aaah...aaah...aaah...*" he husked. A Winchester, with a cracked stock, lay not far from the man, and his six-shooter was still in its holster.

Sloan moved quietly until he was just behind the man and it was then that he saw the wide dark red stain on the left shoulder and side of the man's shirt. He had been badly hit. "Lie still," said Sloan.

The man tensed, then slowly turned his head to stare at Sloan with pain glazed eyes. "Shoot, you sonofabitch," he gasped. There was something vaguely familiar about him.

"Don't play the hero," said Sloan.

"Get to hell away from me!"

The rain pattered down steadily.

"If I do, mister," said Sloan, "you won't live to see the night."

The man closed his eyes. He was about Sloan's age, about the same height, but much more slender, and there was a suggestion of wiry strength in the body. His hat fell off as he writhed and revealed his light blonde hair.

"Let me take a look at that shoulder," said Sloan.

"Go to hell!"

Sloan leaned his rifle against a tree, then swiftly withdrew the man's Colt from its holster. He gripped the man by the right arm and tried to turn him over. The man struggled for a moment then went limp. Sloan swiftly took off the wounded man's denim jacket and ripped back the wet shirt. The slug had smashed into the left shoulder and had made a wide wound probably because the bullet had ricocheted sideways into the flesh.

Sloan staunched the flowing of the blood, then lifted the man to his shoulders and carried him slowly to the house. He made a bed for the man and then dug out his simple medical kit; relic of his days with the Frontier Battalion of the Texas Rangers. He sterilized the instruments, then worked skillfully and swiftly to remove the mutilated slug from the wound.

The rain slashed steadily as he prepared coffee and soup. Now and then he glanced at the taut, pale face of the unconscious man. It was a close thing. The shot that dropped the man had sped with more luck than skill.

Now and then Sloan took his rifle and left the house, peering into the wet woods, scouting along the rise above the trail. But there was no sign of life. Nothing, not even the horse of the wounded man.

Sloan could have let the man die out there in the wet, but that wasn't his way. Maybe it would have been better to have left him alone. But he did not try to kill Sloan, or that was the impression Sloan had. At least he did not *think* he had meant to kill him.

It was almost noon when he tasted the soup and nodded in satisfaction, then something made him turn to see the light blue eyes of the wounded man fixed on him. For a moment the two of them eyed each other. "Don't worry," said the wounded man. He grinned a little and jerked a thumb at the Winchester leaning against the wall beside his bed. "I could have got you in the back any time in the last twenty minutes."

"Why didn't you?"

"You could have let me die out in the rain, Sutro."

Sloan nodded. He walked to the basin and picked the slug out of the water and tossed it to the man who deftly caught it in his right hand. He eyed it. "Nice," he said softly. "How close was it?"

Sloan held up two fingers, about an inch apart.

"You a sawbones?"

"No. I learned a thing or two in the Rangers."

"Arizona Rangers?" The man lifted an eyebrow.

"Texas," answered Sloan quietly.

"Yeh, I might have figured that."

"Now, who are you, mister?"

"I owe you that much anyway. The name is Yarnell. Rio Yarnell."

"Who sent you?"

The man grinned faintly. "Maybe I came on my own."

"Don't lie about it, Yarnell! Did Bylas send you?"

"What do you think?"

"I'm almost positive he did."

Yarnell nodded. "Some joke on him. He sends Rio Yarnell to hurrah Sloan Sutro, and Sutro shoots down Yarnell with probably one of the luckiest shots in history! Some joke on me, too, come to think of it."

"You didn't want to kill me, did you?"

The eyes clouded a little. "I wasn't *told* to."

"And if you *were* told to?"

"You'd be dead, Sutro. I could hardly have missed at that range. Damn Bylas anyway! He said it would be simple enough to shoot up this place!"

Sloan smiled faintly as he looked about at some of the havoc wrought by the heavy rifle bullets. "You did a good job, Yarnell." Sloan filled a bowl with soup and placed it beside the wounded man. "Bylas didn't think he'd scare me out by a hurrahing, did he?"

"No. It was a warning."

When they had finished eating, Sloan rolled two cigarettes and placed one of them between Yarnell's lips. He lighted it. "Always puzzles me why a man will kill for money," he said quietly.

"You're alive, aren't you?"

"Sure, but if Bylas gave you the word, I would be dead now. For money, Yarnell! I can't figure out a man like you."

"You were a lawman. Don't *they* kill for money?"

The rain pattered steadily upon the roof. "There's a difference, Yarnell," said Sloan after a pause. "I think you're intelligent enough to know that difference."

Yarnell inspected his cigarette. "Sure, I know the difference. A man like Bylas pays a lot more to get his dirty work done than honest citizens pay honest lawmen to do *their* dirty work. Mind you, I didn't actually say Bylas had paid anyone to do any killing."

"You wouldn't. If you did talk, he'd pay someone else to make sure your mouth was shut forever. *Los muertos no hablan*"

"The dead do not speak."

"And you may have failed him this time, Yarnell."

The blue eyes flicked at Sloan. "What do you mean by that?"

"Supposing you were to vanish, Poof! Like a puff of wind-driven smoke. No sign, no trace, nothing. Maybe Bylas would do a lot of thinking."

Yarnell glanced at the Winchester.

"You couldn't reach it in time, Yarnell," said Sloan quietly.

"You could have left me out in the rain to die. You didn't. Why kill me now?"

Sloan smiled faintly. "I saw condemned outlaws nursed back to good health so that they could walk up onto the gallows like little men, Yarnell! A curious custom of our enlightened times."

"You talk like a damned college professor!"

"Think it over, Yarnell."

"What is it you want?"

"Why is this land so valuable?"

"I don't know what you're talking about."

"Yes, you do, Yarnell." Sloan straddled a chair and rested his elbows on the back of it, studying Yarnell all the while. "Simon Kelso was murdered on this land because someone wanted it."

There was an odd fleeting look in the hard blue eyes.

"Buck Kelso was driven from this valley because of this land. Bylas nearly euchred him out of it. Buck Kelso died in Vista Springs under strange circumstances."

Again the odd look in Yarnell's eyes.

"What do you know about that, Yarnell?"

The hired gun flipped his cigarette out of the window. Sloan tossed him the makings and he deftly rolled a smoke with one hand and lighted it. He blew out a perfect ring and watched it float toward the window.

Sloan rested his chin on his crossed arms. "A couple of men did a lot of talking in Vista Springs. They had money and they threw it around in the saloons like confetti; buying drinks for every bum in town, talking up a case against Buck Kelso, until the mob broke into the calabooze, dragged Kelso out and lynched him. Lynched him for a crime he did not commit. I found the man who committed that crime. I fought him and mortally wounded him. He confessed in the presence of witnesses before he died. But it was too late for Buck Kelso, wasn't it?"

Another smoke ring. "You're telling the story, Sutro."

"Why did those two men do all that talking? Why were they so anxious to see that Buck Kelso didn't leave Vista Springs alive?"

"Interesting questions."

"Someone wanted Kelso out of the way. It would have made it much simpler to gain possession of this land."

"Do tell?"

"Is it possible that those two men had been sent there by Garth Bylas?"

The blue eyes narrowed. "Jesus, God, but you like to poke that big nose of yours into dark places, don't you?"

"Habit of mine, Yarnell."

"Keep it up. They might bury you on this damned land."

"No one is going to drive me from this land, Yarnell."

"You talk big."

Sloan stood up. "I mean to stay."

"They'll be up here looking for me before long."

"I'll be waiting, Yarnell."

The wounded man turned on his side and looked the other way. "Like I said: 'They'll bury you on this land!' You can't win this fight, Sutro."

"You won't talk then?"

"No!"

"Suit yourself."

Sloan left the house and began his chores.

All that day there was no sign of any other humans about the place. The rain pattered on, died away, then came on again, until that night it drizzled steadily across the meadows and tapped on the roof of the low log house.

The hoarse screaming aroused Sloan out of a sound sleep. Before he had his eyes fully open he had his cocked Colt in his hand. The screaming came from Rio Yarnell, who sat bolt upright on his bed, staring with wild eyes at a corner of the room. "Take him away!" he yelled.

Sloan placed a hand on the wounded man's forehead. It seemed as dry and hot as a stove top.

"Take him away!" husked the hired gun.

"Take who away?" asked Sloan as he eased the man back down on the blankets.

"I didn't know he didn't have a sixgun!"

"Who, Yarnell?"

"Old Man Kelso! It was Bylas who said that the old coot carried a hideout sixgun. But he didn't! I didn't know that until after I shot him down!"

Sloan began to bathe the man's fevered face and forehead.

"Water," said Yarnell in a faraway voice.

Sloan reached for a water bucket and cup. Yarnell pushed the filled cup to one side. "Take it easy," said Sloan.

"Water. Water and blood. Blood for water."

Sloan eased Yarnell down again and the man seemed to pass into either sleep or unconsciousness. "Water and blood," said Sloan thoughtfully. "Blood for water."

"That's right," said Yarnell out of his sleep. "That's the price all right." Then he was gone again.

Sloan rolled a cigarette and sat down on a chair, tilting it back against the wall. He studied the taut, sweat-dampened face of the wounded man. There was a puzzle here. Something deep, dark, and bloody. There was no use in trying to sleep that night, and he knew he'd be haunted until daylight with the unformed pictures suggested by Rio Yarnell.

CHAPTER FIVE

The sun slanted down through the moving branches of the trees and glinted from the rushing waters of the bank-full stream. The fifth trout in an hour had struck hard, and Sloan Sutro set the hook, and expertly flipped the fish out on the wet grass beside the stream. He was removing the hook when his honed sixth sense warned him. He turned quickly, dropping the fish to snatch up his Winchester. A rider was coming through the woods. Sloan stepped behind a tree, stared for a moment, then stepped out into the open to ground the rifle.

She rode quickly toward him, and her hat hung at the back of her neck, but her hair was dark in the fresh sunlight. She drew rein and looked down at him. "Good morning, Mr. Sutro," she said. "I'm too early for lunch, but too late for breakfast."

He smiled. "But more than welcome, Miss Corday!" He glanced toward the house. Rio Yarnell was still asleep. It wouldn't do for her to see the wounded gunman. After all, she did work for Garth Bylas, and he was not sure of her loyalties. "A day off?" he asked.

"It's Sunday, Mr. Sutro! I always ride on Sundays. This always was one of my favorite places. I was born in this valley. I can't wait until Sunday to get out into it and ride and ride, Mr. Sutro."

"My first name is Sloan, Miss Corday."

She smiled. "And mine is Amy." She stared at him as she saw the change on his face. "Is anything wrong?"

"No," he said quietly. He gave her a hand down from the horse. "Did you always live here?"

"Not always. I left for a time. I took nurse's training and liked it, but there was no chance for that kind of work in the Valley. The few doctors they have here don't want a woman in their offices, they're that old fashioned. There isn't a hospital here as yet. I had to come back to the valley."

He smiled. "To marry a Rio Blanco man?"

"I used to think I would. Now I'm not sure."

"Why, Amy?"

She tossed a pebble into the stream. "There are few enough real men in the valley. Men who will stand up for themselves. Garth Bylas and his tribe run the valley. You know that by now. I admire you for your spirit of independence, but I am afraid for you."

"I'll be all right," he said quietly.

She glanced at him quickly. "You can't fight them alone," she said seriously.

"I can try."

She flipped another pebble into the stream. "I think they are looking for one of their men."

"So?"

The dark eyes studied him. "Rio Yarnell," she said quietly. "Have you seen him?"

He did not answer. She came close to him and placed a small cool hand on his right wrist. "You can trust me, Sloan. Rio Yarnell means nothing to me. He is a hired killer. I work for Garth Bylas, but not as a hired gun." She smiled. "I do my work, but that is not to say I agree with Mr. Bylas' policies. You are so alone! Someone must help you!"

"Thanks, Amy," he said.

"If they come looking for Rio Yarnell and find him..." Her eyes searched his face. *She knew all right.*

"Why is this land so valuable?" he asked her.

She looked away. "I'd rather not talk about it."

"Buck Kelso never seemed to think it was worth much. Why are so many people interested in it?"

"Sell it and get away from here."

"You said you would help me."

She shrugged. "Come with me," she said at last. She walked toward the fringe of woods that looked down upon the great valley. She stopped at the lip of the drop with him beside her. "The person who has this land will have great power here in the valley. Buck Kelso's father wouldn't sell the land. He was shot down for his resistance. Buck Kelso himself was stubborn and hardheaded. He was driven from the valley." She glanced sideways at him. "I happen to know that Mr. Bylas was all set to take over this place when you appeared, new owner of the land, a man as stubborn and hardheaded as both of the Kelsos. The owner of this land seems to court death."

"Goon," he said quietly.

She nodded. "You can see where the stream that runs through your land, past the rock formations back there, angles to the west until at last, miles and miles from here, it empties itself into the desert country. It seems like a great waste doesn't it?"

"Depends on how you look at it, Amy."

"I agree. It depends on how a man with a hard business head and a great deal more than average foresight looks at it."

"Get on with it," he said impatiently.

"Garth Bylas owns most of the northern part of this huge valley. Timberlands, some mines, cattle ranges, and possibly sheep grazing land."

"Perish the thought," said Sloan drily.

"That's the Texan talking. But sheep are money and Garth Bylas never overlooks anything that will fill his purse. But that's only part of the picture. Perhaps, the smallest part. When this great valley is developed, and rest assured it will be in time, possibly within the next five years, water will be the most important consideration. Water for cattle, sheep, power and farming. A *great* deal of water, Sloan."

"What does Bylas have to worry about? He has the North Branch of the Rio Blanco running through his backyard. So he has the property, the money, *and* the water."

"Now," she said succinctly. He felt for the makings, waited until she nodded assent, then began to form a cigarette. He lighted it, then waited for her to speak again.

She rested her back against a pine. "Garth Bylas got control of what was then thought to be the most valuable part of the valley, with plenty of water. Simon Kelso sat up here in his little kingdom, hunting, fishing, prospecting, and dreaming, while Garth Bylas bought land, worked hard at improving it, made money and more money and became the most powerful man in this valley."

"Who is to say who was right and who was wrong?"

"That is neither here nor there. Bylas must have this land, Sloan, or become a ruined man."

"I'm still waiting," he said.

"It will be easier to show you, Sloan. Get your horse." She hesitated. "Bring your rifle too."

"I wasn't figuring on going without it."

Sloan walked back to the house and entered it. Rio Yarnell was propped up against the wall, smoking a cigarette. There was an amused look in his blue eyes. "Quite a filly, Sutro," he said.

Sloan saw the field glasses, a relic of his days with the Rangers, lying on the chair near Yarnell. "She's not a filly," he said shortly. "She's a lady, but then you wouldn't know one when you saw one."

Yarnell's hand closed tightly on his cigarette, crushing it. "You like to look for trouble, don't you?" he asked.

Sloan picked up his field glasses and cased them. He slung the carrying strap over one shoulder. "I'm taking a ride," he said.

"With the lady?"

"Yes."

Yarnell grinned. "The gay social light of the Rio Blanco Valley. What happens to me?"

"Depends on you."

The hired gun studied Sloan. "I'm not leaving here," he said. He placed a hand on his bandaged shoulder. "This is keeping me here like a jailer."

"Maybe. But maybe Rio Yarnell doesn't want to go back to his boss and tell him he failed."

"He probably already knows."

Sloan nodded. "They're looking for you."

"I figured as much."

"You can do what you like. Stay or run. Go with them or hide. It doesn't matter to me."

"You running away now?"

Sloan shook his head. "I'm coming back. They can't take my land with them. I have the deed. This is my land, Yarnell."

The hired gun yawned a little. "I won't run. I can't run. I'd just as soon not have them find me here, though." The blue eyes flicked toward Sloan's holster. "I feel damned naked without a six gun."

"You think I'm fool enough to leave you a gun?"

"I'm not going back to work for Bylas, Sutro. Ever. And I'll never work at my profession again."

"Why the sudden change of heart?"

Yarnell flipped his cigarette through an open window. He began to fashion another one, slowly and deliberately. "I'm almost thirty years old, Sutro. I came from a good family that educated me as far as I would go. It seems as though I learned other things more quickly. Poker, faro, skill with a gun and a horse. The fast draw. Cold nerve. I liked money and the things money could do. Being a lawman was next to being a pauper. I cashed in my shooting skill to the highest bidder. It paid off well, much better than I had expected, until just a short time ago."

"What happened then?"

Yarnell smiled grimly as he glanced down at his bandaged shoulder. "I learned a lesson the hard way. Maybe I got careless. I'm a professional, you understand, and I thought I knew my profession inside and out, backwards and forwards. Forgot one thing, Sutro..."

"Yes?"

The hard blue eyes held Sloan's eyes. "No matter how good you think you are, there's always a better man." Yarnell looked away. "I owe you my life. Being around you has taught me what I might have been."

"Meaning me?"

"Meaning you! You ever take a job for the highest bid? I mean a job that was profitable but not quite legal?"

"No."

"That's one thing I mean. Most men would have pulled foot out of this mess by now, wanting no part of the blood price of this damned land. You're sticking it out. Sort of an underdog, but not really an underdog. Sounds loco, but it isn't. I'm kinda curious to see what happens."

Sloan walked into the bedroom, reached up behind a log, and retrieved Yarnell's beautifully engraved Colt. He took it to Yarnell and handed it to him. "Maybe I'm a damned fool to do this. I believe you. *Adios, amigo.*"

"*Adios.*" Yarnell passed a loving hand over the principal tool of his trade. "Don't worry about me, Sutro. They won't find me here. Just be careful when you come back. They just might be waiting for you."

Sloan eyed the fancy six shooter in Yarnell's capable

hand. He tossed a box of cartridges onto the bed. For a long moment, the eyes of the two men met and locked, and it seemed to both of them at that instant, had they met each other at a different time, and under different circumstances, they might have become close friends.

Sloan looked down at the Colt. How many men had died beneath its hired muzzle? A coldness came over Sloan toward this smiling man, with blue eyes like glacier ice. How many men? *The voice of the gun...*

———

AMY CORDAY HAD LED the way across the stream, thence through lush Mountains Meadows and through thick stands of timber, to thread her way through a tangled maze of rock and fallen timber high on the mountain slopes. She evidently knew that country like the palms of her slim and lovely hands. But why did she ride by devious and well-hidden trails when there were much easier and more open ways of traveling?

Was it that dangerous, pondered Sloan as he led his horse up a narrow transverse trail, concealed by scrub trees and brush. Higher and higher, until at last they emerged into a wild tangle of jumbled rock and splintered tree trunks, laced and interlaced with thick and thorny catclaw and wait-a-bit brush.

To the left, far below, was the great Valley of the Rio Blanco with the sun glancing brilliantly now and then from the rippling waters of the North Branch of the river. A thread of smoke arose from a ranch house and a thicker plume of smoke drifted up from the unseen sawmill east of the town.

"Look," said Amy. She pointed above them, to the southeast.

The massive bulk of the mountain range had here undergone a cataclysmic change not too many years past. A huge piece had seemingly been gouged out of the sharp-crested range, leaving a vast hollowed portion, naked and yellowish-white bathed in the bright sunlight.

It was then that Sloan realized that he was standing upon what had once been a solid part of the mountain that loomed high above them, dwarfing them into insignificance. A gigantic collapse of rock had thundered down, smashing thousands of great trees beneath it, leaving a ragged fringe of dead timbers standing above the shattered rock like a man-made *cheval-de-frise* —fantastic and gaunt jungle of wood and rock that almost denied man passage through it.

"Come on," said Amy. She had paused just long enough for Sloan to feel the immensity of the great collapse of a good part of the mountain. It was more than enough to awe anyone.

She threaded her way through the tangle, although Sloan could hardly tell a trail existed in it. They went, climbing high, turning and twisting, almost meeting themselves at times, squeezing through narrow passageways like the guarded approaches to the innermost keep of some gigantic medieval castle. They emerged at length on a wide rock shelf, open to wind and sun, that overlooked a huge trough of a canyon, stippled with trees on the far side, but naked and dead on the nearside.

Far below in the shadows rushed a white-watered stream and the sound of it mingled with the constant and mournful soughing of the windswept pines. The canyon swept in a vast curve to the right, to vanish at length into the gigantic and featureless massif that crept higher and higher, almost imperceptibly, to form the unseen Continental Divide miles and miles to the east in New Mexico.

Sloan slowly felt for the makings and just as slowly rolled a cigarette. It was no place for idle talk, not for a time at least, for the work of the Creator here was such that a man felt almighty puny. Sloan lighted up, then flipped the broken match into the depths. He turned and eyed the huge masses of rocks and boulders that almost seemed to hang suspended in air above them. "Doesn't seem like it would take much for that heap of rock to slide down all the way to the bottom of that canyon," he observed quietly.

"You're getting the idea, Sloan," she said.

"That's the North Branch of the Rio Blanco down there?"

"Yes."

Sloan eyed the vast gap where the landslide had come from, and then far below to where the stream raced along, and he could see the rapids formed where the fallen rock had already encroached upon and narrowed the old channel.

"You see, Sloan?" she asked.

"I can see now where nature has taken a hand. It won't be too long, perhaps another hard winter, before that landslide begins to move, and when it does, it will more likely plug that entire canyon, forcing the North Branch back upon itself. Nothing will get through this canyon, for there will *be* no canyon."

She nodded. "Garth Bylas knows that full well. Without that water, he is nothing. He has the North Branch under his thumb but *not* the South Branch." She glanced sideways at him. "*You* have the South Branch under *your* thumb, Sloan."

He rubbed his lean jaws. "If a man was to dam up the South Branch, to keep the water from flowing into the desert country, he could supply this whole valley with water."

She sat down on a rock and rested her chin in the palm of a hand, looking down upon the water so far below. "I did some research, Sloan. In no other state or territory of the United States is water so vitally important to economic welfare as in the Territory of Arizona."

"Hear, hear," he said gravely. He smiled and tipped his hat to her.

"I mean it, Sloan! It's no joking matter! Garth Bylas

must have control of the South Branch, or he'll lose his position in this valley."

Sloan drew in on his cigarette and blew a puff of smoke, watching it ravel in the clean, dry wind. "Which means that the man who controls the South Branch could supplant him."

She flicked her lovely dark eyes at him. "Simon Kelso was too simple a man to think of such things. Land was land to live upon and enjoy, not to exploit. Buck was wild and careless. He'd have fought for a cup of water or a whole lake on the principle of the thing, not really knowing why. The fight intrigued him, not the results. But now the land is *yours,* Sloan Sutro. What will *you* do with it?"

He flipped away his cigarette. "I haven't the money for such a development," he said quietly.

"But you own the land."

He shrugged. "I figured on living there, to hunt and fish. I wasn't thinking of grand schemes, Amy."

"Another Simon Kelso?"

"What's wrong with that?" he answered her challenge almost angrily.

"There are other men in the valley who would work with you, Sloan. Money could be raised. It could be a cooperative deal, rather than a one-man empire such as Garth Bylas favors."

He slowly rolled another cigarette and lighted it.

"Sloan?" she asked, a little anxiously, as though she had lost his interest.

He turned and looked at her with those hard eyes of his, and once again, an almost delicious feeling of fear for this man swept through her. "It *is* my land, Amy. The water rights are really not mine. *No* one has the right to pen up water and hold it from others who need it." Sloan looked up at that vast poised landslide area. "Bylas controlled the North Branch and looked what has happened. *Almost as though a greater power steps in to see that the water must go to the people, not to one man alone."*

She stood up and came close to him. "But there must always be a man of destiny to carry out the wishes and plans of that greater power, Sloan."

He flushed beneath his tan. This young woman could easily make him feel high or feel low, and he knew for certain that his life would never be complete without her at his side, fighting and loving, working for him and with him, bearing his children.

He bent his head to kiss her.

The rifle flatted off, slamming its crisp report off the towering rock walls like a lively rubber ball. Tango reared and lashed out with his hoofs. The second shot struck the horse between the eyes, and he fell as though pole-axed, driving Sloan to the edge of the brink, half stunned. He looked up at Amy. "Run!" he husked.

"No, Sloan!"

"Dammit!" he yelled fiercely. "Get out of here! This is man's work. *Vaya!"*

She swung up into the saddle and spurred the frightened horse.

"Stay low, Amy!" he called out.

The next rifle shot flatted off and struck a rock a few feet from Sloan driving tiny shards of rock and lead against Sloan's face like the slap of a cholla needle whip. He felt the quick and painful spurting of blood from a myriad of tiny cuts as he hit the rocky ground and drew his Colt.

She was gone from sight now, and even so, Sloan could not have seen her going. The blood had worked stingingly into his eyes, and his vision had blurred. He cursed and wiped savagely at his eyes with a rough shirt sleeve. The rifle cracked again, and the slug whipped cleanly through the crown of his hat, lifting it from his head. He flattened himself and cocked his Colt. There was no use in shooting yet. Sloan Sutro was never the man to gain confidence by exploding gunpowder. But he knew he was trapped. Whoever was shooting at him was more than good and had a fair target. Why didn't he shoot to kill? The answer to that was not in Sloan Sutro's mind as he lay there, clenching the worn walnut butt of his Colt, greasy with cold sweat, waiting for the next move. Waiting and waiting...

CHAPTER SIX

Minutes drifted past. Cloud shadows fled down the slopes, seemingly rising and falling to the swells and dips of the ground. The wind swept across the wide valley, rippling trees and brush, giving them the illusion of being the surge and motion of the ocean. A hawk hung high in the clear sky.

Sloan wiped the blood from his stinging face, cursing the fact that so much blood could come from such insignificant wounds. He peered toward the dead horse, wishing he could get his hands on his full canteen. He bellied out a little toward it, and the marksman must have grinned as he fired for the slug slapped crisply through the canteen, and the water gurgled merrily out of the twin holes to vanish into the thirsty ground. Another shot cracked, and the bullet creased a rock inches from Sloan's head, making him crawfish back into cover. The devil could shoot like one of Berdan's Sharpshooters.

Sloan edged toward a crevice, lying as flat as possible on the sunbaked rocky earth. A faint wisp of powder smoke hung in the air above a brush-shielded ledge. A good seventy-five yards range, too far for his Colt to be accurate. Maybe if he played dead the marksman would move in, confident that he had dropped Sloan, to allow

Sloan a quick shot, but that was hardly likely. Sloan was willing to bet the rifleman could have dropped him easily at the first shot.

The sun was higher now, driving shadows from the rock face. There was no man alive who could creep down that bright slope unseen by the rifleman. Sloan rested his head on the hot ground. In this game, all you had to do was make one false move, and it seemed as though he had done just that.

He raised his head as he heard a faint scrabbling sound somewhere behind him in the labyrinth of shattered rock and splintered trees. He turned, raising his Colt for a quick shot. The sound had stopped. There was nothing to see, but *someone* was back there. It couldn't be Amy, for she would have had to pass Sloan to get there. That meant but one thing. Whoever was shooting at Sloan and whoever was behind him might have been there all the time watching Sloan and the girl.

The rifle cracked again, and the slug slapped hard against a rock, showering Sloan with shards of lead and rock. His hold on his temper slipped, and he thrust his Colt between two rocks and pumped three slugs down the slope. The ricocheting slugs sang eerily through the air, and just when the noisy rataplan of firing died swiftly away against the huge rock face, the soft laughter of a man came up the slope. "Losing your nerve, Sutro?" the marksman jeered.

They knew it was him, then. But he did not recognize the voice. Sloan bit his lip as he worked slowly to reload his hot Colt, trying to keep his shoulders down out of sight. He opened the loading gate and fed three cartridges into the cylinder. He snapped up his head as a boot grated on the ground behind him. He turned, Colt ready, to see a swift movement behind a clump of brush. He rapped out two shots, then rolled over quickly as the rifleman down the slope fired twice himself. Sloan kept rolling until he landed beneath a ledge.

He saw the vague movement again and fired two more rounds. The echoes died away, and the smoke rifted just above his head.

He slitted his eyes and waited. Every movement he made was dangerous. Even now, he didn't know whether or not they could see him. Yet the man down the slope could have killed or wounded him by now; he was that good with the long gun.

A gun flashed from the brush, and the slug keened past Sloan's head. He echoed the shot, and the blast of the big Colt seemed three times as loud in the confined space in which he crouched.

"That's five rounds, Sutro!" came the jeering voice. "One left in the locker! How you goin' to reload, hombre?"

There was a slow and sinuous movement three feet from Sloan, followed by a dry scraping noise. He stared fascinated at the thick body and ugly flat head of a big diamondback rattler. The thick body coiled, and the rattles buzzed like a hive of gigantic bees. The head arose and drew back for the hammerstroke of striking. The Colt leveled and cracked and the heavy .44/40 slug smashed cleanly through the head of the rattler even as it moved forward. The body writhed and twisted and the bloody shattered head dragged across Sloan's left leg. He drew back in revulsion.

It was then that he heard the hard slapping of boot soles on the ground. He jumped to get to his feet, and his head drove up hard against the ledge above him, half stunning him. He staggered out in the bright sunlight, with blood streaming down his face from his lacerated scalp, half stunned and with a hot empty sixshooter in his hand.

"Cover him, Yancey!" rapped out a hard voice.

Sloan whirled and raised his Colt, then realized it was empty. He tried to run to his Winchester. A tall man stepped from behind a boulder with Winchester at hip level. "Stay where you are, Sutro!" he snapped.

Sloan turned to see another man standing behind him. Colt in hand. Sloan drove in at him with flailing fists despite the menace of the sixgun. The man jumped back. "He's gone loco, Sage!" he yelled.

Something struck hard alongside Sloan's skull. He tried to get up while scrabbling for a rock for a weapon. The rifle barrel struck again, and the last thing he remembered was the voice of the man named Sage. "You almost have to kill a man like this to stop him!"

There was a vague memory of being carried downhill on the back of a horse and of hot sunlight striking up into his aching eyes like blades of fire. Of harsh pain flowing in his skull and of an intolerable brassy thirst constricting his throat. He opened his eyes to find himself belly down on a hardpacked dirt floor littered with chaff and manure.

He crept out his dry tongue and touched his cracked and bloody lips. His senses swirled and reeled in a mad rigadoon while he fought to keep them clear. The green bile rose swiftly in his throat, and he fought too to keep that down. He had taken one hell of a beating for sure.

A horse whinnied softly. Sloan raised his head and pushed himself up onto his knees. The horse whinnied again, and for a moment, he thought it might be Tango until he remembered that Tango was dead and would never whinny for Sloan Sutro this side of heaven or hell.

He raised his head and looked about. The barn was big and well built. Here and there, rays of sunlight shafted through cracks and crannies with dust motes dancing steadily in the light. There were half a dozen horses in stalls and they weren't hammerheaded range mounts by any means. Sloan pushed himself up to a sitting posture. There was a bucket beside a post and he crawled to it and thrust a hand in to feel that it was half full. He upended the bucket

on his aching head, sucking in some of the water as it
trickled down his face. He worked around until he could
place his back against a post and felt for the makings. He
was alone in the building. He rolled a cigarette and lighted
it, drawing the smoke deeply into his lungs.

Then the sounds of voices came to him, closer and
closer, until the men were just outside of the barn. The
door slid back on its rollers and three men stood there
looking down at him. Two of them he knew. Yancey and
Sage. The third man looked vaguely familiar and yet
Sloan knew he had never seen him before.

"Nice and comfy, Sutro?" asked the tall rifleman
named Sage.

"Passable," said Sloan.

Sage grinned. He was handsome in a rakish, devil-
may-care sort of a way, with dark hair and mustache, but
with eyes of an almost incredible light grey that stood
out from his tanned skin. Eyes like a damned hawk
thought Sloan. He knew now that Sage could have killed
him at any time upon that mountain.

Yancey rubbed a jaw. "Damned good thing we didn't
run into him up there," he said to the third man. "Bastard
put up a fight as it was."

The third man nodded. He glanced at Sage. Sage
grinned. "He won't bother you." There was the faintest
touch of sarcasm in his tone.

The three of them came into the barn, and Yancey
closed the door behind him. The man walked like a prize-
fighter slightly gone to beef, but still a powerful and
dangerous man to face in the ring or out of it. His nose
had been smashed at one time in his life, and there was
scar tissue around his eyebrows and lips. His eyes were
small and as green and cold as glass.

But it was the third man who interested Sloan. Sloan
narrowed his eyes and studied him. He was dressed in
fine gray broadcloth and wore a flat-brimmed black hat.

He was tall, and he had cold eyes, and Sloan Sutro suddenly suspected who he was.

"I'm Harry Landres," said the man. "You've never met me, Sutro."

"Pleased. I've met your brother Dave."

Landres nodded curtly. "You've met my wife Julie too, haven't you?"

"Yes."

"How did that come about?"

The tone of the man sent a bit of a chill through Sloan. "She was riding up at my place the first day I came there." There was no use in lying. Landres probably knew that anyway.

A nerve worked at the left hand corner of the man's mouth. "That must have been interesting, Sutro."

"I thought it was. She's very pretty."

The nerve twitched again. "They say you just don't give a tinker's damn for anything you say."

Sloan grinned a little. "I'm a Texan," he said.

Landres spat. "They say a Texan is considered just as good as a white man as long as he behaves himself."

In the pregnant silence that followed, Sloan Sutro got slowly to his feet and wiped the palms of his big hands on his levis. He wet his lips and leaned a little bit toward Mr. Harry Landres. "Maybe you'd like to say that *man* to *man,* Landres, without being backed by your two yahoos."

Neither one of the two *yahoos* moved, and Sloan almost got the message from Sage that it would be all right with him if Landres met Sloan face to face. Might be interesting at that. Yancey balled a granite fist and spat lightly on it, and the green eyes studied Sloan speculatively.

Landres wasn't moved. He was safe enough, and he knew it. "Sitting in a saloon drinking with a man's wife isn't exactly ethical, is it, Sutro?"

"Not in my book, Landres. Happens, I didn't know she was married."

"You're a damned liar."

Sloan looked wearily at him. "Send those two yahoos away, Landres," he almost pleaded, "and say that once again, will you?"

Landres spat again, trying to play the part of the man. "You're in no condition to face anyone, Sutro. Fact is, if you don't act better, you might not be in any condition to face anyone again."

"Hear, hear," said Yancey.

Sloan shrugged. "Ask your brother. I think he'd say that I was outright surprised when he told me who she was. I just didn't know. Besides, the woman was drunk. Beyond that, if I was interested in another man's wife, do you think I'd take her into the best saloon, right in the middle of her hometown, in the same building as her brother's office, in broad daylight to play games with her? Don't be a damned fool, Landres!"

Sage inspected the nails on his slim hands. "By Christ, Mr. Landres, he's got something there."

"Shut up, you!"

The curiously light eyes narrowed. Then Sage shrugged. He leaned indolently against a post and studied Sloan.

"What is it you really want me for, Landres?" demanded Sloan.

"You were trespassing."

"My God! I get a good cayuse killed. I get hell scared out of me by your two yahoos there, then get dragged down here like a side of beef, just for trespassing? Come, come, Harry, my boy!"

Landres flushed. "They didn't sell that big mouth of yours short, Sutro. That's a certainty!"

Sloan held out his hands, palms upwards. "One of my failings, Landres."

"What were you fooling around up there for?"

"Sightseeing."

"Who was with you?"

"I was alone."

Landres turned to Yancey. "All right," he said shortly.

Yancey grinned. He came forward slowly and smiled benignly at Sloan. "Mr. Landres wants you should talk nice and clear, Sutro."

"I told him all I know."

Yancey smiled again. He came forward. He was a head shorter than Sloan, but about twice as broad, with thick, short arms, that hung away from his sides to end in ham-like hands with thick stubby fingers. He closed his fists. "Once more," he said gently.

"No."

The man moved so fast and so viciously Sloan was flat on his back on the litter, staring up into the flat, expressionless face of the man before he knew it, and the crisp, solid blow had hardly hurt him as much as the impact on the packed earthen floor.

Landres smiled coldly. "*Now*, Sutro?" he asked.

There was a trickle of blood coming from the side of Sloan's mouth. He shook his head.

"Get up," said Yancey.

Sloan knew better, but the Texas blood in him didn't. He was up and down in an instant. This time Yancey had hit him twice, first in the gut, then on the jaw, a perfect one-two, and both blows had stung like the slash of a blacksnake whip. This man could cut a man to ribbons or kill him with one punch.

Sage was just behind Landres. He shook his head, then opened his mouth, to mimic talking. He wanted Sloan to talk before he got cut to pieces.

Sloan sat up and wiped the blood from his mouth. He looked up at the patiently waiting Yancey with his head tilted to one side. "Stand still," he said whimsically. "I can lick one of you but not *both* of you."

"I'm standing here alone," said Yancey with a stupid look on his flat face. "I don't need any help to lambast you, Sutro!"

"Hardly fair to beat a man with a sense of humor like that, Landres," Sage observed.

Landres came a little closer. He was getting braver now. "What were you doing up there? Who was with you?"

Sloan's silence was the signal for Yancey. Sloan knew well enough Landres would not have him killed. Not yet, anyway. Garth Bylas must know there were subterranean rumblings in the valley about the killing of Simon Kelso. There were others who had died mysteriously, from the hints given to Sloan by Buck Kelso. Even Buck Kelso's death had a mystery about it.

When Yancey was through, Landres bent down on one knee to look at Sloan. "What happened to Rio Yarnell?" he demanded harshly.

"I don't know such a person."

"You're lying! He went up to your place. He just vanished up there. You must have dry-gulched him! You couldn't face Yarnell and gun him down! Where is Rio Yarnell, Sutro?"

"I don't know."

Landres looked at Yancey. The man came forward like the well-trained machine he was, and Sloan got the impression that the man had nothing personal against Sloan. It was a job, nothing more.

"Let's call this quits, Landres," said Sage.

"*Mr.* Landres!"

"Mr. then," said Sage wearily. "I can't stand and watch any more of this."

"You've killed men, Sage," sneered Landres. "The sight of blood unnerving Sage Spencer?"

"Take it easy," said the gunman. His mouth worked a little.

"Get out!" yelled Landres. "Yancey can do the job! Get out, damn you!"

Sage Spencer didn't want to go, for two reasons, first that he didn't want to see Sloan get beaten to a pulp, second, that he hated to take orders from a yellow whelp like Harry Landres. But Sage was paid well. Not by Landres, but by Garth Bylas, and Bylas, despite his scorn for the weakling that had married his sister, would still back the man up. Sage turned on a heel and left the barn. The door slid shut with a creaking of finality for Sloan Sutro.

The two men watched Sloan, and he knew what was in their merciless minds. He had seen a cowpoke in El Paso years past who had been badly beaten by unscrupulous lawmen in another town to make him talk. The man walked around and seemed normal until you looked into his vacant eyes and listened to his inane talk. A living dead man. A shudder crept throughout Sloan Sutro.

"Get up," said Yancey. He moved his feet about in a curious sort of shuffling dance. "I ain't never yet hit a man who was down."

"Marquis of Queensbury rules, Yancey?" said Sloan.

"Who's he?"

Sloan got up and stood there with his hands hanging by his sides, wondering if the whole damned thing was worthwhile. "Runs a cantina in Nogales," said Sloan.

"Very funny," said Landres. He passed between Sloan and Yancey, and Yancey stepped back and turned his head to one side to spit. In that split instant, Sloan Sutro came to life, and he moved faster than the diamondback he had killed on the mountain. He hooked up the empty wooden water bucket, a solid affair of thick wood and heavy metal strapping, gripping it tightly as he swung it up to full arm's length and then brought it down like a fly fisherman making a cast, with twice the speed forward as that back. The bucket came down cleanly, thudding atop Yancey's round skull with a soul-satisfying crunch, driving his hat down around his cauliflower ears. Yancey went down fluidly to his knees, his hands, then his flat face, and lay as still as a Christmas goose.

Landres yelled. "Get up, damn you!"

Sloan Sutro gripped Landres by his arm, tapped him lightly on the chin, then thrust a hand swiftly inside the man's coat to withdraw his snub-nosed Colt from its half-breed holster. He flipped the Colt across the floor. Landres dashed after it and bent to pick it up, but a well-planted underslung bootheel smashed squarely against his rump, and he half leaped and half flew clear over the gun. Landres yelled in terror. He turned to scrabble for the gun, and another bootheel crushed down on his wrist. Landres looked up into the coldest pair of gray eyes he had ever seen beyond those of a timber wolf.

"Now, Mr. Landres," said Sloan gently. "What was it you said about Texans? Let me see? Was it something about a Texan being just as good as a white man if he behaves himself?"

"Yancey!" yelled Landres.

"Get up," said Sloan softly, and the whimsical smile on his battered and bloody face was more frightening to Harry Landres than that of a demon. Sloan bent down and pulled Landres to his feet, but the man broke loose and fled to the rear of the barn.

Sloan shrugged. He picked up the Colt and slipped it into a pocket. He walked back toward the front of the barn, casually spitting a little blood onto the broad back of Yancey. Sloan set the catch on the door, then wedged a two by four against it. He turned to see Landres trying to reach Yancey's Colt. "Don't, Landres," he said quietly.

The outstretched hand drew back. Landres wet his lips. He backed across the barn until his back hit the rear wall. Sloan walked to Yancey and took the Colt from its holster. He emptied the sixgun and tossed it to Landres. "Here, Harry," he said. "Catch!"

Landres let the useless gun strike the wall beside him. "Look, Sutro," he said swiftly. "I'll make it up to you."

Sloan came closer. "You will?"

"Sure! Money! All the money you'd ever want!"

"From your beloved brother-in-law, eh?"

"Well..."

Sloan smiled again, and Landres started for a ladder that led up to the loft but his coattails were just within reach of Sloan, and the man was pulled back ignominiously to hit the floor at Sloan's feet. He got up just in time to get a one-two, not as hard and efficient as those that Yancey had dealt with Sloan but highly satisfactory for a man in Sloan's condition. Landres went down. "Get up," said Sloan. He shuffled his feet. "I ain't never yet hit a man who was down."

Landres got up, and then Sloan went to work like a man chopping wood for exercise, hitting Landres with rights and lefts, neatly timed to snap his head back and forth, until he went down against the wall, with his breath coming harshly in his throat.

Sloan knew he should make a break out of there. He was armed now, and he had his pick of horses. But he didn't know just where he was. Probably on the Bylas ranch. "Get up, Landres," he said.

"I can't," moaned the man.

"Get up!"

Landres got to his feet, and the Colt nestled against his belly while two eyes bored into his. "Now you and I are going to take a little ride from here, Mr. Landres. One false move from you, and I'll let you taste some of your own lead."

Yancey moved a little, and the light of hope came into Landres' cowed eyes. "Tie him up," said Sloan. Landres got a reata and lashed Yancey's thick arms behind him. Sloan inspected the knots and nodded. "Get two horses," he said to Landres.

The man led out two fine horses and saddled them quickly. His hands trembled and his head shook. He was scared half to death.

"Go open that door!"

Landres walked to the door, removed the wedge, undid the catch, then slid the door open. Sloan was right behind him with the two horses led by his left hand. A tall man was standing fifty feet from the front of the barn with a Winchester in his hands and a thin smile on his lean face. Sage Spencer.

"I've got a gun on Landres," said Sloan.

"I can pick you off from here, Sutro."

"Don't try. Landres will be dead before I hit the dirt."

Sage smiled again. "I get my wages from Garth Bylas," he said.

Landres tried to talk. He held out a hand toward Sage. "For God's sake, Spencer," he husked. "Don't shoot!"

"*Mr.* Spencer!"

"Mr. Spencer, then."

Sage eyed Sloan. "Stupid, isn't it?"

Sloan shrugged.

A minute fled past and then another. The windmill beyond the barn suddenly whirred into life as the wind shifted and grew stronger.

"Well, Sutro?" asked Sage.

"You'd better listen to Mr. Landres," said Sloan. "*No one is going to get me helpless again around here, Spencer.*"

"I know what you mean." Sage eyed Landres. "What happened to you, Mr. Landres?"

By the tone of his voice, Sloan suddenly knew that the tall marksman had been outside all the time Sloan had been dusting off Landres. Sage had figured he held all the aces, and maybe he had wanted Harry Landres to get a little of the punishment Yancey had been handing out to Sloan.

Then, almost magically, two thick arms slid around Sloan's arms and chest, and a slightly sour breath came to him along with a hardy dry voice. "Just put down the gun, Sutro," said Yancey. "That reata was long past its prime, hombre."

Landres smiled, then the smile vanished as he felt the snub-nosed Colt against his kidneys.

"What do they call a thing like this, Sutro?" asked Sage coolly.

"Impasse, I think."

"A good word."

Sloan nodded. "I don't want any killing. Rio Yarnell is still alive. You can take my word on that. I haven't killed anyone in this fight...*yet!*" He could see the cold sweat trickling down the back of Landres' neck, and he could also feel Yancey's arms tightening a little. His breath was getting shorter. Landres swallowed hard.

"What do you want to do?" asked Spencer quietly, looking at Landres.

Landres tried to talk, but it was hopeless. Nothing but a dry croaking came from his throat.

Yancey was starting to exert his power now. The man was like a grizzly. Spots suddenly danced before Sloan's eyes, and before he quite realized it, he knew Yancey's arms could squeeze him into semi-consciousness.

"Now!" screamed Landres as he whirled and struck savagely with the edge of his left hand at Sloan's eyes. Sloan tilted his head to one side, and the blow struck Yancey, startling him just enough so that he relaxed his grip, allowing Sloan to throw himself sideways. He saw Spencer snap up his rifle. Sloan fired at him from the hip as he swung with all his strength to break free from the cursing Yancey. Spencer fired. There was the sound of a stick being whipped into thick mud, and Yancey stiffened.

The big man fell slowly sideways, releasing Sloan. A second shot cracked from Spencer's deadly rifle. The slug tore through the slack of Landres' coat. The man screamed and scuttled back into the barn.

The horses reared and plunged, getting in between Sloan and Spencer. The rifleman darted to one side and went down on one knee, peering through the wreathing powder-smoke. Sloan swung up on the nearest horse and spurred him directly toward Spencer. The man rolled to one side firing as he did so. The horse struck him and flung him helplessly to one side.

Sloan lay along the racing horse's neck. Spencer fired twice and the slugs whipped past Sloan's head. He saw a woman sitting a horse between him and the gate that led to a road. There was no way to pass her. Sloan turned the horse savagely, set him at the fence, lay low as he cleared the top rail, then raked him from stem to stern with his spurs as the frightened animal plunged into the woods. Sloan looked back to see Julie Landres standing in her stirrups, watching him with undisguised admiration on her lovely face, and then he was gone.

CHAPTER SEVEN

I t was pitch black before the rising of the moon, and a cold wind keened through the Valley of the Rio Blanco as the lone horseman reined in on a wide rock shelf to look down upon the meadowland that was his. There was no light to be seen from the low log house. The place seemed as quiet and deserted as the day he had arrived there, not so long ago in time, but a long, long time in his mind.

Sloan Sutro turned in the saddle and rested his hand on the cantle while his eyes tried to pierce the darkness behind him. He had been steadily on the run since he had broken free from Landres and his two gunmen. Somewhere beyond the North Branch, he had taken a wrong trail, and darkness had trapped him high on the rimrock overlooking a wild and tangled canyon country to the east of the Rio Blanco Valley. He holed up that night, and during the next day, he followed half a dozen blind trails, and once, he found himself on a ridge looking down on a party of horsemen, led by Sage Spencer. They were obviously looking for someone, and he knew well enough who it was. That had forced him to hole up again. It was hardly sensible to try and fight half a dozen hardcases while he was armed only with a snub-nosed

Colt that had an accurate range a little farther than he could spit.

Now it was Tuesday evening. He was faint with hunger and still a little weak from the bloodlettings he had suffered. He had to have food and a rifle. He slid wearily from the saddle and led the equally weary horse into the timber. He tethered it and walked silently over the soft grass until he reached a place where he could see the house and barn from behind a projecting shoulder of rock not far from the stream.

There was a quiet and eerie quality about the place. Now and then he had an uncanny feeling that someone was watching him from the darkness. Someone who was there in spirit only. Buck Kelso had said his father haunted the place after death as much as he had been there during life. It wasn't hard to believe. But there would be no reason for Simon Kelso's ghost to be a malignant one, toward Sloan at any rate.

He drew out the short Colt and worked his way quietly toward the log house, stopping every now and then to look and listen, testing the night with his senses. But still there was no sign of life; no indication that the place was not wholly deserted. He crawled past the base of the huge rock formations that formed a wild backdrop behind the buildings, then paused to study the barn. If Rio Yarnell was about he was keeping almighty quiet. "Just be careful when you come back," he had said. "They just might be waiting for you."

He crossed to the barn and flattened himself against the side wall, eying that part of the house he could see from there. Odd that the two burros had not scented him and made him welcome with their friendly but un-melodious braying.

He worked his way to the back of the barn, gripped the edge of a rear window and let himself gently down to the earthen floor inside the building. He padded through it to the front door. The door was slightly ajar and through the gap he could plainly see the dark shape of the house. There was the faintest suggestion of moonlight high in the eastern sky. He looked back over his shoulder but the interior of the barn was thick in darkness. A mouse scuttled for shelter.

Sloan rubbed his unshaven jaws. His belly cried for food. His hands needed a better weapon than a snub-nosed Colt. He needed a good horse between his thighs. He stood there for another five minutes until he could stand it no longer. He took his courage into his hands and slipped through the gap in the door and crossed like a fleeting shadow to the rear of the house, feeling every instant as though a gun would crack from the outer darkness and drive a slug between his shoulder blades. A board creaked drily as he stepped up on the sagging rear porch.

He looked right and left, then behind him at the dark bulk of the barn, before he gripped the rear door handle and lifted the latch. It squeaked a little as he opened the door and swiftly stepped inside, Colt at hip level, right elbow tight against his side and hard eyes peering in a line with the gun barrel, ready to press trigger and fire in less than an instant.

It took him three minutes to learn that the house was empty. It took him another three minutes to open a can of embalmed beef and heap the beef onto thick crackers . The contents of the can vanished in no time and he finished his hasty meal with a can of tomatoes and another of peaches. But all the time he ate he peered from one window to another, then back again.

The moon was making itself known on the western slope of the great range. If he was going to leave at all, now was the time to do so, for anyone watching the house would easily have Sloan pinpointed when the moon rose higher. He had too vivid a memory of his experiences the night Rio Yarnell had hurrahed the place. And where *was* Yarnell?

He found the hired gun's cracked stock Winchester and spent ten precious minutes binding the split at the small of the stock with baling wire and rawhide thongs. It would serve until he found a better one. He filled a sack with canned food, bacon, crackers, and coffee, slung it over his shoulder, then stepped out onto the back porch.

"Just stand where you are," the cold voice said from the shadows at the west end of the porch.

Sloan froze. He held the rifle in his right hand and there was hardly time to drop the food sack, lever a round into the Winchester's chamber, to turn and fire at the unseen man who stood there.

"You Sloan Sutro?" asked the unseen.

"Yes."

"Drop that rifle."

The Winchester clattered to the porch and Sloan let the sack fall too. His Colt, or rather *Landres'* Colt, was in his holster, but there wasn't a chance to draw and shoot.

"My name is Seb Wister," said the man. "Sheriff Seb Wister. I'm looking for a man, name of Rio Yarnell. Have you seen him?"

"He was around," admitted Sloan. He glanced quickly at Wister and saw the dull shine of a badge on the tall man's coat, but the face was hidden beneath the brim of the hat. A sixgun was in Wister's right hand and it was aimed at Sloan. The man could hardly miss at that range.

"Where is he now?"

"I don't know," said Sloan, truthfully enough.

"His horse came back to Mr. Bylas' ranch. There was blood on the saddle, Mister."

"So?" asked Sloan.

Wister shifted a little. "Last thing anyone knew he was up this way hunting deer. He didn't come back. His horse did."

"What has this to do with me."

"Seems like you were the last person to see him alive."

Sloan wet his lips. "Alive? Is he dead then?"

"We don't know, mister. We do know you consider yourself quite a hard case."

"I take care of myself," said Sloan.

"Maybe you took care of him, too?"

Sloan looked directly at the lawman. "No," he said. "Where the *hell* was Rio Yarnell! If he had died, they'd have to have his corpse to pin the murder on Sloan. They could do that easily enough.

"You have any explanation as to how that blood was on his saddle?"

"Maybe it was deer blood," said Sloan.

"I don't think so."

"Can you prove it?"

Wister spat. "Damn you," he said sullenly. "I didn't come all the way up here to split hairs with a murderer, Sutro."

"Don't call me a murderer, Wister!"

The sheriff glanced about almost as though expecting to see someone else. "Happens I can," he said quietly.

"Then you *have* found Rio Yarnell?"

"No."

The wind picked up as the moon began to fill the valley with cold silvery light, and Sloan could see Wister's features now. Lean faced and tanned, big nosed, with tightly compressed lips beneath a neatly trimmed dragoon mustache. The very picture of a law officer, according to the books.

"You have no right to accuse me of murder, Mister unless you can prove it."

"He *can,*" said another voice from the other side of Sloan, and this one he recognized without turning to look at the newcomer. It was the voice of Dave Landres.

Landres came to stand in front of Sloan. The moonlight glinted on a badge on *his* coat too. "Deputy sheriff Landres," said he with a touch of dryness in his voice. "We're arresting you for murder, Sutro."

"Build up a case, Landres," said Sloan sarcastically. "You'll damned well have to prove it."

"We can."

Wister walked up to Sloan and held the gun on him while he removed the snub-nosed Colt from Sloan's holster. "Sloan Sutro," he said in a louder voice, "I hereby arrest you for the murder of one Ellis Yancey, shot to death by you in front of three witnesses last Sunday on the Bylas' ranch. I hereby warn you that anything you say from now on may be used against you."

Sloan stared uncomprehendingly at the lawman. "Ellis Yancey?" he said quickly. "I didn't kill Ellis Yancey!"

"No? Mr. Harry Landres and Mr. Sage Spencer say you did. Mrs. Landres saw the shooting, too."

Sloan looked at the dark impassive face of Dave Landres. "She didn't see a damned thing! *Spencer* shot at me and hit Yancey!"

Wister spat casually. "That's not what Landres and Spencer say."

"Why should they? It's damned easy to cover this thing up. They want me out of business. This is as good a way to do it as anyway! I didn't kill Ellis Yancey!"

"Hear him talk," said Landres coldly. He half closed his eyes. "I can see a rope around your neck already, Sutro."

The wind whispered evilly about the eaves of the house, hinting and muttering to Sloan Sutro of the thing that would happen to him. He touched his dry lips with the tip of his tongue. There wasn't a thing he could say to make them believe him, nor would it be any better when he tried to convince a jury.

"Don't get any ideas, Sutro," said Wister.

Sloan flicked his eyes toward the barn. He was a better-than-average sprinter under normal conditions. But it was hardly possible to beat a pair of soft-nosed forty-fours to the shelter of the barn.

Landres leaned against the wall of the house. "Mr.

Bylas is very upset about you, Sutro. Says he made a nice offer for this land. Says he's still willing to give you that price for the land. Now, if you were to agree to that, turn the deed over to us, and take your money, maybe it could be arranged for Yancey's death to have been accidental rather than deliberate."

Sloan looked quickly at Wister. The man's face was as impassive as that of an Easter Island statue.

Landres slowly began to roll a cigarette. "Mr. Bylas will be fair about this, Sutro. How about it?"

Sloan knew they had him cold. Whichever way he tried to work it they would have him checked and checked again, and the checkmate would not be by the use of the usual pieces but by the use of hot lead.

"Sutro?" said Landres.

Sloan looked at him. "You've arrested me for murder," he said quietly. "Take me into town and jail me. That's all you have to do as an officer of the law."

Landres lighted up, and the flare of the match revealed the sardonic humor in his dark eyes. "Listen to him, Seb," he said.

An idea came through to Sloan. A cold, grisly, evilly repellent thought. No matter what he did or said, he knew right then and there *they never meant for him to leave his land alive.* The silver stars they wore were nothing but shields to cover men who were tools of Garth Bylas. He might have a chance if they took him into town and jailed him. Here he knew he was doomed. Bylas had offered money for the land and would have the deed, and the money. They'd never allow him to escape from that country. He had been doomed by Garth Bylas.

The Mexicans had an apt phrase for such a proceeding as he expected to face. *Ley del fuego.* Law of the fire. Let the prisoner escape, or let him *think* he is escaping. When he runs, the voice of the gun speaks. The report reads: killed while attempting to escape. It saves time and money. Whether the man is innocent or not, does not seem to matter. "Let God sort the souls," the executioners say fatalistically.

"Sutro?" said Landres again.

The wind suddenly thrashed through the trees, swaying and buffeting them, as though in bitter anger at the fate of one, Sloan Sutro, a man who had stubbornly and perhaps too foolishly tried to stand alone against the powers of the Rio Blanco Valley. It is far better for a man to die in the warm sunlight with a smoking gun in his hand than to die at night on a windy mountainside with a bullet in his back, to be known henceforth as a man who died beyond the law.

Many men do not actually fear death itself; it is the *way* of death that makes heroes or cowards out of men at the very end.

"Gawd dammit!" snapped Wister, at the end of his patience. "You want the deal or not?"

There were ghosts prowling that mountain meadow in the windy darkness. Simon Kelso and Buck Kelso, and possibly in a short period of time, they would be joined by a third ghost, that of Sloan Sutro. Three men who had died because of that land and because of Garth Bylas.

Sloan looked at Landres and smiled thinly. "You and your brother are a precious pair, Landres. Two little men playing at being big men. Without Garth Bylas and his drunken sister, you Landres men are nothing but third-rate citizens in this valley, or any other place for that matter."

Landres hit him cleanly. Sloan lay flat on his back. He had hoped that Landres would strike him, and in the quick scuffle, Sloan might have been able to get Landres' gun. But the man had been too fast.

"Get up!" snapped Landres viciously.

Sloan got slowly to his feet. "Now what?" he asked almost pleasantly. "How do I get it? Belly or back? You or Wister?"

"Keep laughing, Sutro! Smile! Shoot off that big

mouth! Throw your Texas brag! But in the end, it will be us that will laugh!"

"The deed," said Wister impatiently.

Sloan wiped the trickle of blood from a corner of his mouth. "You go to hell!" he said savagely.

Wister reversed his pistol and tapped the butt against the palm of his other hand. 'Talk," he said thinly.

Sloan knew well enough what would happen to him if he refused to give them the deed. Once Bylas had the deed, it would be easy enough for him to make the transaction legal. Why not? He ran the valley; Sheriff Wister was under his thumb. Bylas ruled by money and by his hired guns.

Wister suddenly swung up the pistol. He stepped closer to Sloan.

"It's hidden," said Sloan quickly.

"Where?"

"In the house."

"Move then!"

Sloan turned and opened the door. There was no chance for him, as there had been when Spencer, Landres, and Yancey had him cornered in the barn on the Bylas' ranch. He felt the muzzle of the gun nestle against the small of his back. He walked into the house and into the living room, then reached up to slide a hand along the place where the low roof met the wall, but his hand did not encounter the stiff envelope within which he had placed the deed. A cold trickle of sweat ran down his sides. That was where he had left it. No one else knew where he had hidden it. No one! But perhaps Rio Yarnell had known of it. He had been in the house when Sloan had hidden it.

"Well?" demanded Wister.

Then suddenly, Sloan's finger touched paper. As much as he hated losing the deed, there was a feeling of intense relief within him. Better turn over the deed and take a chance of living rather than to stand another savage beating. He turned and held out the deed toward Wister. Wister snatched it from his hand. "Cover him, Dave," he said out of the side of his mouth. He lighted a match and scanned the paper. He nodded. "All right, Dave. This is it, sure enough."

The match flickered out, and although the moonlight was coming through the dirty windows, Sloan could not see the two hard faces looking at him from beneath the shadow of their hat brims. There was no need for him to see those faces. He knew what was etched on them. Death for one Sloan Sutro...

"Outside," said Wister.

When Sloan stepped off the rear porch, his back crawled between the shoulder blades. Any minute now...

"Walk," said the lawman.

He walked past the barn and into the filtered shadows of the woods, with the moonlight streaming down through the treetops. The pines swayed steadily in the breeze. Suddenly an eldritch cry came riding on the wind like a night demon.

"Cougar!" said Wister.

"You sure?" asked Landres.

Sloan glanced back at the man. His face was plain in the moonlight. There was something written on it. The man was afraid. Not of guns or men, but of the unknown.

"Come on, Dave," said Wister.

Landres wet his lips. "You sure that's a cougar, Seb?"

"What else would it be."

"You've heard stories about this place."

"You mean them haunts? Hawww! Dave, you ain't afraid of ghosts, are you?"

Landres flushed. "Well, Rio Yarnell always claimed Old Man Kelso prowled around here."

"Sure he did! He lived here, didn't he?"

"After he was dead?"

Wister's eyes narrowed. "By God," he said in a dry voice. "I believe you're scared of haunts at that!"

Sloan raised his head. "Buck Kelso's been back too," he said quietly.

"Shut up!" snapped Wister.

"Wait," said Landres. He came close to Sloan. "You saw him?"

"No, but I've heard him."

"Like *that* sound?"

"Something like it," admitted Sloan.

Landres wiped the cold sweat from his pale face.

"Come on," said Wister. He shoved Sloan forward.

Landres did not want to go, but he couldn't stay back and let Wister carry on with the dirty work. Besides, if word got back to Rio Blanco that Dave Landres was afraid of haunts, he might be laughed out of town, fast gun or not. A man like Dave Landres would rather die under the gun than to be laughed at.

The cougar cried again, faintly and hauntingly.

They were well in the woods now. Any minute, any *second,* and the gun would crack, and Sloan Sutro would die. He had developed a split-second timing in his life, and that was why he was still alive. To gamble and live, that was the secret, but the timing was all important.

Sloan whirled, swinging up an arm. The arm struck up the Colt and then struck Wister across the face. In that second, Sloan sprinted forward, driving his toes deep into the soft earth, head down, arms and legs pumping like pistons. Then suddenly, he veered from side to side just as Wister's gun cracked. Thank God he had not veered into the slug. Wister fired again, missed in his haste, and cursed in his anger.

Sloan hurdled a log and jumped behind a tree. The gun flatted off again, and bark flew from the tree inches from Sloan's head. Sloan sprinted again, keeping the tree between himself and the cursing gunmen. A gun cracked. Sloan hooked a toe under a dead branch and fell headlong.

"Got him!" yelled Wister. "Not bad in this light, eh, Dave?"

Sloan bellied along, keeping behind a log. He heard the soft thudding of feet as Wister came through the moonlit woods, hastily reloading his revolver. Then he paused not twenty feet from Sloan peering about, cocked pistol ready for instant action. Sloan was looking directly at Wister, hoping that the crooked lawman could not see him. He knew better when he saw the Colt come up and steady as Wister aimed at him.

A shot slapped out in the woods, but no slug hit Sloan Sutro, nor had Seb Wister fired the shot. The lawman fell heavily, and his Colt pitched from his hand. Sloan turned quickly. There was no sight nor sound of anyone. Nothing except for the faint trace of gunsmoke filtering upward through the leafy branches.

"Seb?" called out Dave Landres.

Sloan worked his way close to the log.

"Seb? Where are you?" called out Landres again.

There was no answer from Seb Wister. There never would be. His eyes were wide open, staring up at the moonlit sky, but they saw nothing.

"Seb?"

Sloan worked his way to the end of the log, peering about for a sight of Wister's Colt.

"You got him, didn't you, Seb? Seb! Dammit! Answer me!" called out Landres.

Wind in the pines. Thrashing of boughs. Soughing of leaves. Nothing more.

Sloan heard soft footfalls. Then he saw Dave Landres standing not far from the body of Wister. His cocked pistol was in his hand. Cautiously the gunman approached the body and looked down at it. He looked up again, and cold fear was etched on his lean face. He peered about, trying to probe the hidden secrets of those dark and mysterious woods. Then he knelt beside Wister and hastily removed the deed from the man's coat. Sloan was just getting up to make a try for Landres when the cougar shrieked eerily through the night.

Landres turned and ran, hurdling a log. A branch knocked off his hat, but he didn't stop. Sloan jumped to his feet, saw Wister's gun, snatched it up, and raced after Landres. But it was no use. He heard the crisp slapping of leather against horsehide, followed by the startled whinnying of a horse, then the steady thudding of hoofs as Landres rode like a centaur for the trail. Something was riding with him. Something unseen and grisly, whispering strange and alien things into his ears. Once more, the cougar shrieked. Then Landres was gone from sight.

Sloan turned and peered into the woods. Some of Landres' naked fear seemed to have settled within him. Yet Wister had died by a bullet fired by a flesh and blood person, certainly not ectoplasm. Dave Landres was gone, fleeing down the mountainside lashed on by sheer panic. Seb Wister, the would-be executioner, was dead; Sloan Sutro, the intended victim, was still alive, and there was still no sight nor sound of his savior.

Sloan flitted from tree to tree like a phantom, until at last, he felt, rather than saw or heard, the presence of someone. Then he saw a man seated on the ground, a Colt lying on his lap, back resting against a tree, and cold sweat dewing his pale face. Sloan walked toward him, pistol ready and cocked. "Yarnell," he said quietly. "It was you, then?"

The man nodded, and the effort brought out a fresh dewing of sweat on his agonized face.

"Why?"

Yarnell looked up. "I once told you I owed you my life."

"Is that why you killed him?"

Yarnell moved, and the effort seemed like agony to him. "What's the difference? He's dead. You're alive. I said I was kinda curious to see what would happen around here. Besides, I never liked that two-faced Wister."

It was a rough job getting Yarnell back to the house. When the job was done, the man passed out. Sloan went back into the woods and carried Wister's body to a small cave in the rock formation behind the barn. He covered the mouth of it with rocks. His hands shook as he rolled a cigarette and lighted it. He was in deep now. Already accused of the death of Yancey, he knew that Landres would report that Sloan had also killed Seb Wister while the law officer was performing his sworn duty. Killing a man like Yancey was bad enough, but to kill a lawman was certifying your own death sentence. Every other lawman within hundreds of miles would gun him down like a mad dog.

Bylas would soon have the deed. For Sloan to try and get it back would be madness. Trust Bylas to work out some way of making it look legal. Sloan had made a helluva mess of things.

As he walked slowly back to the house, deep in thought, the lonely, haunting cry of the cougar drifted from the heights as though to mock him.

CHAPTER EIGHT

During that long wind haunted night, the life of Rio Yarnell hung in the balance, seemingly sustained by the stubborn faith of Sloan Sutro that the man would live. Every fiber in Sloan seemed to cry out to him to pull foot out of there and head for the tall timber, to vanish until such time as he could continue the fight for his land. But he could not leave Rio Yarnell.

Just before dawn, the first drops of rain fell on the shake roof of the house and found their way through the shattered windows. By the first vague light of the false dawn, a steady drizzle was falling on the Mountain Meadows country, veiling the sight of the Rio Blanco Valley from Sloan Sutro as he prowled the woods overlooking the valley and the winding trail that led up to his land.

There was no sight of men, but Sloan knew that it was just a matter of time, and a damned short time at that before the hue and cry would sweep up from the valley to cover his land. If they found him there, it would be short shrift. Shorter shrift perhaps than Buck Kelso had received.

He went back through the drizzle, hunched in his worn slicker, desperately anxious to get out of there to run anywhere, for a time, at least. But he could not move Rio Yarnell. Not yet.

He entered the house and took a long chance, making a fire to heat coffee and fry bacon for himself and to heat thick soup for the sick man. Yarnell ate slowly, with an effort, but he did manage to get the food down, and when he finished, Sloan rolled a cigarette for him. He smiled faintly. "Feel like a weakling," he said.

Sloan shook his head. "I should be so weak," he said.

Yarnell closed his eyes and drew in on the cigarette. "You'll have to get out of here," he said.

"I know that."

"You stayed for me; I know. Maybe it would have been better if you had pulled out. If they find me here, they'll kill me anyway, Sutro. I know too much."

"They'll think it was me that killed Wister. Even if they believed otherwise, it's too good a chance to miss. It's a perfect way to kill me and get away with it, Yarnell."

"You can always pull out."

"No."

Yarnell nodded. "I knew you'd say that."

Sloan rolled a cigarette and lighted it. "Trouble is, Landres has my deed. I couldn't stop him. You know well enough that with that deed in Bylas' hands and me hiding out for two murders I did not commit, he'll have me run down and wiped out. With the deed in his possession, he can work it out in his usual *legal* way to get possession of this land. It looks pretty black, Yarnell."

The hired gun nodded again. "You said *two* murders."

Sloan quickly explained what had happened at the Bylas ranch.

Yarnell whistled softly. "Your life isn't worth a plugged centavo, *amigo*. Why don't you pull foot? Fast! Now! I can take care of myself."

The rain slashed against the house. Sloan eyed the weak man. "You know what would happen to you if they found you here."

"What difference does it make to you?"

Sloan drew in on his cigarette. For a moment, their eyes met and held. The same fleeting thought occurred to both of them in that instant. The thought they had experienced once before. Had they met each other at a different time and under different circumstances, they might have become close friends. The plains' Indians have a double word for it. Brother-friends. Closer than brothers, closer than friends.

"We're even up," said Rio Yarnell softly. "You save my life. I saved yours. Let's shake on a double debt paid off. Then you pull leather out of here, *amigo!*"

Sloan shook his head.

"A fool there was," said Yarnell softly. He accepted another cigarette from Sloan and a stiff slug of whiskey in a water glass. Sloan poured himself a hooker too. He sipped at the amber fluid and felt new strength seep into his tired body.

The hired gun sucked in on his cigarette and blew a reflective puff of smoke toward a dripping window. "You once were curious about a number of things. I didn't answer your questions then. I will now. I don't know what will happen to me, but whatever *does* happen to me, you'll be here to carry on the fight against Garth Bylas. Maybe this information will help you. That is if you're still fool enough to stick it out in this damned valley."

"I am."

"I killed Simon Kelso. I was always sorry for it. It haunts me. No other killing I ever did haunts me like that one does."

Sloan remembered the man's fevered ravings. "I know," he said.

The hard blue eyes flicked at Sloan. "Bylas conned me into believing the old man carried a hideout gun. He didn't. How was I to know? I thought it was me or him, and the old man could fight like a buzzing rattler with a gun or tongue. I shot him and then found out he was unarmed." Yarnell's voice died away, and then he looked at Sloan. "Jesus, God, Sutro," he said in a strained tone, "You must believe me."

"Goon."

"You said Buck Kelso died in Vista Springs under strange circumstances. That a couple of men did a lot of talking about him in the saloons until they riled up the mob and had them lynch Kelso. Those men were paid by Garth Bylas to do the job."

"Can you prove that?"

"Take a good look at me, Sutro. A good *long* look. *Ever see me before?*"

There always had been something familiar about the man, and then Sloan knew where he had seen him before, although just fleetingly. In Vista Springs, just before Kelso had been lynched. "You!" he said accusingly.

Yarnell closed his eyes. "Yes, Sutro. I was one of those two men. No one knew me there or the hombre with me. He lit out after the job." Yarnell smiled faintly. "Said he was scared of you. He had good reason to be. Maybe I would have been smarter had I gone with him. Too late. *Too late...*"

"Blood for water," said Sloan. He emptied his glass. He eyed the weak man.

Yarnell opened his eyes. "My conscience bothered me. I couldn't stop thinking about the things I'd done."

Finally, I prepared a full report of my work with Bylas. The killings and the hurrahings, all the dirty, underhanded filthy things that man is capable of ordering his hired guns to do, and what they do for his filthy money!"

"Take it easy, Yarnell," said Sloan. He eyed the sick man expectantly. He might have stumbled onto something here. A weapon to topple Garth Bylas from his bloody throne!

Yarnell nodded weakly. "I wrote out that confession and had it signed by two friends of mine. Men there in town. Well respected men who have long wanted to get rid of Garth Bylas but who have never been able to buck up against his will and his hired guns. *Especially* the hired guns. The confession is legal, Sutro. It will stand up in any court in the land. Sim Grosset, owner of the big general store in town, was one of the men who witnessed it. Sim is a notary public. The other man is Heck Watt, owner of the livery stable. Both of them hate Bylas but have never been able to strike back at him. If they had tried to use that confession against him, they would have been drygulched. Another thing, as long as I am alive, they would not dare to say that it was in existence. For as surely as you are standing there, the confession would put a rope around my neck."

"It's rather useless then, isn't it?"

Yarnell shook his head. "No, it is the best weapon a man could have against Bylas." He looked up at Sloan. "As far as I am concerned, it can be used at any time by the right man. That man is you, Sutro."

"And what about you? The noose will still dangle for you, Yarnell."

The tired blue eyes seemed calm and resigned. "Yes," said the hired gun. "But it doesn't matter, Sutro. I might not live to see it used. This wound is a bad one. No offense to your doctoring. I might have already been dead, but for that. Even if I survive the wound, I don't think I'll be around long."

"You'll hit the out-trail then?"

Yarnell closed his eyes and nodded slowly. "Yes, I think I will hit the out-trail."

"You can't stay here. You must see a doctor."

"I told you that Bylas would have me killed on sight."

"No."

The eyes stabbed at Sloan. "I know him!"

"You don't know *me*."

Sloan went into swift and skillful action. He got his horse and rigged a sling seat on one side, counterbalancing it on the other side with a kyack filled with blankets, food, and other necessaries. It took time and patience to get Rio Yarnell from the house and into the sling seat. He led the horse to the east, through the gray drizzle, until at last, he reached a faint trail, the one he had used to approach his land the day before. He led the horse up the slope and then tethered it to a tree while he faded back down the trail to a place where he could see his holding. A faint thread of smoke seemed to hang listlessly from the big chimney.

He stood behind a tree and scanned the area with his field glasses. Just as he was about to turn away, he saw three horsemen top the trail and draw rein two hundred yards from the house. Rifles rested across their upper thighs, and the rain glistened on their slickers. Even as he watched, they rode on toward the house. Dave Landres, Sage Spencer, and another man. In a few minutes, they had dismounted and were Indianing up on the house. Sloan couldn't help but grin.

He turned quickly back and hurried to the horse. In a swift gray downpour of cold rain, he led the horse deeper and deeper into a wet, thick tangle of trees, rocks, and fallen timbers until not even a bloodhound could have trailed him.

———

THE CAVE WAS warm and dry. Sloan had dared to make a fire of dry wood he had found sheltered beneath a rock overhang. Once the rock floor of the cave was warm, he put out the fire and covered the rock with blankets and other padding, onto which he eased Rio Yarnell. The man was unconscious once more. His face was so thin and pale it seemed as though the very skull was trying to force its way through the flesh rather than to wait for the certain decomposition of death.

Sloan had heated food on the fire. He tried to feed

the man but could not bring him around. It was already dusk. The mouth of the cave was around a right angle bend from his simple camp, and beyond the mouth was a high ledge of rock which would shield any light. He lighted a candle and placed it behind a rock so that the light shone partly on the face of Rio Yarnell.

It seemed like hours before the wounded man at last opened his eyes. He looked about the cave. "Nice," he said. "Reminds me of the bridal suite in La Fonda."

"You had better eat."

Yarnell shook his head. "Where are we?"

"In the hills somewhere east of the valley."

"On Bylas land?"

Sloan's eyes narrowed. "Damned if I know. I was in too much of a hurry to get *out* of the valley without bothering to think of *where* I was going."

"Followed?"

"I'm not sure. Dave Landres, Sage Spencer, and another man arrived at my place shortly after we left. Another five minutes delay..."

"You can still go on running, Sutro."

"No."

The blue eyes had an amused light in them. "Never say die, is that it?"

"Something like that."

"What will you do now?"

"I want the deed to my land."

"Yes."

The hard gray eyes held Yarnell's blue ones. "I want that confession you signed. Where is it?"

"Maybe I'm a damned fool in letting you know where it is," hedged Yarnell.

"If you live, and I think you will, you can always turn state's evidence."

The blue eyes closed. "Yes," said Yarnell in a faraway voice.

"Where is it?"

The eyes opened. "You'll love this. It's in the bunkhouse on Garth Bylas' ranch. Beneath a board under my bunk. Bylas has as many as ten or twelve men staying in that bunkhouse at times. Tough men, Sutro. They won't just let you walk in there and calmly remove that confession."

"Why didn't you leave it with Grosset or Watt?"

Yarnell smiled faintly. "I may be a damned fool but not *that* much of a damned fool."

Sloan slowly rolled two cigarettes and placed one between Yarnell's dry lips. He lighted both smokes and then teetered on his boot heels, listening to the faint beating of the rain outside the isolated cave. "All I have to do," he said thoughtfully, "is to go into Rio Blanco to get back my deed beneath the noses of Bylas and his merry boys, then ride casually out to his ranch, enter the bunkhouse, say good evening to more of the boys, take the confession from beneath your bunk, then ride out again. Then, quite casually, of course, I have to find someone in authority to give that confession to. In a country where the sheriff is dead, supposedly killed by *my* hand, and where the deputy sheriff is under control of Mr. Bylas."

"Simple, ain't it?" agreed Yarnell.

Sloan nodded. He reached for his slicker and shrugged into it, then reached for the Winchester.

"Where are you going?" asked Yarnell.

Sloan looked down at him and smiled faintly. "To get that deed and get that confession."

"You're plumb loco! They'll shoot you to doll-rags!"

"They'll shoot me anyway, Yarnell."

"The Texas Ranger way!" jeered Yarnell. "Charge hell with a bucket of water, eh?"

Sloan leaned on the battered rifle. "Listen," he said. "You stay here, *amigo*. Not that I think you'll be *going* anywhere in your condition. There is enough food for at least a week. You have your six shooter. I'll leave the horse for you."

"Why, you aiming *not* to come back?"

Sloan walked toward the mouth of the cave. "Maybe *they'll* see to that, Yarnell. *Adios, Amigo!*"

"*Vaya con Dios, amigo!*"

He led the horse closer to the cave and sheltered it beneath a rock overhang. Water had filled the hollows, and there were patches of grazing in the thin soil that covered the rocks here and there. He slapped the horse on its wet rump, then padded swiftly down the dark and shallow canyon toward the north. He wasn't sure where he was.

It wasn't until he came out into the open that he realized he was on the heights above the North Branch of the Rio Blanco, not far from where he had been ambushed and captured by Sage Spencer and Ellis Yancey. Through the slanting veils of rain, he could see the faint and far-off yellow lights of the town. To his right, far below, across the rushing river, were the lights of the Bylas ranch. So near and yet so far. But the deed must come first. Without it, he had no legal way of claiming his land, and he'd never give up that fight.

As he worked his way down the wet slope, thunder pealed in the gorge of the Rio Blanco, and chain lightning etched its eerie way across the mountain tops to illuminate in ghastly light the sheer wall of the great canyon and the terrible masses of rock high above it, seemingly hanging there by a thread. A thread that might snap at any time. If it did snap, it would be the end of the Garth Bylas and his kingdom, providing he did not retain possession of the deed stolen from Sloan. The only way he would retain the deed would be to kill the lean, hard-eyed man, who even now, all alone, with a battered rifle in his big hands, was striding downhill, through the wet and clinging brush, toward the very stronghold of Garth Bylas, the town of Rio Blanco.

CHAPTER NINE

There was one person and one only who might be able to help Sloan Sutro. He had not seen nor heard anything about Amy Corday since she had fled from the heights above the Rio Blanco the day he had been captured by Spencer and Yancey. Amy had worked long enough in the office of the Rio Blanco Company to have a good idea where such an important document as the deed to the old Kelso land might be kept.

Amy had told him she lived alone in her parent's little house not far from the company offices. The rain was still slanting down when he paused in thick shrubbery across the street from the little house to study it. The house was unlighted. She probably was not there, for it was too early for her to be in bed.

He quickly crossed the street and passed around to the rear of the house. He tried the rear door and found it open. He entered and looked about in the darkened house, softly calling her name, but there was no answer. There was evidence that she had not left the house, not intending to come back. He walked to the rear of the house and stepped out onto the rear porch. There really wasn't any place for a young woman to go in Rio Blanco for an evening's pleasure unless it was to a church social. She had told Sloan that she did not date anyone in town, and he knew well enough such an attractive young woman would hardly suffer for lack of dates if she had a mind to accept them.

Then he remembered something, and his eyes narrowed. She had also told him that occasionally she was required to work evenings in the office, usually alone with Mr. Jonas. At the end of each month, there was certain work to be caught up, and Mr. Jonas required her to work with him. The fat slug probably had other ideas, although Amy had told Sloan that Jonas was married, *really* married, she had said with a dry smile.

Sloan remembered the first time he had been in the office and had brashly asked Amy for a luncheon date, only to be held off by Mr. Jonas.

He rubbed his bristly jaws, then walked back into the house. He hastily scribbled a note for her and placed it on her bed. As he did so, he saw the butt of a pistol protruding from the shelf of a small nightstand on the far side of the bed. He rounded the bed and picked up the weapon. It was a Colt forty-four. He held it close to his eyes and saw the engraved initials on the butt strap. E.S.C. Amy had said her father had served a number of times as a Rio Blanco special police officer. Edward S. Corday. Sloan examined the weapon after he emptied it. Its action was as smooth as silk. He loaded it with fresh cartridges from his own belt loops, then slid the Colt into his holster. Now he felt like a whole man again.

He left the house and padded up the wet alleyway. The house was further out on the same street upon which the main door of the upstairs office of the Rio Blanco Company was situated. He reached the area behind the big frame building. From somewhere to his right came the noise of a player piano and the subdued voices of men, and he realized he was within a few feet of the open rear door of the Bijou, situated below the Rio Blanco office.

He leaned the rifle against the wall at the bottom of the long wooden stairway that ascended to the second floor of the building and padded silently up it. The office did not seem to be lighted from below, but when he reached the landing at the top, he could see a faint glowing of yellow light from within.

He pressed his face against the wet and streaky glass. There were two lights in the office. One at the big roll top desk of Ernest Jonas, and the other at the desk of Amy Corday. His heart leaped a little as he saw a familiar dark head bent over work on the desk. There was no sign of Jonas.

He studied the big dark areas of the office, but still, there was no sight of the man. Sloan took a long chance. He tried the door. It was locked. He tapped lightly on the glass. She raised her head and stared toward the door. Sloan tapped again, more urgently.

Amy Corday had courage. She stood up and walked toward the door until she was close enough to see the lean whiskered face of the man she loved. She quickly opened the door and kissed him. "What are you doing here?" she demanded. "They're looking all over the valley area for you, Sloan."

"Where is Jonas?"

"He went for coffee. So he said. I think he went to have a drink."

"How long will he be gone?"

"I don't know."

"Dave Landres has the deed to my land. Did he give it to Bylas?"

"I don't know."

"Where would Bylas keep such a thing?"

"There is a safe in his office."

"Do you know the combination?"

She smiled a little at that. "I thought you *knew* Garth Bylas."

He walked past her, taking off his wet slicker. He dropped it on the floor behind a nearby desk. He eased the Colt in his holster. "I've got to get that damned deed!" he said. "I'm sorry, Amy."

She came to him. "Let me try," she said. She led him toward the big corner office usually occupied by Bylas. She entered it and knelt on the floor in front of the safe. She took a hairpin from her hair and began to work on the door. Suddenly there was a sharp click, and she opened the door, turning to look at him with a triumphant smile. "Never underestimate the power of a woman," she said.

"I learned that from my mother," he said drily. He knelt beside her and began to riffle through the papers in the safe. Suddenly he raised his head. That honed sixth sense of his had warned him of danger. He stood up. "Get back to your work," he said quickly. He turned on a heel and strode toward the door.

"No shooting, Sloan," she said. "Let me bluff it out."

He faded into the darkness at the rear of the office, and as he did so, he heard the door of the safe shut almost at the same instant that he heard the door at the bottom of the main stairs open. A heavy tread sounded on the stairs.

She left Bylas' office and turned to wave a folded paper at him, with a smile on her lovely face. There was no doubt but what she had stayed a moment longer, with cold courage, to find that most important piece of paper. She had hardly seated herself at her desk when the shadows at the top of the stairs were thickened by the portly form of Mr. Ernest Jonas. The man crossed to the gate that let one into the office proper and rested his soft white hands on it. The lamplight glittered from a ring and shone dully on the heavy gold chain that rested against his firmly rounded paunch.

"Quiet, isn't it, Miss Corday?" he said at last.

Amy Corday looked up. "Yes. It always seems quieter inside when it is raining outside."

"Quite different now from the hustle and bustle of the day's commerce," he said. He leaned forward, and the light glistened on his soft wet lips. "An opportune moment for you and I to have a cozy little chat, Miss Corday."

"That had better be done during business hours."

He waved a plump white hand. "In my capacity as office manager for the Rio Blanco Company, Miss Corday, I keep no special business hours. The company comes first, you know."

"I'm sure Mr. Bylas would be more than pleased to hear that, Mr. Jonas."

He opened the swinging gate and stood close to her, at the side of her desk. "I am afraid that Mr. Bylas doesn't quite appreciate my loyalty to the firm."

"I am sure he does, Mr. Jonas."

"Has he ever mentioned that to you?"

"Mr. Bylas hardly knows I exist."

He smiled. "I know you exist, Miss Corday."

She leaned back in her chair. "I think my work is done, Mr. Jonas. Shall I leave my desk lamp on?"

For a moment, he did not move nor answer. Sloan could almost smell the rutting fever in the man clear across the wide office. "There is no need for you to leave, Miss Corday," said Jonas softly. "It was only through my forgiveness and generosity that I allowed you to continue to work here after your association with that Sutro fellow."

She looked sharply at him. "Just what do you mean by that, Mr. Jonas?"

He leaned a little closer. "I happen to know who was riding in the hills with him the day Ellis Yancey was foully murdered on the Bylas ranch."

"You do?" she said coolly.

"I do."

"How did you find out?"

"Sage Spencer told me. He told me not to tell anyone else. Sage prides himself on being a gentleman despite his bloody record. He was in his cups at the time, he told me. I am almost sure he does not remember doing so. It so happens, Miss Corday, that I have an almost infinite capacity for liquor, and it does not have quite the same effect on me that it does on most men; therefore, when others *talk* too much, Ernest Jonas *listens*."

"How admirable," she said coldly.

"Mr. Bylas might be interested to know that you were with Sutro that day."

"And you'd tell him?"

He hesitated again, then waved his hands in little circular motions. "Certainly not! That is to say unless you are not, shall we say, a little more than nice to me, Miss Corday. There, I've said it at last!"

"You certainly have," she said.

"Your job, Miss Corday," he murmured. "Remember that I have the power to have you discharged."

She stepped back a little as she stood up. "I think I had better leave, Mr. Jonas."

He straightened up. "Sloan Sutro will not be back, Miss Corday. Not to protect you in the case of any eventualities due to your unfortunate association with him."

"Why do you say that?"

He shrugged. "He murdered Ellis Yancey. He shot down Sheriff Wister in cold blood. Men are looking for him, Miss Corday, and I assure you, they will find him!"

"Sloan Sutro did not murder those men."

"So? You have proof?"

"I may have."

His eyes narrowed. "What do you mean?"

"Nothing," she said hastily.

He placed a hand on her arm. "Come, come," he said. "Is there something I should know?"

"No!"

"Be nice to me, Miss Corday. Be very nice."

"Let me pass, Mr. Jonas."

He shook his head. "Supposing Mr. Bylas finds out that you know something about those murders?" He eyed her speculatively. "Do you know what might happen to you?"

"I am not interested."

"You had better be," he warned. He leaned close to her again. "Now, you had better be nice to me. It is high time that you realized that being friendly to me is a matter of fine discretion on your part. I'm a reasonable man..."

"Just exactly what do you want?"

"A little kindness. The friendship of a lovely young woman for an older man, whose married life, shall we say, is not exactly a bed of roses."

"Just *friendship,* Mr. Jonas?"

He pursed his soft wet lips. "Well, as a matter of fact, I had thought of something a little more intimate than that. I thought that perhaps... That is to say..."

"*An affair,* Mr. Jonas?"

Jonas licked his lips quickly. "The word is hardly suitable, Miss Corday."

"Take your hands off me, Mr. Jonas!"

He grabbed her, and she struggled.

Suddenly Jonas jumped back and clapped a hand to his soft jowls. Blood sparkled in the lamplight and ran down onto his white shirt cuff. "Why damn you!" he spat out. He caught her full handed across the side of the face, and her hairpins flew in every direction, losing her lovely dark hair.

Then a folded paper fell to the desk from her ripped blouse. He stared at it, then snatched it up. "Where did you get this?" he demanded. "Who did you get it for?"

"For me, Jonas," said Sloan quietly from the darkness.

Amy hastily covered her upper body as Jonas slowly turned to look toward Sloan. "Sutro?" he asked softly.

Sloan did not move.

"Sutro?"

No answer.

It was quiet except for the harsh breathing of Ernest Jonas and the steady ticking of the big wall clock, and the soft pattering of the rain on the windows. Then Jonas made out the lean hawk-face of Sloan Sutro.

Sloan did not move. He wanted no outcry from the man. He must get close enough to hit him once for the long count, for there could be no gunplay.

"Look, Sutro," said Jonas, extending a shaking hand. "I had a little too much to drink. I..."

"Shut up," said Sloan.

Jonas backed away, pushing against the gate with his plumply rounded buttocks, while Sloan closed in on him, trying not to panic him. He had to get close enough for one telling punch. Just one.

"You can't get out of this town alive, Sutro," said Jonas quickly. "Look, I'll pay you well for this deed."

"What about your *loyalty* to Bylas?"

"Damn him! I'd like to beat him at his own crooked game. I'll give you a certified check for seven thousand dollars."

"No."

"Eight?"

"No!"

"Ten then! That's the highest I can go."

"You couldn't go high enough, you scum! Give me that deed!"

Jonas wet his lips and nodded. He extended the paper with his left hand, and as Sloan reached for it with his right hand, a small, silver-mounted derringer came out of its hiding place and seemed almost buried in Jonas' soft, plump right hand. The hammer snicked back and was echoed by the soft, satisfied laugh of Ernest Jonas. "You damned fool," he said triumphantly. "You think so damned much of yourselves, you scum smelling of sweat and manure! Well, you didn't outsmart Ernest Jonas, Sutro!"

The office manager held the aces. He could yell or shoot. Either way, Sloan knew he'd have one hell of a time getting free this time. Even if he could outdraw that soft-nosed slug from the double-barreled stingy gun in Jonas' hand, the gun reports would have Bylas or some of his men down on him.

The clocked ticked on.

"You can have the deed, Mr. Jonas," said Amy. "Let him go, for God's sake! He'll leave the valley, I'll see to that!"

Jonas shook his head. "No," he said quietly. "Men like him never quit. It would be him or me. I might have a chance to outsmart Garth Bylas. I'd have no chance for my life if Sutro went free."

"So?" said Sloan softly.

"Get next to your lover, Miss Corday," sneered Jonas.

She came close beside Sloan, but there was no fear in her beautiful eyes.

"There are two slugs in this little gun," said Jonas. "One for you, Sutro, and one for Miss Corday. I can hardly miss at this range. I can't afford to let either one of you live. If I kill you, I can always say I found you looting the office."

"A double murder, Jonas?" said Sutro. "What price murder?"

"I have standing in this community! I am a man of responsibility and reputation! In time I can deal with Bylas about this deed. I can cover up my disloyalty, as you'd call it."

"I believe you would," said Amy.

Draw and shoot! What did he have to lose? The thoughts raced through Sloan's mind.

The door swung open at the bottom of the stairs.

"Jonas? You up there?" It was the voice of Garth Bylas.

Jonas was startled. In that instant chance, Sloan swung from the hip, driving Jonas back toward the head of the stairway. The derringer cracked, and the slug rapped into the ceiling.

"What the hell!" yelled Bylas. "Dave! Spencer!"

Jonas jumped back and missed his footing. For a second, he swayed on the edge of the top step, then he tumbled headlong like an empty barrel and smashed into Garth Bylas.

"Hide!" snapped Sloan to Amy.

"I won't leave you this time, Sloan!"

He wet his lips, swung her about, hit her neatly on the point of the jaw, caught her before she fell, then carried her across the office and placed her behind a wall cabinet. He spun on a heel and ran to Jonas' desk to turn out the light. He sprinted across the office, heading for the back door just as three men appeared at the top of the stairs.

Sloan jerked open the door just as a shot cracked out. The slug shattered the window and a shard of glass struck his face with stinging impact. He jerked back his head and as he did so he slipped on the wet landing and fell sideways down the long flight of stairs struggling desperately to grip the slippery railing until, at last, he fell heavily at the bottom. The three men appeared on the landing, and a gun cracked. The slug ripped a splinter from the bottom step driving it into Sloan's gun hand as he reached for his Colt.

Then the three big men were on him. A boot ground down on his gun wrist, and he looked up into the cold face of Dave Landres. Sage Spencer ripped the Colt from Sloan's holster. The third man was the biggest of all of them. He smiled in cold satisfaction and drew back a big boot. "We've finally got the Texas sonofabitch *exactly* where we want him," said Bylas. It was the last thing Sloan remembered.

CHAPTER TEN

Sloan Sutro shivered as he opened his eyes. A spit of rain came through the barred window above his battered head. He slowly sat up on the cot and looked toward the door, and he knew well enough where he was. In *the calaboose* of Rio Blanco. He reached for the full water bucket, raised it, and drank deeply; then, his eyes looked across the bucket into the eyes of Dave Landres, who stood beyond the barred doorway. Sloan slowly placed the bucket on the floor and stood up, reeling a little in his dizziness. He placed a hand against the damp wall.

Landres began to roll a cigarette. "Where is Seb Wister's body?" he asked.

"Up on the ranch," said Sloan.

"Where?"

"I put it in a cave in the rock formation behind the barn, and closed the mouth with rocks."

"Why?"

Sloan eyed the man. "There's a cougar loose up there. Wolves, too, for all I know."

"That the only reason?"

"What other reason would I have?"

Landres lighted the cigarette. "Hide the body and not get the law to prove you killed him."

"I didn't kill him."

"You said the same thing about Ellis Yancey."

"I know well enough I can't prove it, not with the three *witnesses* against me, that I didn't kill Yancey."

Landres blew a reflective puff of smoke into the cell and idly watched it drift toward the open window. "You're in one hell of a bind, Sutro. Two murder charges. Maybe three, for all I know, because no one knows where Rio Yarnell is. Do you?"

Landres shrugged. "Then there are a few other charges. Resisting arrest. Robbery."

"What do you mean by that?"

"You were caught in the act in the office of the Rio Blanco Company, weren't you? Then you resisted arrest again. You're a bear for punishment, Sutro. Maybe we can even pin the death of Ernest Jonas on you."

"Do," said Sloan politely. "Might as well get hanged for three murders as one. How did he die?"

"Broke his fat neck."

"Of course, you'll have to *prove* all these accusations."

Landres inspected his cigarette. "You don't think Garth Bylas is going to let this thing get as far as a trial, do you?" He looked up at Sloan with his head tilted to one side and eyes half closed. "People might get ideas that something *underhanded* was going on!"

"You don't say!"

Landres grinned. "I have to hand it to you. I wonder if anything would ever make you crack?"

"Like ghosts make yew crack, eh, Landres?" Sloan grinned back at the flushing Landres.

"You won't be so damned lippy when they put the noose around your neck!"

"You said Bylas would never let me go to trial."

"I wasn't talking about an execution *after* a trial, Sutro."

The picture was clear enough. Bylas had used that device before, sending Rio Yarnell and another hired gun to Vista Springs to talk up a lynching against Buck Kelso. It had worked well enough, as Sloan knew.

Landres flipped away his cigarette and began to roll another. "Seems like there is a great deal of ill feeling here in Rio Blanco against you, Sutro. Ellis Yancey had many friends. Seb Wister was a good sheriff. Rio Yarnell was well liked, or so it is said." Landres looked up at Sloan, hoping to see naked fear in those hard gray eyes, but in that, he was disappointed. "Well, anyway, I have deputized a few men to help me with this mess, now that I've taken over as sheriff. Seems like we'll have to take you back to the scene of the crime, like city cops do, to have a re-enactment of the sudden and lamented death of Seb Wister."

"Why not take the Yancey murder first?"

Landres lighted his cigarette. "Seems as though that was on Bylas land."

Then Sloan knew well enough that if he was taken up to his land by Landres and his deputies, that he'd never leave that land alive. It was better to get rid of him up there than on Bylas land. People might talk. *Ley del fuego!* Not trials for enemies of Garth Bylas. It was too chancy.

Sloan shivered in the cold, wet wind that swept into the cell.

"Nervous?" grinned Landres.

"What time does this execution take place?"

Landres sucked in on his cigarette. "That is hardly the word. I figured on taking you up there sometime tomorrow. That is, *unless* the cruel mob takes over, as they did in Vista Springs, resulting in the sudden death of Buck Kelso."

"And the talkers are busy in Rio Blanco right now, spending Bylas money in the saloons, stirring up the drunks for a lynching to cap the evening's drinking?"

"You figure it out. Anything you want?"

"Sure, Landres! A sixgun and a Winchester and half a dozen *honest* men to back me up."

"Haw! That's good. What a humorist! Well, they say sometimes men die with a smile on their lips. I'll be waiting to see if that might possibly be true."

When Landres left, Sloan dropped onto the cot and felt for the makings. He could hear Landres in low conversation in the sheriff's office at the front of the jail. Sloan rolled a cigarette and lighted it. He could hear the rain pattering on the roof, and there was a subdued roaring noise coming from somewhere. It was not the wind.

It took him some time to realize that it must be the North Branch of the Rio Blanco roaring past after its constriction in the narrow gorge to the east of town; the gorge that was constantly menaced by that tremendous pile of loose rock and timber hanging high above it in the landslide area. The steady rains would fill the water courses. They would also seep beneath that gigantic mass of rock and perhaps loosen it. If it should start sliding, nothing on earth could stop it from plunging down and filling the gorge of the Rio Blanco from rim to rim like a tightly fitting cork.

He was on his third cigarette, idly blowing the smoke up toward the window, when he heard a soft brushing noise just outside of the window. He sat up and tilted his head to one side to listen better. Then something scraped on the window ledge. He looked up to see a slim hand, and he stood up to look into the wide and frightened eyes of Amy Corday. He placed a finger to his lips. She nodded. Then she passed a pair of guns between the bars, two matched double-barreled derringers. "It was all I could find," she whispered tensely.

"They will do."

"You won't have a chance, anyway, Sloan!"

He looked back over his shoulder. "I won't go alone,"

he said grimly. He looked at her. "Do they know you were up in the office?"

"No."

"Who has the deed?"

"Mr. Bylas."

He passed a hand between the bars and touched the bruise on her chin. "I'm sorry," he whispered.

She smiled bravely. "You were right. I can't fight beside you like a man, Sloan."

He slid the twin derringers into his boot tops. "You'd probably be dead by now if you had been a man. You've done better as a woman, Amy." He smiled. "Thank God you *are* a woman!"

"Enough of a woman to love you forever, Sloan."

"You talk as though I won't be around long."

"What can you do now?" she asked fiercely. "You're trapped any way you look at it. You won't live to see tomorrow night!"

"I've been in seemingly hopeless situations before this."

"Not like this, Sloan! You don't know those men! You have to die, Sloan! They won't let you live! You're doomed!"

"Can you get help?"

"Who here would face *them?*"

"The law? Can you get word out of the valley?"

She shook her head. "The telegraph wires are down. The South Branch has flooded over its banks and blocked the south road from the valley. The closest town to the north, through the pass, is thirty miles away! The nearest army post is sixty miles from here! You're all alone, Sloan!"

He shook his head. "I have you," he said quietly.

"Wait!" She ducked down out of sight. Sloan sat down and began to roll a cigarette just as Landres stopped in front of the cell. "Who were you talking to?" he asked.

Sloan lighted up. "Came from the next cell," he said.

Landres walked to the next cell. "Keep quiet in there, damn you!" he snarled. He came back to Sloan's cell. "Better get some rest," he advised with a sly grin. "You might need all you can get." Then he was gone.

Sloan stood up and spoke over his shoulder. "Go to Sim Grosset and tell him they plan to either have me lynched or taken to my place and shot while attempting to escape, or so they will say. Tell Grosset I know about Rio Yarnell's confession."

"What do you mean, Sloan?"

"Vamonos!" he snapped. "There's no time to lose!"

He heard her feet squelch in the pasty mud of the alleyway. He wasn't through fighting, and he wouldn't be until they killed him, one way or another. As long as he was alive and armed, with a woman like Amy Corday fighting for him, he'd make the riffle yet. Or so he hoped against hope.

————

But the cold gray light of the false dawn showed there was no sign of help for Sloan Sutro. He could hear low voices in the office, the grating of boots on the dirty floor, and an occasional low laugh. Then Dave Landres came to the door with a sixshooter in his hand. "Come on, Sutro," he said, "We're all taking a little ride."

"The lynching is off, eh?"

"The mob didn't feel up to it, probably due to the rain. They were fed plenty of liquor. Funny thing. Sutro, I don't think any amount of liquor in the town would have worked them up enough. It was different in Vista Springs, I suppose. Buck Kelso wasn't exactly the most lovable of people, so I suppose he provided good sport for the mob."

"Maybe the people of Rio Blanco are a little sick of Garth Bylas and his machinations."

"Maybe. But it won't matter to you. Besides, they're sheep, too afraid to buck Bylas and his boys."

"You ought to know."

"Yes. Now shut up and get into your slicker."

Sloan snubbed out his cigarette and put on his worn slicker. He put on his hat and walked to the door. He could feel the weight and hardness of the two little stingy guns in his boots. It was well that he had placed them there, for the first thing Landres did was to pass a quick hand over Sloan's body feeling for hideout weapons. He did not feel the boots.

The rest of them were waiting in the stove-heated office. There was no mercy in the hard eyes of them. There was no need to ask what type of men the three of them were. Hardcase was stamped on their faces, and the Bylas brand was probably on their rumps as well. Dave Landres was buttoning his slicker. He jerked his head at his three deputies. "Jim Marcus, Todd Durkin, and Bob Slade. Good men and true." He grinned. "You ready, Sutro?"

Sloan shrugged. "As ready as I'll ever be."

Durkin opened the wide front door and pushed Sloan through it. The rain pattered lightly on the wooden roof over the board sidewalk. Five horses were tethered to the hitch rail in front of the jail. Sloan mounted a raw-boned claybank. It was then that he noticed that the street, which should have been empty of life in a cold gray dawn like that, was beginning to be lined with men, and a few women, who came from doorways and from side streets, to stand silently in the misty rain, watching the men who had come from the jail.

Dave Landres' face tightened beneath the low pulled brim of his hat. He swung up on ta his black and kneed it away from the hitching rail. He looked at his three men. 'Take out your Winchesters," he said.

"Nervous, Landres?" asked Durkin. He grinned.

"Damn you! I'm in charge here! I don't want any trouble."

"Who's going to buck up against us?" asked Durkin. He spat to one side. "Them sheep won't try to stop us. Besides, ain't we *lawmen* now?"

"Jesus," said Slade quickly. "I think you really believe that, Durkin."

But even so, the four *lawmen* glanced from side to side as they began their slow ride to the south, toward the wooden bridge that creaked and moved a little in the hard-driving current of the North Branch. When they drew abreast of the big general store of Sim Grosset, it was noticeable that quite a few hard-faced men were standing beneath the dripping wooden awning, watching the five horsemen. Sim Grosset stepped out into the street. "Landres," he said sharply. "Where are you taking that man?"

"What the hell is it to you?"

Heck Watt, all six feet four of him, lean and laconic, straightened up from the post against which he had been leaning. "If Sutro is as guilty as you say he is, why bother to take him up there for a re-enactment?"

Landres was obviously puzzled. "What do you mean?"

"It's damned poor weather for a man to be taken up there. Worst rains I've seen in years. Why today, Landres? It isn't like you to spend a day outside in this kind of weather when all the saloons are warm and dry."

"What the hell do you mean?"

Sim Grosset came close to Landres' horse and looked up at the deputy sheriff. "The people of this town seem to think there is no need for such a thing, Landres."

Landres touched his thin lips with the tip of his tongue. "There was some talk of a lynching," he said thoughtfully. "Of course, I couldn't allow the mob to take over, could I?"

Watt spat expertly at a tin can in the street. "If you let the mob take over, as you say, Landres, there might be someone else heading for a noose other than Sutro there."

"He's guilty as hell!"

"That's your say so. There ain't been a trial yet. Not even an inquest."

"Why bother?" jeered Jim Marcus. "Save the county money!"

Now the men on the sidewalks began to move out into the street until there was a semi-circle of them between the five mounted men and the creaking bridge. The rain pattered on the mud and on the slickered shoulders and low pulled hats. None of the waiting men had guns in their hands. It was a silent resistance to law and order, such as it was in die Rio Blanco valley. Those men knew well enough that to face Landres and his 'deputies' with guns in their hands might lead to bloodshed and plenty of it. They knew how to handle guns themselves, but not with the cold killing speed of Landres and his men.

"Get out of the way," said Dave Landres.

None of them moved.

It was then that Sloan saw Amy Corday standing beneath the awning of Grosset's General Store. She held her soft lower lip between her even white teeth, and her face was as pale as death. This might be the last cast of the dice for the man she loved. It wasn't easy to stand there and see another horseman beside the five who sat their mounts in the street. The Rider on the Pale Horse, for he was there as surely as the others were. He knew where to be when he was wanted. He had never failed yet in the history of the world.

Landres walked his horse forward, followed by his men, with Sloan forced along between Durkin and Slade, while Marcus brought up the rear. The crowd did not move. "Get out of the way," said Landres coldly.

"You men had better do as Deputy Sheriff Landres says," said a strong voice from the west side of the street.

There was no mistaking the authoritative voice of Garth Bylas. All eyes swiveled to see the man standing there hunched in his slicker, a cigar clenched between his strong teeth. Behind him, at either side, stood Harry Landres and Sage Spencer. Spencer was as cool as the waters of the Rio Blanco, while Harry Landres, for all his front, seemed to emanate the green, sickening aura of fear.

"No," said Grosset. "There's no need for Landres to take this man from here. At least, today."

"He's the law here," said Bylas.

"Sure, sure," said Heck Watt courageously. "After *you*, Bylas."

The rain slashed down a little harder, and a peal of sullen thunder sounded in the gorge of the Rio Blanco.

Bylas slowly worked his cigar to the other side of his wide mouth. "You've got a hell of a nerve, Watt," he said softly. "Just what do you mean by that?"

"Everybody knows you run the law here," said a gray-haired man standing just behind Grosset.

Bylas snorted. "Who are you to talk, Brady?" he demanded. "You owe me money. Half of you owe me something one way or another. You, Jensen! If it wasn't for me, you wouldn't own the pharmacy! You, Morris! When you're on your feet, you stand in a mob. If it wasn't for me, you'd of been in the jail for nonpayment of debts! You men want me to go on? Half of you work for me one way or another. If I close my sawmill, the mines, the businesses I own; if I stop buying from you merchants, this damned two-bit town will go broke. I'll see you starve before I open my businesses and accounts again."

"That may be," said Sim Grosset calmly. "Go ahead. With no law and order and no wills of our own, it won't matter."

"Listen to him!" jeered Harry Landres.

Sage Spencer eyed Sloan. The man held his deadly rifle in his hands, and Sloan seemed to know that if he made a break, Spencer would kill him before his horse went twenty feet.

Heck Watt raised his head. "This man hasn't had a trial," he said steadily. "We've heard all kinds of stories. We don't know if he's guilty or not. In fact, we don't know a damned thing other than that he refused to sell his land to you, Mr. Bylas."

"Tell them, Dave," said Bylas quietly. He relighted his cigar and waited expectantly.

Landres leaned forward in his saddle. "Sutro shot Ellis Yancey to death on Mr. Bylas' ranch. Rio Yarnell went up to Sutro's place to do some deer hunting. He hasn't been seen since. Sheriff Seb Wister went up there with me to confront Sutro. In the fight, Sutro shot Wister to death and damned near got me into the bargain. Isn't that enough?"

"I didn't kill either one of those two men," said Sloan. "Rio Yarnell is not dead."

"Where is he?" demanded Landres.

"I don't know."

Bylas laughed harshly. "Take him along, Dave," he said.

Then Amy Corday came out into the muddy street and looked at Landres. "Sloan Sutro did not kill Ellis Yancey," she said. "I followed Sloan when Ellis Yancey and Sage Spencer took him to the Bylas ranch where Harry Landres was waiting. In the fight that followed Sage, Spencer shot at Sloan Sutro and hit Ellis Yancey instead of Sloan Sutro."

"You'll swear to that in court?" demanded Landres.

"Certainly," she said.

"Damn her," said Bylas.

Sage Spencer looked steadily at the girl with those icy eyes of his. She did not flinch. In a way, there was almost a light of respect and admiration in his eyes.

"It's just her word against mine, Spencer's and my wife's!" cried out Harry Landres.

"Speak for yourself," another voice chimed in. The slurred voice of a woman. They all looked at Julie Landres, who stood swaying in the middle of the street behind the horsemen.

"Shut up, you!" yelled Harry.

She shook her head. "No," she said firmly. "It's as Amy Corday says. I'll swear to that in court!"

"I ought to break your damned neck!" yelled Harry.

"Shut up, you spineless pup," said Bylas out of the side of his mouth. "All right, you men! Supposing that *is* true! What about Sutro's murder of Seb Wister? Where is Rio Yarnell?"

"Right here," a faint voice called out.

This time they all turned to see a lone man in the center of the trembling wooden bridge. It was Rio Yarnell, afoot, leaning against the side of the horse which had carried him into the hills, away from death at Sutro's place.

It was almost quiet there in the muddy street, except for the occasional stamping of one of the horses and the steady pattering of the rain, undertoned by the sullen roaring of the swollen river.

Rio Yarnell swayed a little. "I killed Seb Wister," he said clearly. "If I hadn't, he would have murdered Sutro. Now, Bylas," he added loudly. "What else can you pin on Sloan Sutro?"

Grosset smiled quickly. "All right, Landres," he said. "The only charge you have on Sutro now is that so-called charge of robbery. Certainly the man was in the office of the Rio Blanco Company. *But did he steal anything?*"

Landres was taken aback. He looked at Bylas. Bylas nodded. Landres moved his horse forward. "Rio Yarnell!" he called out. "I hereby arrest you on the charge of murder, in that you shot and killed Sheriff Sebastian Wister, of this county. I warn you that anything you say may be used against you."

"Come and get me, you bastard," said Yarnell thinly.

Landres looked again at Bylas. Again the man nodded. Landres spurred his horse forward, followed by his men, and Sloan Sutro as well. The crowd parted in sudden panic.

Luckily for Sloan the crowd was between him and that deadly rifle muzzle of Sage Spencer's. This was his chance. He slammed his horse suddenly against that of Bob Slade who rode on his right, meanwhile reaching into his boot top for one of the stingy guns. Jim Marcus, who rode at the rear, stood up in his stirrups and swung his reversed rifle at Sloan's head. Rio Yarnell fired twice, and the two slugs rapped into Marcus' chest, driving him back from his saddle.

Bob Slade cursed. He turned his rifle to get a clean shot at Sloan and died with a soft-nosed .41 caliber derringer slug in his heart. Sloan slid from his saddle when he saw Sage Spencer raise his rifle. Sloan fired quickly and missed Todd Durkin, who was leaning from his saddle to get a shot at Sloan. Sloan jumped behind Slade's rearing, plunging horse and snatched the second derringer from the other boot.

Men yelled and cursed as they broke for cover out of the line of gunfire. Dave Landres spurred directly at Yarnell. The hired gun fired from the hip, and Landres' fine black fell heavily at the very edge of the trembling bridge, catapulting Landres forward. The deputy landed on one knee and swung up his pistol. Todd Durkin raised his rifle to shoot at Rio Yarnell. The swaying gunman fired twice, and Durkin went down for good, landing almost on Sloan, driving him to his knees in the churned mud, while the little derringer flew out of his hand and sank into the rushing river.

Then Landres' sixgun rapped three times, and the slugs struck Yarnell. Instead of falling backward, he clutched the rail of the bridge and fired once at Landres. Landres jerked as the heavy slug tore into his gun arm. He dropped his Colt. Yarnell staggered forward, dying, and wrapped his arms about Landres, pulling him to the railing of the bridge. He fell over, dragging Landres with him. "Come on in!" he yelled just before he went under. "The water's fine!"

The Rio Blanco closed over both men and carried them away to their deaths.

Sloan snatched up a Winchester and turned to face Bylas, Harry Landres, and Sage Spencer. There was no sign of them, nor was Julie Landres anywhere in sight. It was then that he saw them at the far end of the street, walking quickly toward a side street, with Julie stumbling along between them. Then they were gone.

"Don't follow them. Sutro," said Sim Grosset. "Bylas will be heading for his ranch. It would take a battalion of cavalry to get him pried out of there."

Sloan grounded the rifle. "He's on the run, Grosset," he said quietly. "You know about the confession. We'll need it to break him forever."

"Sure, I know about it. I notarized it. But where is it? Yarnell is dead. He's the only one who knows where it is if it still exists."

"It does," said Sloan. "Yarnell hid it in the bunkhouse on Bylas' ranch."

"Might as well be in the middle of a den of diamondbacks."

"We'll need it," said Sloan stubbornly.

"Who'll go and get it?" asked Heck Watt.

There was no answer from anyone. Then Sloan looked up. "I will," he said.

Sim Grosset wet his lips. "Seems as though this county hasn't got a sheriff or a deputy anymore," he said. "It's early in the day. Time for a fast election if you men have a mind."

There wasn't any doubt but what the citizens of Rio Blanco had a mind to have an election.

"I nominate Sloan Sutro for the unoccupied office of sheriff of this county," said Heck Watt.

"I second that nomination," said Brady quickly.

"Any other nominations?" demanded Grosset, "Nominations are now closed! All those in favor of Sloan Sutro for sheriff of this county signify by saying yea."

There wasn't much doubt about that either.

Grosset glanced at Brady. "There's a star in the office at the jail. Go get it, George."

Sloan shook his head. "You can't do this, Grosset," he protested. "Not without the rest of the county having their say!"

Grosset smiled. "This *is* the county, Sutro. Rio Blanco County's population is practically centered here. Besides, I doubt if there'd be any opposition. We've been trying to get rid of Wister for years and Landres as well. That was taken care of by providence."

George Brady hurried through the crowd and handed the star to Sim Grosset. Sloan unbuttoned his slicker. Grosset eyed the dark patch on the vest, then expertly pinned the star right over it. He took Sloan's hand. "Call out a posse," he said.

Sloan shook his head: "There's been enough bloodshed. I've seen this thing through so far, almost alone. I aim to finish the job that way."

Lightning flashed across the streaming skies and illuminated the masses of rock piled high above the river gorge. Thunder rumbled sullenly in the canyons.

No one argued with Sloan Sutro about his decision to go to the Bylas' ranch alone. After all, he *was* the new sheriff. It was *his* job, wasn't it?

It was Amy Corday alone who walked to the sheriff's office with Sloan Sutro, and when the door closed behind them, he drew her close and kissed her wet lips again and again. He knew she didn't want him to go. She knew that no matter what she said or did, he would go anyway. But these few last moments would let him surely know that she loved him with all her heart.

CHAPTER ELEVEN

The drums of the Thunder People pealed continuously through the canyons while eerie sheet lightning flickered over the valley of the Rio Blanco. Although it was getting close to mid-day, the ominous sky, hung with thick gray clouds that scudded swiftly before the cold wind, gave the valley an aspect of approaching dusk.

Sloan Sutro tethered his horse in the thick and dripping woods to the west of the big spread owned by Garth Bylas. As he did so, the flashing lightning illuminated the streaming sky, etching in sharp and eerie relief every rock and tree and particularly that area where a vast piece of the mountain top had been gouged away in times long past, piling up the huge masses of rocks and boulders, detritus and shattered tree trunks. Silvery streams of water, appearing like silken threads at a distance, poured down the mountainside, winding here and there, appearing and disappearing, but always plunging downward, until at last they all met and flowed in a wide and shallow fan down the last great talus slope to pour into the swollen Rio Blanco.

Sloan drew his Winchester from the saddle scabbard and levered a round into the chamber. He padded through the wet and clinging brush. The continuous roaring of the flooded river drowned out any sound he might make, and indeed almost every other sound except that of the thunder.

Sloan paused at the edge of the woods and peered around a thick-boled pine. Beyond the woods was the big barn of painful memory to Sloan. The low white painted bunkhouse was sited right at the very edge of the river. If the confession was in there, as Rio Yarnell had said it was, it would be the lever that would topple Garth Bylas from his throne of power forever.

Sloan seemed to flit like a ghost through the under-brush until he was close beside the wall of the bunkhouse. Thus far, he had seen no signs of life about the place. It was then that he noticed that the raging river had undermined the bank and that the bunkhouse was settled at a slight angle. If the storm kept up, the whole bank might eventually cave in. Even as he stood there, the building seemed to sink a little.

Sloan flattened himself against the wall and peered over his shoulder into a window. There were no lights in the building, no sign of life. This was a stroke of luck. Rio Yarnell had said that Bylas had as many as ten or twelve hardcases staying in that bunkhouse at one time. But the fact that they were not in the bunkhouse did not mean that they were not somewhere around the place.

He walked to the front of the building and stepped up on the sagging porch. As he did so, he felt the building move a little. He looked back over his shoulder. There was no one in sight through the misty veils of rain. He tried the door handle and then opened the door, step-ping in quickly, Winchester at hip level, swinging back and forth to cover the dim interior.

There were no signs of occupancy in the bunkhouse, although some of the bunks still had mattresses and blan-kets on them. It was possible that Bylas' men were out working against the flood somewhere up river. It had been getting worse by the hour.

He went from bunk to bunk. There were at least twenty of men in the building, and he had hardly a mind to examine the flooring beneath each one of them. The floor was at a slant from the sinking, and he could hear the scouring action of the rushing water as it worked fiercely at the soft bank.

A sudden flashing of lightning revealed deeply carved letters in a nearby bunk post. "R.Y.," said Sloan quickly. He knelt on the floor and felt the boards. It was no use. They all seemed firmly fastened. He took out his sheath knife and pried at each board in turn until one of them gave a little. He lifted it up and groped in the cavity beneath it until his hands struck a thick envelope. He withdrew it, swiftly cut the cord that bound it, and took out the folded paper contained in the envelope. The next flashing of lightning showed him he had found what he had come to find. He replaced the confession in the envelope and slid it inside his shirt.

He stood up, and at the same time, he heard a floorboard creak. He turned swiftly to see a heavy-set man walking toward him with a rifle in his hands. "Who the hell are you?" demanded the man. He peered closely at Sloan. "By God!" he said. "You're Sutro!"

Sloan jumped forward and gripped the rifle by the barrel, forcing it to one side. Even as he did so, he saw another figure darken the doorway. "What's up, Kraft?" demanded the newcomer.

"It's Sutro! Go get Spencer!"

But the newcomer slapped his hand down for a draw. There was nothing else Sloan could do but to drive his knife into the forearm of Kraft. The man cursed and dropped the rifle. Sloan backhanded him, and as Kraft staggered sideways, the building lurched and slid a little toward the river. Sloan dived forward and caught the second man with a shoulder in the gut, slamming him up against the wall. Once again, the building trembled, lurched, then slid a little. This time it seemed to be teetering on the weak bank of the river. The floor was at an ominous slant.

Kraft pawed for his sixshooter. Sloan gripped the second man by the slicker front and hurled him down the slanting floor against Kraft. The two big men fell heavily and struck the far wall of the building, adding their weight to the unbalanced weight of the lower end of the bunkhouse. The building slid and grated. Sloan seemed to be climbing a hill as he fought to reach the door. His hands gripped both sides, and he forced himself up and through it. He heard the men yelling as the building slid in a steady motion toward the roaring stream.

Sloan dived for the edge of the porch flooring, gripped it, and pulled himself up and over it to land heavily in the mud as the building slid all the way into the raging Rio Blanco, swung lazily about, then smashed against some boulders. There was a last despairing scream from within, and then the building sank lower and lower until only the roof was above the frothing waters.

Sloan ran to the shelter of a grove of trees and then stopped to look about. There was no one else in sight. He wiped the cold sweat from his face and felt for the confession to make sure he had not lost it.

He had enough now to break Garth Bylas. But Bylas still had the deed to Sloan's land. The game was not over as yet. There were a few debts to be paid off as well.

It took him the better part of an hour to scout the area of ranch buildings. The barn was empty and the rest of the outbuildings were devoid of humans. But a low scarf of smoke hung over the big log ranch house. It was darker now and the gorge beyond the ranch seemed almost shrouded in night. The rain pattered steadily down.

There was only one place they could be if they were

on the ranch at all, and that was in the house. He could figure on Garth Bylas being there, backed by Sage Spencer and possibly Harry Landres, weak as he was. But a cornered rat can fight in desperation, if not in courage.

Sloan eased through the dripping shrubbery and saw a wide window before him. It was partly open, and the lace curtains, soaked in the rain, had plastered themselves on the broad sill. Sloan took off his slicker, then checked his Colt and the double-barreled derringer he carried in his left boot top.

He looked back over his shoulder, then stepped on the hewn stone foundation edge and shoved aside the wet and clinging lace curtains. The room seemed empty, but it was too dim to make sure. Even as he let himself in he had a quick idea of whose room he was in, for the unmistakable mingled aura of perfume, powder and feminine flesh met him, mingled with the faint and fruity odor of whiskey.

Someone sat up in the wide and untidy bed. "That you, Harry?" demanded Julie Landres in a slurred voice.

Sloan moved a little closer to the bed.

"Harry?"

"Yes," said Sloan in a low voice.

"What's the matter with you?"

He came a little closer. She held out a shaking hand. "Don't touch me again, Harry! Go get another bottle. That's about all you're good for!"

Sloan bent quickly over her and clamped a hard wet hand across her soft mouth. "Hello, Julie," he said.

She stared up at him with wide and frightened eyes. Damn, but she was beautiful even if she was a lush.

"Now, Julie," he said softly, "I've come here for the deed to my land. I want no outcry from you. Understand?"

She nodded and tried to pull his hand from her mouth.

"Thanks for agreeing to witness that I did not kill Yancey," he said. "You sure you won't cry out?"

She shook her head, and he removed his hand. She immediately squared her lovely mouth to scream, but she, as well as others in that valley, had no idea of how fast Sloan Sutro could move. His right fist clipped her neatly and knocked her back on the bed.

"Some other time, Julie," said Sloan with a hard grin.

He bound her and gagged her, tip-toed to the door, placing his ear against it to listen. The subdued murmuring of voices came to him. He turned the door handle gently and eased the door open a crack. He could see into a hallway and just beyond the hallway into a large living room. The bittersweet odor of burning wood came to him. A pair of booted feet protruded into his vision but he could not see the owner of them. A big, broad-shouldered man stood with his back to the fireplace, his hands back beneath his coat, holding it up a little, revealing a nickel-plated Colt in an ornate leather holster. It was Garth Bylas, and there was a worried look on his broad face.

"Where the hell is Ben Kraft?" demanded Bylas. "I sent him to the bunkhouse more than an hour ago."

"Wouldn't surprise me any if he didn't run off like some of the rest of them did," said Harry Landres in a panicky voice.

"You scared of one man? Sutro's too smart to come busting up here looking for trouble."

"You don't smell so good in Rio Blanco, Garth. Supposing those people come up here to back Sutro's play?"

Bylas turned and spat into the fireplace. "I never did smell so good in Rio Blanco. You can't make a cake without breaking eggs. Sure, Sutro got out of that mess in town this morning. Damned bad luck that he didn't stop a slug in the process. Sage couldn't get a shot at him. Well, Sage won't miss him this time."

Landres stood up and walked to the table to pour a drink. "Maybe he's pulled out, too," he said sourly.

"Not Sage," said Bylas. "I'll bet on Sage."

"You just bet on him then! I can't stand this tension, Garth! I want to pull out."

There was a sneering look on Bylas' face. "Go on," he said. "You're no damned good for anything. Why Julie ever married you is beyond me! Well, go on! *Vamonos!*"

Landres turned and tossed down his drink, then wiped his mouth. "I got to get Julie," he said a little thickly.

"If she goes with you, she'd be a bigger fool than I thought she was."

"She's my wife, ain't she?"

Bylas laughed softly. "Sure, Harry. She's your wife, all right. In name only! Haw!" Landres' face worked. He dropped a hand to the holstered Colt he wore. "Damn you, Bylas," he snarled.

The big man straightened up. "Don't you try anything on me, Landres," he said coldly. "But you won't; you gutless wonder. Go get Julie. Pull tail! Beat it! Don't come back sniveling to me when I whip Sutro and get this whole damned valley to heel again. Hear?"

Landres poured another drink, downed it, then walked a little unsteadily toward his wife's bedroom.

Sloan stepped back, drawing his Colt. As Landres entered the room, Sloan shoved the door shut with his foot, then swung the heavy Colt, laying the barrel neatly just above Landres' ear. As Landres fell, Sloan caught him. He dragged him to the bed and dumped him next to his unconscious wife. Sloan took Landres' Colt from his holster and thrust it under his own belt. He tiptoed back to the door again and eased it open. Bylas was standing by the fire, hands behind his back, staring moodily into the flames.

Sloan eased through the doorway and stepped into the carpeted hallway. He moved as silently as a cat across the living room floor until he was five feet from Bylas. He cocked the Colt, and the crisp double-clicking made Bylas suddenly raise his head. "Harry?" he said. He turned, and his face went pasty white. "Sutro!"

Sloan nodded. "Where is Sage Spencer?"

"Out on the road. Waiting for you."

"Where is the deed?"

"I haven't got it."

Sloan smiled thinly. "Don't pull that on me, Bylas. I know what it means to you."

The hard eyes flicked down and saw the star on Sloan's vest. Bylas laughed. "You know that damned tin star isn't legal on you, Sutro."

"What difference does it make? I want that deed."

"I haven't got it!"

Sloan's trigger finger tightened.

"You can't bluff me, Sutro," said Bylas. "Have a drink. Maybe we can talk business."

"No. The deed doesn't matter in a sense. I have a signed and notarized confession, written by Rio Yarnell, implicating you in a number of murders and other dirty dealings, Bylas. I'm taking you back to Rio Blanco."

Bylas laughed again. "How far do you think my men will let you go?"

"Two of them died in the bunkhouse, Bylas, drowned in the Rio Blanco, when the building slid into it. Harry Landres is out cold in his wife's room. That leaves Spencer. Who else can you call on?"

A nerve worked in Bylas' face. "That confession isn't worth a cent."

"It is all right. Besides, there are a lot of little people who've always been afraid of you and your hired guns who'll talk now, Bylas. They'll sing like canaries, and the song won't be pretty."

"Look out, Bylas!" cried the voice from the hallway.

Sloan whirled and dropped to the floor as Sage Spencer fired his Winchester from the hip. Sloan fired upward and missed. He rolled over and over again toward the far wall as Spencer slammed two quick shots where Sloan had been. Three shots echoed the gunfire of the Winchester. Three slugs rapped into Sage Spencer's chest in an area that could be covered by a playing card.

Powder smoke drifted thickly in the big room. The front door slammed back against the wall, and boots thudded on the porch. Sloan rolled up to his feet and ran for the door. Just as he reached it, a gun cracked flatly from the edge of the porch, and the slug struck Sloan in the left bicep, smashing him back into the room, sick with the frightening numbness of the heavy bullet in his flesh.

Sloan went down on his knees, dropping his Colt. Another shot slammed through the open doorway and struck the big Argand lamp on the marble-topped table, smashing the oil container. The oil dripped swiftly to the thick carpeting and splashed into the fireplace. Instantly a hungry runnel of flame raced across the carpeting and caught on to the oil-soaked fringe of the heavy tablecloth.

Sloan forced himself to his feet and ran out onto the porch to see Bylas hanging onto the reins of a rearing, plunging horse. Sloan hurled himself at Bylas and drove him into the thick wet shrubbery. They fought savagely with the wet leaves slapping against their faces until, at last, Sloan drove a fist hard against Bylas' temple, half stunning him. As Bylas went limp, Sloan thrust a hand into the man's coat and withdrew his heavy wallet. Bills fell into the mud as he pawed into the contents to find at last his precious deed. Sloan stood up and felt for his Colt.

Bylas came up from the ground and butted Sloan to one side. "You'll never take me in!" he yelled. He ran for the horse and swung up into the wet saddle, but the maddened animal bucked and threw him, then ran for the road. Bylas wiped the blood from his face and stared wildly about, then set off at a staggering pace up the road toward the gorge of the Rio Blanco.

Thunder rolled and pealed, and lightning flickered eerily.

Common sense told Sloan Sutro to let Bylas go, but his stubbornness would not let him. He started after Bylas through the slanting rain, staggering now and again, almost falling, but still moving on.

There was a thunderous pealing in the gorge now, and above it came an ominous rumbling and grating sound, as big and loud as the preliminaries would be to the ending of the world.

Sloan stopped and raised his head. The lightning seemed to lance at him. Chain lightning zigzagged through the silvery sheets of cold rain. The rumbling noise came again as though the very bowels of the earth were in violent upheaval. The vast masses of rock high above the narrow gorge seemed to move a little.

Sloan ran on through the rain. "Bylas!" he yelled. *"Come back, Bylas!"*

The man kept on through the semi-darkness and the rain.

"Bylas!" yelled Sloan. "Come back! Landslide! Landslide! Come back!"

Bylas stopped beside a huge boulder while his chest rose and fell with his spasmodic breathing. His face was white in the darkness. "Get back, Sutro!" he shrieked madly. "Take the damned valley! Take everything! You won't put Garth Bylas in Yuma Pen! I've got money in Mexico! An ace in the hole! Get back, damn you!" He punctuated his words with two shots.

Bylas ran on, turning twice to shoot, then to hurl his empty pistol toward Sloan. He spun about and ran like a frightened deer through the wet darkness to enter the gorge of the rushing Rio Blanco. Even as he did so, the first rocks had begun to fall into the gorge.

Sloan turned and ran, forgetting his pain and weak-

ness, spurred on by the grating and rumbling of the shattered rock high above him. The ranch house was now a
mass of leaping flames despite the downpour of rain.
Sloan passed it at a dead run. There was no time for
anything else.

Now there was a sustained roaring from the slide as it
began to gain momentum, sliding slowly and inexorably
into the gorge of the Rio Blanco in a shattering, thun-
dering uproar that arose even above the pealing of the
thunder and the sharp crackling of the almost continuous
electrical discharges that rent the gloomy skies. The wind
seemed to pick up as tons and tons of the loosened rock
plunged headlong into the gorge, and the shrill crying of
a maddened man deep in the gorge was drowned out
beneath masses of huge rocks and riven timbers.

Sloan ran on and on as the rock kept falling, not
daring to look behind, until he reached the woods where
he had left his horse. Then, and only then, did he look
back and the impact of what he saw was enough to make
him close his eyes and look quickly away. An entirely new
landscape had been formed in a matter of terrible
minutes. The mountain now no longer towered high
above the river gorge. *There just wasn't any river gorge.*
Nothing but fallen rock and splintered tree trunks,
soaked with the steadily falling rain, where the river
gorge had been, where the ranch buildings had been.
There was nothing left of the gorge, of the ranch, *nothing*
at all.

Sloan slowly mounted the horse, then checked to see
if he had both the confession and the deed. He badly
needed a drink and medical attention. He touched the
horse with his heels and kneed it out onto the muddy
road that led into the town of Rio Blanco.

The drink could wait, he thought, and the medical
attention could come from a girl with midnight blue eyes
who had been a nurse and who had just lost a job as a
receptionist in the now silent office of the Rio Blanco

Ranching, Mining and Development Company. But before that, she had been a girl born and raised in the lovely and fertile Valley of the Rio Blanco. A valley she had loved and still loved.

The Valley of the Rio Blanco would be the home of Amy Corday for the rest of her life as far as Sloan was concerned, requiring only the changing of her last name from Corday to Sutro. Now that the Voice of the Gun was forever stilled in that remote and wildly beautiful part of Arizona.

TAKE A LOOK AT LAST MAN ALIVE AND NOW HE IS LEGEND:

Two Full Length Western Novels

Owen Wister and Spur Award winning Gordon D. Shirreffs pens incredible, true-to-life tales of the American west that are sure to please even the most discerning consumer of Western fiction.

In *Last Man Alive*, Lorimer had escaped the massacre at Big Hatchet thanks to pure blind luck—probably the only luck he'd ever had in his life. But the money was gone and the Indians sure hadn't taken it—they considered money bad medicine.

The Army thought him a thief and a coward, the Indians wanted him dead just because they didn't like survivors, and Lorimer had nobody on his side but his outcast half-breed...

In *Now He Is Legend*, Ross Starkey is a tormented drifter who lives by the gun and rides wherever the money is—to range wars in the north, to revolutions south of the border, to any outlaw renegade who has the right price to pay for his services. Now Starkey wants out, and there's only one thing that stands in his way—a man they call the Tascosa Kid. The coming showdown will be unlike any Starkey has faced...

"The joy of reading Shirreffs' work is in his mastery of pacing and his tough, gritty prose." – **James Reasoner, author of Outlaw Ranger.**

AVAILABLE NOW

ABOUT THE AUTHOR

Gordon D. Shirreffs published more than 80 western novels, 20 of them juvenile books, and John Wayne bought his book title, Rio Bravo, during the 1950s for a motion picture, which Shirreffs said constituted *"the most money I ever earned for two words."* Four of his novels were adapted to motion pictures, and he wrote a Playhouse 90 and the Boots and Saddles TV series pilot in 1957.

A former pulp magazine writer, he survived the transition to western novels without undue trauma, earning the admiration of his peers along the way. The novelist saw life a bit cynically from the edge of his funny bone and described himself as looking like a slightly parboiled owl. Despite his multifarious quips, he was dead serious about the writing profession.

Gordon D. Shirreffs was the 1995 recipient of the Owen Wister Award, given by the Western Writers of America for "a living individual who has made an outstanding contribution to the American West."

He passed in 1996.